Can't Go Home

A Novel

Angelisa Stone

Dedication

This book is dedicated to my youngest son, "the middle child." I know that you often feel overlooked or inferior, which breaks my heart. You inspired me to create Dre, the loving, sensitive, and charming character that he is. You have so many exceptional qualities that your dad and I couldn't be more proud of. You bring us joy and laughter, happiness and fun, making each of our days brighter.

My Wish

I have a wish for all the people who really want more out of their lives, but are too afraid to fulfill those dreams, those fantasies, and those goals. *Can't Go Home* is for those people who are "living a lie," because that's what friends, family, and all of society expects of them. Our lives are buried with details and mundane tasks that hinder us from achieving our wildest dreams and from being true to ourselves. My wish is that we all end the days of being who everyone else wants us to be. Be proud of yourself. Take pride in your dreams—they're yours and yours alone. That's my shiny-penny wish for you. Now go make your dreams come true.

PART ONE

Blissful Ignorance

Her name is Kathryn Denise Howell. She used to go by "Katie" when she was in high school, even into college, but when she moved here, she became "Kathryn" to her new friends and co-workers. It's amazing what you can learn from social networking and even just from random people on the streets. When I scrutinize her, she looks like a "Katie." She has one of those angelic, "girl-next-door" faces, the kind that when you look at her, you just know that you'd never be able to lie to such an innocent and naïve face.

I understand why she'd choose to go by "Kathryn" now; it's more mature, more professional, and demands respect. As for me, I already respect her; I respect the fuck out of her. She solidified my opinion of her the moment I heard her speak.

The problem is when I actually meet Kathryn and talk to her all I'm going to do is lie like crazy to her. Basically, I doubt anything I ever say to her will be the truth. The feel-good, glowy, little angel on my shoulder keeps whispering that I should most definitely stay away, should move on, should forget I ever heard her on the phone. I should walk away and do her a favor. A big fucking favor.

But, I can't. The evil devil in my pants won't let me. Kathryn got to me—and to him. She got to us bad. Despite my better judgment, Kathryn Howell will be mine, come Hell or high water. I know I sound like a creepy-ass stalker. I'm not a stalker in the "cut 'em up and eat 'em sense." I'm a stalker in the "I know what want, and I'm going to get it" sense. Normally when I see a woman I want, she's mine within in the night, sometimes within the hour. My life has been a series of wanting and then quite easily getting. But lately, what I want and what I have are two very dissimilar things, even very different from what I used to have. It's all changing, and quite fucking frankly, that's just fine by me.

Now the hard part: I have to meet her first. I also have to let go of my guilty conscience, because I'm going to hate lying to her. Well, I guess I must also renege on that promise to myself that I'm going to swear off women. I did swear off women—all women. How was I to know that I was going to overhear Kathryn Howell's phone call, a phone call that put me over the edge and certainly made me want to know her? I decided that I'd scrap the "no women for Dre rule." Let's be honest. That rule sucks anyway.

My infatuation for her started nearly a month ago. Yes, it's an infatuation, possible borderline obsession. Cue the flashback music; let the picture fade and get all blurry until we zoom in on an angry Kathryn Howell on her cell phone, putting someone, presumably her boss, right in his place.

The day in question was crazy hot, unbearably sweltering, which is usually the case in Charleston, South Carolina in mid-September. I was standing under the awning of a local tourist seafood joint when Kathryn parked her bright yellow Volkswagen

Bug at the meter in front of me. Normally, a girl like her wouldn't have caught my eye, but I was dying in the heat and too bored and tired to look away. Nice huh?

When Kathryn got out of her car, let's be clear, I wasn't knock-my-socks-off floored by her beauty or presence. I actually looked at her and thought, "It's too hot to have that much hair." Kathryn has long, dark, wavy hair that is thick as it is long. Nobody should have hair like that in the south. It probably adds about 10 degrees to the body temperature. And nobody wants that.

I don't want it to seem like Kathryn isn't beautiful, because she is. Kathryn just didn't "look the part," the part that I am normally drawn to and tend to sway toward. Most of the women I've dated could grace the cover of a *Victoria's Secret* advertisement, a *Maxim* centerfold, or *Sports Illustrated* swimsuit edition. Typically, I like my women tall, lean, blonde, and a little on the "easy" side. Who doesn't really? I sound like an ass, don't I? I never claimed not to be, which is why I feel slightly guilty for honing in on Kathryn Howell, chartering places I have no business exploring in the first place.

When Kathryn circled around to the parking meter, she rummaged through her large, knockoff designer purse for change, pulling out a handful of coins. Immediately, I loved that she was walking around with a fake handbag. From where I come from, that was unheard of, grounds for societal ridicule and possible emotional torture.

Quickly, she put two quarters into the meter. But then, she did something that made me perk up and pay attention. She put three more coins into the meter next to it, buying time for the car parked next to hers. A random, selfless act of kindness is pretty unheard of these days.

At that point, I became intrigued. People didn't normally surprise me, especially in this day and age. Sure, the South is supposed to be filled with southern hospitality and kindness. But the truth is, when nobody is looking, southerners are just as selfish and rude as any Yankee on the other side of the Confederate lines.

Kathryn continued down the street, adding quarters to the parking meters until all of the change in her hand ran out. Stunned, I watched her walk every step of the way until she walked into a quaint little Italian restaurant on the corner. It was at that point that I decided I needed to at least talk to her. I wanted to meet a woman who put that much energy, selfless energy, into a random act of kindness. Who did that? My curiosity was piqued, but that was all that was interested—at the moment.

I casually walked over to her meter to see how much time she "bought" herself, wondering how long it would be until she would return. Seeing that I only had less than 30 minutes before she returned, I stopped in to a restaurant to gain sanctuary from the heat with an ice-cold drink. Plus, I promised the owner I'd fix the floorboards on their deck in the back—a task for me that would take less than 15 minutes.

In Charleston, 30 minutes wasn't enough time for lunch downtown; Southerners like a long, leisurely lunch. Kathryn must have been just picking up food, so I knew I didn't have too much time to screw around if I wanted to approach her.

I finished my drink, replaced a few rotted out two-by-fours, and was patiently waiting for Kathryn's return. Finally, she emerged from the restaurant, carrying bags of takeaway food. I saw my chance and knew that it was now or never. As I began to approach her with my "I've got this smile," an older, smarmy man pounced, offering to help her.

Shockingly, she shot him a look that clearly said, "Back off Buddy, I don't need your help." Wow, I'd dodged a bullet. My approach would've been regarded as offensive and chauvinistic. Kathryn Howell wasn't a damsel in distress who needed a man to swoop in and save the day.

I trailed behind her, determining my next move, when her cell phone rang. I laughed when she said, "Dang it," and put the bags of food down on the ground, next to her car. What adult woman says "dang it?" She took her phone out of her bra—her bra? And answered it.

"Kathryn Howell Seaside Literary Agency—"

Bingo! At least, I knew her name and where she worked. I had time. I didn't need to accost her then. I could figure out my plan of action before I approached. Now remember, at this point, I was just intrigued, wanted to get to know her more. It's this phone call that just came through on her phone that put me flying over the edge and dying to have her.

I listened, impressed, to her conversation. "Yes sir. Yes sir. I understand," she said, nodding as she put the food into her car. "Of course, I follow. You want me to pick up a dozen roses and a necklace from the jeweler here and drop it off to a hotel prior to coming back to work."

Kathryn rolled her eyes and leaned against her car. Then she floored the fuck out of me. "How about his? How about I pick up the roses and the necklace and drop it off at your house—to your wife—with a note that says, 'I'm sorry I'm a cheating bastard; I'll stop—"

The caller on the other end apparently cut her off, because she stopped abruptly and let him finish. Kathryn shook her head aggressively and said, "No, you listen. Fire me if ya want. I'll have a new job tomorrow morning."

Kathryn looked around, realizing for the first time that she was yelling. She lowered her voice an octave and continued "I'm one heck of a literary agent, and you know it. Your flailing agency needs me more than I need it … and I'm pretty darn close with Beckie Foster, our HR director." With that, she hung up her phone, reached inside her car, and then put more quarters into her parking meter. Damn, this woman was good.

The people who I know, people I've known and admired my entire life, don't do things like that, standing up for the underdog. They don't speak up for those who can't speak for themselves; they mostly just turn the other way, ignoring the pain and problems of others. They certainly don't take it upon themselves to right the wrongs of the world; ultimately they just add to them. At least in my experience that's just what people do.

I wondered where she was off to, now that the meter was full of change again. Then for the final time in that short time, she shocked me again. Kathryn Howell got into her car and drove off, leaving a full two hours on the meter for the next person who parked in that spot.

I needed to meet her. I had to meet her. I was going to meet her.

Granted, I said that I was swearing off women for the time being. I've actually been *womanless* for over a year now. And when I say *womanless*, I mean without any female companionship at any time, zero, zilch, nada. I mean nothing. Let's get really real here, I haven't even experienced any form of pleasure in over a year either—not even the manual kind. Before you even think to ask, I don't have a problem; there isn't an issue. I just know that right now, at this time in my life, a woman, a relationship would complicate my life even more. And let's lay it all on the line, my life is a total cluster-fuck of chaotic shit right now.

But I cannot deny it; I'm going to fight the good fight to meet and woo one Kathryn Howell, literary agent, and quick-witted wonder, right into bed, her bed. And today's the day. I'm currently standing outside of the Seaside Literary Agency awaiting our "chance" encounter.

Kathryn goes to lunch at approximately 1:10 p.m. every day, except for Friday, when she skips lunch and leaves work at 4:30 p.m. instead of 5:30 p.m. I've spent the good portion of the last month studying my new favorite subject: The Social Behaviors of Kathryn Denise Howell. I'm just eager to add "anatomy" to the lesson plan.

Kathryn exits the old, pale mint green building today at 1:15 p.m., later than normal. She looks cute in a bright orange tank top and tan skirt. Her hair is piled on her head in some knotted, bun thing. (If I had that much hair, I'd chop it off.) Kathryn is probably a little shorter than 5'5" and curvier than my type. She's got really muscular legs, too muscular, I think.

Lately, when I've been looking at them, I've thought about how she could probably snap my head off if she gets too excited when I go down on her. (I plan to chance it anyway.) Her stems are nice though, shapely, strong, and look really smooth. I want to touch them—tonight.

My plan is to casually ask her for directions to Battery Park, seem perplexed, and then use my Dre Donley charm to convince her to show me the way there, while making it seem like her plan all along. We'll go to the park, talk, laugh, and then I'll persuade her to meet up with me tonight. Finally, I'll nail her and get her out of my system, so I can focus back on the shit storm that has now become my life. It's probably not the greatest plan or well-devised plan, but it'll work. Bedding a girl isn't all that tough. Women are usually pretty easy—even when they're trying not to be. Kathryn Howell looks like she needs it too, so it's a win-win. I'm doing her a favor and vice versa.

Kathryn is quick to her car, so I have to pick up speed to catch up to her. As soon as I approach her car, she closes the door and turns the key in the ignition. It doesn't start. She tries again. The engine won't roll over; her battery is dead. Perfect. Here's my shot; I can ditch the lame "lost tourist" routine.

I walk over to her car and give her my best line. Wait for it, and go: "Car won't start?" just as she opens the door. (Brilliant, wasn't it?)

"Yeah it will; it's just a fun game I like to play, pretend the car doesn't start and trick strangers on the street," she says sarcastically, and starts rummaging through her purse. "It's really fun. You should try it sometime."

"As much as I'd like to play games with you, Sugar, I'd rather help you out," I say as I take her phone from her and disconnect the call she was making. Clinched it. Kathryn's blue eyes are staring up at me in awe. I've seen this look a hundred, no scratch that, a thousand times, right before a chick agrees to go home with me.

"Oh wow, hot stranger, should I take my panties off now or would you like to do it for me?" she asks, rolling her eyes, and grabbing her phone back as she gets out of her car. "I have a freaking dead battery. I need jumper cables and a jump—not that kind—and I'll be good to go."

Kathryn turns her back on me, and dials the call again. I stand there speechlessly, contemplating my next move. Kathryn taps her nails on the hood of her Bug. Her nails aren't painted or manicured, bitten down to the nubs. How could this girl have entranced me so? Then she says, "Hey there, it's Kathryn. I'm not gonna be able to make it today; my car won't start."

Waiting a few seconds, Kathryn then responds, "No. No, I'm fine. Just tell Jose to write another 1000 words this week, and we'll work on all of it next week," she turns around and frowns when she sees that I'm still standing next to her. Then she says, "No, I'm sure. You're too sweet. Thank you," and ends the call. Kathryn puts her phone back in her purse and starts walking back to her office.

"Wait a minute," I say, before I even realize I'm stopping her. "Aren't you going to get your car jumped?"

Kathryn turns around and looks at me, almost like it was the first time she actually saw me. She walks in closer, definitely crossing over into my personal space. "Why do you care?" she asks, eyeing my suspiciously.

Kathryn's got me, because I really have no idea. Why do I care? What is it about her that has me so drawn to her? This was not going so well. I was definitely not on my game. Maybe that's the problem, I never saw her as a challenge, but this is the hardest I've ever had to work. And I mean ever.

Stammering, I say, "I thought I could help you find someone with cables and jump your car for you."

"Well, that is awfully nice of you, kind sir," she says in the most fake Southern accent I've ever heard. "I wouldn't know the first thing about jumping a little ole car."

Shaking her head and frowning, Kathryn adds, "I mean how could a woman even attempt to put the color-coordinated jumper cables on the positive to negative chargers all by her silly old self?" Kathryn flutters her eyelashes and then fans herself, dramatically. Holy shit. She doesn't want me. She's not at all charmed by me.

Game on. "Positive on positive. If you put the positive on the negative," I say, walking in closer, our bodies nearly touching, "sparks will fly." I hear her gasp. Nice, there it is. I got her.

"Oh will they?" she asks, countering me. "From my experience, something that heats up that quickly … fizzles out … like that," and she snaps her fingers in my face. Shit, this girl is good. Kathryn may need laid way more than I do. She is one big ball of pent up sexual frustration. I love it.

Right before she enters her office, she turns and says, "Hey Casanova, you wanna help me? Be here at 5:30 p.m. tonight with jumper cables, so I can jump my car … by myself … and go home on time … by myself."

It's 5:31 p.m., and Kathryn Howell hasn't left work yet. How do I know? I'm sitting on the hood of her car, waiting for her. See, I've got a few connections in Charleston, and the main receptionist at the Seaside Literary Agency was putty in my hands when I told her that she had beautiful hair, as I twirled it around my fingers. She willingly and eagerly retrieved Kathryn's keys from her purse when Kathryn was in a meeting with her boss. I cannot wrap my brain around the fact that women can fall all over you, even when they know you're interested in someone else. It's beyond me.

As for the car, all I had to do was check under the hood for what kind of battery she needed, swing by an automotive store, get a battery, and replace it. I returned the keys to the secretary. (I also gave that dim-witted receptionist a sweetgrass-woven rose. Never make enemies when unnecessary.) Now I'm awaiting Kathryn's arrival—and appreciation. And I am really ready for her appreciation.

When I see her come out the door, my face lights up; hers grimaces. I decide to strike first, "Hi honey, how was work?"

Kathryn shakes her head, and says, "Where are the jumper cables, big guy?" Big guy? She has no idea—yet.

"Didn't get any," I say, shrugging my shoulders, pretending not to care.

"Then, why're you on my car?" she inquires.

"Seemed like a great spot to rest … cozy and all," I say, sliding to one side of the hood of her VW Bug. "Care to join me?"

"Listen, I need to get home. I'm not sure what game you're playing at, but I'm not interested."

As she starts scrolling through her phone, a truck pulls up next to hers, and an older man rolls down his window. "Do you think I'm close enough?"

Kathryn looks relieved. "Nah, you need to pull in front of my car … I'll go ahead and pop the hood." She unlocks her car, and turns to me, "Could you at least move, so we can get my car jumped?"

I nod and hop down off her car. As she leans inside the car to pop the hood, I turn to the man, and say, "Thank you sir for your help, but the car's fine. She doesn't need it jumped." He eyes me, and waits for her confirmation or explanation.

"What're you doing?" she asks, looking at me. "Warren, don't leave. It won't start."

"Why don't you give it try, before you spend all that time moving his car and hooking up the cables," I suggest. Kathryn glares at me, squinting her eyes suspiciously.

"Alright Casanova, what'd you do?" Kathryn asks, as she slides into the driver's seat. She puts the key into the ignition, turning it as the car hums and comes to life. Still glaring at me, she leans out of the car, and says, "I'm sorry to hold you up, Warren. Thanks for offering to help." Warren looks at me, shrugs his shoulders, and waves to Kathryn before pulling out of the space.

Kathryn kills the engine, gets out, closes the door, and walks over to where I'm standing. "First of all, thank you. I'm not sure what you did, but you obviously did something."

I start to cut her off, when she raises her finger to hush me. "Secondly, I'm not sleeping with you." Kathryn quickly shakes her head, lowers her shoulders, and says, "Third, I'd like to buy you dinner to thank you for your help."

Kathryn walks around to the passenger side of the door, and opens it, motioning for me to get in. I have to be honest; I've never had a girl open a door for me. I'm not too sure I like it. I can almost feel my balls shrink up and hide.

"Fourth," she says, after I'm in, "I have pepper spray in my purse, and I will blind your ass if you try to kill or rape me." Kathryn taps her purse as if to emphasize what's inside. Then she walks around to the other side of the car, gets in, and says, "And finally, I'm not sleeping with you."

"That was number two," I remind her, smirking.

"And it's **also** number five … repetition for emphasis," she says, and pulls out of the parking spot. "Where to, Car Fairy?"

"Seafood. I'm hungry for some seafood," I reply, turning toward her. "You pick the place," I say, smiling at her.

"Perfect," she says, "I've got a coupon for Sam's Seafood Bucket."

Damn, she's cute. "By the way, I do have a name."

"I'm sure you do," she says and turns up the radio.

The hostess leads us to a table on the patio, overlooking the marina. It's as hot as balls, but I'm not about to complain. Every single one of my senses is in overdrive. I can't stop looking at Kathryn, especially the fullness of her ass, the curve of her hips, the swell of her breasts. Have I ever liked a nice, round ass before? Damn. This chick's got me all mixed up.

All I can think about is getting her in bed, which makes walking behind her difficult and discomforting. When the air conditioning was cranked in the car, I was getting wafts of her scent, making my mouth water. I'm not sure if cinnamon sugar and vanilla is an actual scent, but that is exactly what she smelled like. My thoughts kept wandering to my tongue on her skin, behind her ears, down the back of her neck. I was more than thankful that the air conditioning was blasting me in the face; I needed a cool down.

Honestly, I could've done without the sense of sound though. A Taylor Swift song came on the radio, and Kathryn belted it out like she was auditioning for *American Idol*. The only time anyone would ever see or hear her on *Idol* is during the outtakes—when those poor people get axed in line before the real auditions even begin. Sight and scent were becoming my new favorite senses, but I'm not an idiot, I know that once taste and touch get in the game, they'll take the ball right past the goal line. Score!

After ordering drinks and all-you-can-eat crab legs, Kathryn leans across the table and says, "So Car Fairy, what'd you do to make it start?"

Deciding that I was done with this topic and ready to move on to different questions and answers, I simply say, "Got ya a new battery."

"How'd you get under my hood without my keys?" Kathryn asks, truly confused.

"A magician never reveals his secrets," I say, winking at her, as I take a drink.

"Holy smokes, seriously, how many women have you slept with?" Kathryn asks, not batting an eye at the intrusiveness of her question.

"Excuse me," I choke on my drink, buying time to make sure I heard her correctly. "What'd you say?"

"How many women have just full out fallen for this whole mysterious, sexy stranger thing?" she asks again.

"You think I'm sexy?" I inquire, raising my brows.

Kathryn leans over, grabs her purse, and takes out a small mirror. Opening the case, she holds it in front of me, and says, "I had no idea you didn't own one of these. This is a mirror. Mirror. Take a look." She shakes the mirror in front of me. "People pay big bucks to look like you, Casanova."

Kathryn retracts the mirror, closes the case, and stirs more sweetener into her unsweetened tea. The whole time, I am staring dumbfounded at her. This is not the type of girl I'm used to. Kathryn is straightforward, honest, and as intriguing as Hell.

Before I can answer, she says, "So, why're you pulling out the big guns on me?" She takes a sip of her tea, frowns, and adds in straight sugar this time. After tasting it again and grimacing, she calls the server over and orders a large sweet tea. Now that's some funny shit. There are no false pretenses with this woman.

The server glances at her briefly, looks at me, and says, "We have the sweetest tea here; it just melts on your tongue. It really whets your appetite." Then she licks her lips and leans over, smiling at me, giving my line of vision a direct assault on her cleavage.

Kathryn begins laughing, loudly with a snort, and says, "Sweetie, it's liquid. It doesn't have to melt. And it's wet, so it's going to wet anything it touches."

Kathryn shakes her head, takes a deep breath, exhales, and says, "Write your number on the check when we leave, and make sure to put a big heart over whatever "i" is in your name, but for the love of God, please keep your panties on until I leave."

The waitress leaves quickly and a few moments later a different server returns, dropping off her sweet tea quickly and quietly. I'm not sure what is happening, but I can feel myself being captivated by this woman. I'm tempted to ask her if she even knows the definitions of demure, dainty, or coy, because she is none of those things. But yet, she is the most "womanly" woman I've ever encountered.

"Aright, back to my question, the one before Allie with an "i" drenched us in her drool," she says, cracking open a crab leg and pulling out a huge hunk of meat. Meanwhile, my crab legs are coming out in aggravating little strips. I'm enthralled by her talent, envious of her expertise. Not to mention, fucking starving.

After dipping the meat in butter and putting it in her mouth, she questions, "Why am I getting the 'full court press' treatment?"

"Ahhhh basketball fan?" I ask, nodding appreciatively.

"Not at all. I just know my clichés and analogies. Stop avoiding the question," she commands.

"Can't a man see a beautiful woman and want to help her out, spend a little time with her, get to know her?" I ask, reaching for her hand. She quickly puts her hand on her lap. "Why does there have to be some hidden agenda?"

"There doesn't have to be. But in this case, the agenda is so hidden, people are going to find Jimmy Hoffa, before they figure out what you're up to," she says. "I don't play games. I don't act all giggly and giddy for some hot guy on the street. So, I'd like to request the same honesty in return."

"Why do you keep talking about how hot or sexy I am?" I ask, truthfully curious.

"Are you kidding? Guys like you don't talk to girls like me … unless you're asking who my friend at the bar is that looks like Blake Lively," Kathryn replies honestly, a slight frown forming on her face.

"Do you have a friend who looks like Blake Lively?" I ask, joking.

"Yeah … actually … Syd's prettier … if you can believe that," she admits, rolling her eyes.

I love her honesty. She almost makes me want to be honest and upfront with her … almost. But this isn't horseshoes, so almost doesn't count.

However, I do decide a little truth here might actually pay off. "I've been stalking you." She rolls her eyes again and sighs, revealing her annoyance. "No truthfully," I continue, "last month, I heard you tell someone on your phone that you wouldn't be an accomplice in his extra marital activities."

Kathryn's eyes widen, recalling the incident. "I come from a long line of lying and cunning women. I loved your abrasiveness, your honesty. I've been wanting to meet you."

"Did you purposely disconnect my battery?" Kathryn asks, eyeing me with caution.

"No, my big plan was to ask you for directions to Battery Park. I got lucky with your dead battery," I confess.

"Directions? Really? That was the best you had?" she says, shaking her head. "I'd have thought you had better game than that, Dre," she scolds.

I laugh, throwing my head back. Kathryn's funny. I like that. "Yeah well, it's been a long month. Plus the heat fucks with my mind—wait—did you just call me 'Dre?' How'd—"

"My secretary has the biggest mouth on the planet. I knew the plan the second you got my keys," she admits, matter-of-factly. "We have a ton of connections at Seaside, Dre Donley, handyman."

"I thought you didn't play games?" I ask, smirking.

"I don't play, Dre. I win," Kathryn states, flawlessly cracking open another crab leg.

~ Kathryn ~

Dre Donley is known around the city as "the gift from unknown." Everyone knows his name. Every guy wants to be him; every woman wants to bed him. However, nobody really knows him, other than his name and occupation: spur-of-the-moment handyman. Dre shows up when someone's in trouble, helps out, doesn't take any money, and then leaves. He's said to be pretty polite, gentle, and grateful. I'd known all of this, prior to letting him into my car. I'm not some dumb bimbo who lets crazy pervs jump into her vehicle for a quickie rape or trial appendectomy.

I've known what little there is of Dre's story since I moved to Charleston less than six months ago. It was impossible not to ask around about the sexy guy who's always seen loitering around area businesses and parks, sharing stories and laughing with the locals. I've even seen him give a few impromptu tours to visitors, pointing out Rainbow Row, Battery Park, and the College of Charleston.

I like to pretend to have him all figured out. I'm not too sure what people's viewing interests are, but I'm fairly certainly that he's an angel pretending to be a handyman. I saw it on a TV show once, and now I'm convinced that's what's going on. He's angelic and good—serving our world, bettering us as a whole. Definitely making the scenery more visually pleasing. Not too far-fetched, eh? It's the only I explanation I can muster up. Why else would someone be as sweet as sugar on a succulent strawberry if he weren't a gift from God? (Ever since I moved here, I've been trying out my southern similes and alliteration. It's just not working for me.)

But yesterday doesn't fit into his whole "super hero" persona. Sure, Dre got me a new battery and all that chivalrous jazz. But something important doesn't add up. Nobody has ever described him as "cocky" or "flirtatious."

Actually, most of the females in these parts talk about how unattainable and uninterested he is, which is why I'm perplexed as to why he was coming on so strong … to me. It just does not add up. I even used the calculator on my phone to do the figuring. Or I secretly snapped two pictures of him when he wasn't looking to send to my mom. Tomato. Tomahto.

Don't get me wrong; I'm flattered, full-out freaking flattered. I may or may not have squealed the second he got out of my car after dinner, especially after he said that he'd see me again "sooner, rather than later." I may have even called my best friend, Sydney, and gushed about how dang hot and sexy and kissable and touchable he was—although I didn't kiss him or touch him.

In my mind I did though, a couple of times. I wasn't ignited by his sense of humor, intelligence, or generosity; it was good old physical attraction that sparked my engine, and the new battery helped a little too. Granted, Dre was pretty witty, obviously very

20

generous, and seemed oddly intellectual for a handyman, possible angelic handyman.

Dre Donley is the kind of good-looking that makes "hot" sound like a cliché or an understatement. He's not short, nor is he too tall. (I'm only 5'2", so everyone towers over me. It's hard for me to judge height.) Anyway, he's just normal height, whatever that means. His body, his body is sublime. Crap, if I plan to write a book someday, then I need to work on my adjectives. Alright here goes: God-like, perfect, sculpted, chiseled. No, I'm not doing him enough justice.

Ya know when you see a body builder and think "Ew, lay off the roids and protein shakes?" Well, his body is not like that—at all. Ya know when you see a nerdy type, and you think "Awww, can I carry that gallon of milk for you?" It's not like that either. Well imagine some cosmic force shoving them together, pounding them as one, creating the perfect body.

Dre's muscles were clearly defined in the thin t-shirt he had on. But in no way was I afraid his shirt was going to disappear as his biceps "Hulked" right out of them. I could just make out the curves and shapes of each muscle on his pecs and abs. Not that I was really checking him out. Whatever, I was checking him out—a lot. Even his jeans did that sexy, hanging-on-his-hips thing that makes you just want to take a quick peek at the scrumptious little "V" that starts right below his belly button, illustrating the most direct and quick route to euphoria.

But it's not his body that gives you the sense of total euphoria, it's his bluish, greenish, yellow speckle-y eyes that stare right at you, through you even, that make you just want to rip off your clothes, his clothes, the dude standing next to you's clothes—whatever you're into. And trust me, I was into Dre.

Dre's eyes are his golden ticket, but even his hair is like the backstage pass that goes with the VIP ticket. It's that light brown, dark blond "come jump me hair." It's a little longer than it should be, like he's a month or two overdue for a cut. It's got that messy, run-your-fingers-through-it look that makes you want to rip it out as you scream his name. Not that I thought about it—too much.

And his smile, even it's adorable and devilish at the same time. His grin is crooked and impish, but his teeth are million-dollar choppers, pearly white and straight as soldiers at inspection. Dre's look is polished, but messy; perfect, but flawed. Man, I really do need to work on my descriptions and adjectives if I ever do plan to write a book. Can I just say; he's as hot as all get out?

So yes, I am replaying the entire day's events in my head as I'm waiting for my ever-tardy best friend to show up for our lunch date, a lunch date that she's pretty much missed now as I take the last bite of my grilled chicken salad. (630 Weight Watchers points) Regrettably, I can't even eat a full dinner tonight since I inhaled two slices of bread, bread she would've stopped me from devouring had she been here on time.

I've been trying to take off my "college" weight since, well, college. I'd like to say I put on the infamous Freshman Fifteen, but I've always been a bit of an overachiever, so I doubled that fifteen for good measure. I'd also like to say that I drank those excessive pounds onto my body from partying too much, but I'd be lying if I did. I gained all my weight, because my mom is a crazy, neurotic freak-job. I know all 20-something girls think that about their mothers, but I'm not kidding. No exaggeration here.

When I was little, my mom was terrified that I'd follow in her foodsteps, not footsteps, actual FOODsteps, and get fat just like she did. My mom, mother extraordinaire, bamboozled me as a toddler and young girl. Every time I wanted a cookie or ice cream or cake or a brownie or anything delicious that a young child throws head-banging tantrums for, my mom gave it to me. Anything.

However, before she gave the coveted scrumptious delectable to me, without my knowledge, she dribbled Tabasco sauce or anise flavoring (that stuff that makes things taste like black licorice) on it, destroying its taste, forcing me to gag and vow profusely to never try it again. I couldn't believe how many kids loved those God-awful foods and begged for them constantly.

I spent my elementary and high school years oblivious to her shenanigans and only ate fruits, vegetables, whole grains and lean meats. You know, basically healthy, bland foods, foods that you're supposed to eat. I was trim, fit, and had a smoking little body, a body that I'd kill for now.

I went to college and one drunken night, my roommates and I got pizza and wings, foods I'd tried and loathed in the past. That night after some serious hard drinking, I fell in love with bar food. But I didn't know what true love was until I met that creamy, icy dessert. Ice cream and I have been inseparable ever since. It's amazing that I only gained 30 pounds, considering I was making up for 18 years of lost edible euphoria. What mother does that to her daughter? Mine, that's whose!

In all honesty, I wish I'd never fallen to the other side. I'd still have my tight little body, and my Weight Watchers app wouldn't be getting more use than my Facebook and Twitter apps put together. But I digress, my mom tried. She put forth an effort. In hindsight, she probably should've modeled better behaviors, taught modification, and maybe even emphasized physical activity on occasion. Instead, I'm sitting at a table in a café, alone, licking the salad dressing from my fork, computing calories, wishing I could order the key lime pie.

Finally, Sydney walks in. Heads turn; she smiles only at me. Syd notices the eye-popping stares and spinning heads, but she never lets on. That's part of the game. Play it aloof, and they'll come crawling. Tossing her hair to one side, she leans down and kisses each of my cheeks, European aristocrat-style. "Darling, you look gorg," she says, fluffing my hair.

I, by the way, do not look "gorg." I may have forfeited my typical getting ready time this morning, while I was on the phone with my mom, recapping my dinner with Dre. Therefore, my hair is frizzy, and my makeup is less than minimal, more like nonexistent. "Gorg" would definitely not describe Kathryn Howell today.

"Now Katie, have you finally accepted that tall, blonde, and beautiful wants you?" Sydney asks, beckoning our server.

Oddly, we now have a male server, who is taking over for the frumpy, middle-aged server who brought me my iced tea and salad. Strangely, two days in a row, my servers have swapped out. Yesterday, because I was a snide, jealous bitch, and today, because this dude thinks he might get somewhere with my best friend. Bless his little heart. I wish I would've gotten "Allie with an i's" phone number for him.

Sydney pauses to order wine, a cheeseburger and loaded cheese fries—quite the combo meal. (I've never once seen her eat a fruit or a vegetable, unless catsup counts as a vegetable.)

"Or are you still droning on to whomever will listen about how there's no way he could be interested in someone like you?" Sydney asks rudely.

Did I mention that Syd is a total bitch? I mean, a card-carrying, certifiable bitch. I know so many people who have those sweet, doting, thoughtful best friends, who are there for them in a second's notice. Sydney is not one of those friends. Actually, I am that friend to her—not vice versa. If you asked Sydney what the definition of a friend was, then she'd probably say someone who'd lend you her best pair of jeans and stilettos.

"Stop calling me 'Katie,' unless you want me to start referring to you as 'Ivy'," I threaten.

"Okay, fine. I just think you're acting like seventh grade 'Katie' did when Todd Lenz held hands with Kim Ritzman at the basketball game," Sydney recalls.

"Hello? This is nothing like that," I argue. "First of all, Todd was obviously not into me; he was making out with Kim by the third quarter. And Dre, well, I don't know what heck is up with him … at all."

"You let Todd get away … and right into that skank's arms. No way he could've wanted that bucked teethed loser. If you wanted him so much, you should've gone after him," she explains.

"You can't call a seventh grade girl a skank … anyway … I don't even understand how that is even relevant right now," I claim.

"Duh … sometimes, I think I should be the one with a Master's in English," she jabs, rolling her eyes.

Sydney pulled a full four semesters in college with a 1.9 GPA when she decided that college was only for "ugly people who couldn't get by on their looks." Hey, I warned you; she's a bitch.

Continuing, Syd says, "Seventh grade Katie didn't think she was good enough for Todd. And now … now … 24-year-old Kathryn doesn't think she's good enough for Dre."

The server brings Syd's wine, and pours her a glass while simultaneously staring straight down her blouse. I'm actually impressed that he didn't spill the Merlot in her lap. "I'm just saying, Hon, if we're going to have a party, can it **not** be one of your 'woe-is-me-pity-parties?' They're so lame and such a buzz kill."

"Buzz kill? That's your first sip," I counter.

"Oh that's right. I'm sorry I'm late. I had a lunch date with my director. A liquid lunch … in his office … on his desk." Sydney laughs, throwing her head back as the men in the restaurant gawk and probably adjust themselves.

"You're telling me that I sat here by myself for lunch while you were getting drunk and screwing your director … again?" I ask incredulously. When would I ever learn?

"Don't get all pissy. You need to lighten up and start getting in the game," she says. "Katie … I mean 'Kathryn,' I'm sure there are men out there, maybe this Dre guy, who want to do you too. You just have to grab the ball and slam dunk it." Did she really just say "maybe" guys want to have sex with me? She's unbelievable.

Sydney turns sideways in her chair, hiking her skirt up around her thighs, crossing one long leg over the other, revealing more leg than both of mine put together. "Watch this," she commands. Sydney leans over and feigns buckling her already-buckled high-heeled, strappy sandal. As she sits back up, she lightly trails her hand back up her leg and then finally flips her hair over her shoulder. Within five seconds, the busboy and server are at our table refilling our waters and clearing my plates. "You have to sell the merchandise. You want this Dre guy, then make him want you."

"I never said I wanted him," I add quietly, looking at my empty iced tea glass.

"You never said you didn't either," Sydney says.

Sydney and I have been friends since fifth grade. I had just moved to town, and the teacher paired us up as "bonding buddies." Sydney's job was to show me around and introduce me to other students. My job was to bail her out of trouble when she got caught on the playground explaining to four other students what the word "foreplay" meant. (Her definition back then: doing four dirty things before you had sex.)

At recess on my first day at Reynolds Elementary, Sydney told me to stay in the big climbing tires while she stood outside with her friends. I was under no circumstances allowed to exit the tire without her approval. I went into the tire, and did as I was told. Sydney was the "Queen Bee," and she was holding court outside of the tires. When she and her friends were talking, one girl said she heard the word "foreplay" on the bus and wanted to know what it was. Sydney explained what it was and that was that.

After recess, all the girls blabbed, and Sydney was called in to the office. I knew then what I had to do. I knew the importance of getting in with the "cool kids" at school. Or at least I thought it was important at the time. Truthfully, the "cool kids" are just like everyone else: afraid, shy, awkward, and dying to fit in and be accepted.

Anyway, I raised my hand and took the fall for Sydney, my soon-to-be best friend for life. My new teacher sent me to the office, where Sydney was already waiting to see the principal. I confessed that it was me who defined the dirty word. Sydney said that it was she. We fought about it in front of the balding, paunchy principal. I told him that I just wanted to fit in, so I told the dirtiest, coolest thing I knew. Syd said that I just wanted to be her and steal her growing popularity. He didn't know what to do, so he let us both off the hook and sent us back to class with a very stern, very fake warning. Our friendship was sealed.

Our friendship has faced some rugged terrain from time-to-time. In tenth grade, I shrunk her lime green cashmere sweater after I put it in the dryer on high heat for two hours. Also in tenth grade, Syd kissed the guy I was crushing on in the hallway right in front of me. (Coincidentally, the sweater incident happened a few hours after the kissing betrayal. I'll never admit that it was intentional.)

In eleventh grade, Syd told everyone at a party that I'd never seen a penis. (I hadn't.) With in three seconds flat, five penises were whipped out and flapping in the wind. I was mortified—and quickly educated.

In twelfth grade, Sydney walked in on me making out with her older brother one weekend when he was home from college. All of Syd's friends had to swear to never touch Kyle. I made the vow, but he was way too hot to care about that silly promise. (He's married and has triplets now, completely off the market.)

Then, in college, I got the grades Sydney wanted, and she got the bar maid job I applied for. (Sydney didn't even apply for it. She got the job, simply because she walked in with me when I turned in my application.) I stayed in college, graduating with Bachelor's and Master's degrees. She did not. It's been a battle of the best friends for nearly fifteen years.

But all-in-all, we've remained friends, best friends through it all. I was there, holding her when her father was diagnosed with Prostate Cancer, crying with her, tear for tear. I was even there when he went into remission. We celebrated with Tequila and nachos, shot for shot, chip for chip.

Sydney was there for me when I discovered that my father had been cheating on my mother. Syd was actually the mastermind in getting them back together and into counseling. Syd saved my parents. I owe her. Our friendship has withstood the test of time, and we're still here, bickering like enemies and loving each other like sisters. But man, sometimes she is such a witch. Like today.

"What can I do to make you see how hot you are?" Sydney asks, leaning in closer to me. Okay, maybe she isn't so bad.

"It's not that I don't think … I mean, I know I'm not butt ugly. But Syd, this guy … he's … I don't know how to explain it," I respond.

"Who does he look like?" she asks. Sydney likes when people are compared to famous people. If you can piecemeal a visual description from multiple celebrities, then she's satiated. For instance, saying something like "The girl had Sandra Bullock's hair, Megan Fox's eyes, Julia Roberts' mouth, Leighton Meester's wardrobe ..." would make Syd's day and paint the perfect picture for her. She's very visual.

"I don't know who he looks like ... like ... I don't know. Like every hot fantasy, I've ever had." I admit truthfully.

I'm stalling, because I know she's going to freak when I tell her. Sydney won't be able to handle what I've already come up with. I spent a good portion of last night thinking about it—figuring out his perfect physical "movie star" description.

"Alright, I already thought about it, because I knew you were going to ask me again. But, you can't think I'm delusional, okay? Promise?"

"Scout's honor," she says, using the wrong gesture, unless of course, the Scouts are really mad at the world these days.

"Dre looks like a triple combination, a twisted delightful perfected version of ..." I stall, knowing she's going to laugh at me and not believe me.

Syd glares at me, motioning for me to continue. "Okay ... okay ... Paul Walker." Sydney's eyes widen. "Taylor Kitsch," I add, while Sydney, licks her lips vulgarly and suggestively, "and Wilson Bethel."

"Fuck me now! Are you serious? Why didn't you do him on the hood of your car as soon as you saw him?" she squeals, a little louder than necessary. Heads whip around over to us, gawking at her profanity. We slink down and lean in a little closer.

"I know! That's what I'm saying. This is … this is … unchartered territory for me," I admit, taking out my credit card to finally pay the server who's been circling us and eyeing my check booklet.

"Syd, I've never scored this high before. But believe me, I want to get in this game." Her face lights up. She's always urging me to meet guys and hook up.

Analyzing it more, I say, "I want to win the whole dang tournament, take home the championship trophy … four years in a row. Retire the jersey and call the game."

"Not that you put any thought into it," Syd laughs, switching my card out for hers. "It's only fair; I made you eat alone." Okay, maybe she isn't the biggest bitch ever.

"Thanks," I say. "Yeah, I sure haven't thought about it at all.

- Dre -

As I get out of the shower, Rory tosses me a towel. I wrap it around me quickly, knowing what's coming.

"I don't fucking get it. I work out all the damn time and can't bulk up. You carry some old bitch's groceries, and you look bigger the next day," Rory whines.

I don't know what his deal is. Rory's ripped; he's just not huge. Neither am I. And girls always flock to him, especially older women. Rory loves cougars; that's his thing. "Hurry up too, we gotta get going."

"You need more protein, and more reps," I offer.

For the past year, Rory and I've been working out at his hotel's gym right before lunch hour. Vacationers tend to exercise in the early morning hours before they hit the beach or the Market. Some people work out late in the evening, right before dinner. Other than that, the fitness room is a ghost town. Typically, we have the room to ourselves, avoiding the questions and complaints of all the hotel guests.

"I can't do any more reps without my arms falling off. I couldn't even raise my hands to jack off yesterday," he jokes.

"Dude, too much information," I say, pulling a shirt over my head. "Your masturbatory practices are not of any interest to me. Not now. Not tomorrow. Not ever."

Changing the subject, "Alright, so what're you gonna do? Ya gonna see her again?" he questions.

"I have to. Can't get her off my mind," I confess. "I'm sure that once I fuck her, she'll be out of my system."

"Whatever you say, Bro, whatever you say," Rory says, waving me off.

"What?" I ask, raking my hands through my hair.

"Dre, you haven't as much as looked at a girl since you got to Charleston last year, and now ... now, you think fucking some chick is going to 'cure your month-long, obsessive crush?" Rory asks.

"This is more than "baby Dre" wanting to come out and play. This chick got under your skin. This is more than just your pants talking." Rory argues.

"Ro, it's not. I'm not getting serious. This is just going to be a one-time hook up and out ... pun intended ... And who're you calling 'baby Dre,' Tiny?" I jab, knowing that I just fueled a fire I'd never put out.

"Tiny? Awwww fuck no. You know what they say about black men ... that ain't no myth. Do I have to show you again?" he asks, unbuttoning his pants. "Don't make me show this Kathryn chick why white men just don't add up. She'll lose interest in you the second this thing's free."

"Okay, okay, okay … just leave that anaconda under wraps. Ain't no one safe with that thing out in the open," I joke, backing away from him.

Rory Carlson (Reginald Briar Carlson Jr.) and I have been friends since college. He was one of the only black guys in our fraternity. Thinking back on it now, they were probably trying to hit some minority-required quota. I didn't exactly pledge the frat with the highest levels of tolerance.

Man, college seemed like ages ago—not just five short years ago. Rory was the only friend I made worth keeping. As soon as he graduated with his Business and Hospitality degree, he moved back to Charleston to take over one of his dad's hotels. So my party-animal, crowd-surfing, best friend was now the general manager of one of the five-star, old-fashioned hotels in downtown Charleston.

Rory can handle the job. He exudes charm and has a mind for business and marketing. He however has the title of general manager, but he's really a glorified bellman. Rory's dad, Reginald Briar Carlson Sr., doesn't trust him to handle anything, other than luggage and dinner reservations for tourists. It's sad really, because the hotel has that air of history that tourists love, but does need the updates and innovation that Rory would bring to the table. His dad won't hear of any of it. Yes, Rory is getting a big fat paycheck, but his ego is taking a demotion.

"Wanna sandwich?" Rory asks, as we enter the hotel's large, dilapidated kitchen. The place is definitely in need of some updates and a few stainless steel appliances. Despite its age, the hotel offers the finest cuisine and guest services, complete with all the upscale amenities. I sound like a goddamn advertisement for the joint.

"Seriously, do ya have to ask?" I say, grabbing the bread from the shelf.

"I don't understand," Rory admits. "Why don't you just bring her here, wine her, dine her, and—"

"Don't finish that sentence!"

"Dude, I was just going to say 'and see where it goes.' Relax man, I'd never disrespect your woman," Rory states.

"She's not my woman," I argue again. "Plus, I don't think she's a hoity-toity kind of girl. She wouldn't fall for this shit."

"Fuck. All girls fall for this top-shelf romance. This is the shit that makes their panties disappear into thin air," Rory boasts as he spreads mustard all over both of his sandwich buns. "You bring her here, and you're in a honeymoon suite by midnight and 'getting her outta your system' by 1:00 a.m. guaranteed," Rory challenges.

"I'm not bringing her here," I finalize, adamantly. "I just want to be with her. Talk to her; just ya know, hang out," I admit. Rory raises his eyebrows at me, questioningly.

"Okay fine, and nail her after that," I relent. Rory's fists pump in triumph. He's really had a problem with my newfound chosen abstinence. Abstinent Dre is much different than the Dre he went to college with.

"Do you hear yourself?" Rory questions. "Saying shit like 'talk to her' and 'hang out.' Dre, you're kidding yourself. This ain't just about fucking some bitch and sneaking out an hour after she dozes off." Rory takes a bite of his sandwich, smearing mustard on the sides of his cheeks. Maybe his dad's right; maybe a little refinement wouldn't be such a bad idea.

"She's different. That's it. Total physical attraction. Nothing more, Man, I swear," I say, wondering whom I'm trying to convince.

"Alright buddy, nothing more, got it," Rory says, rolling his eyes. "Hurry up and eat, I've got a meeting in ten minutes with the board of trustees; whatever the fuck that means."

"Little late getting back from lunch, eh?" I ask as Kathryn gets out of her car.

"I didn't realize my stalker was keeping track of the time clock," she says, uncapping her lip-gloss.

Fuck. She is not going to put that on in front of me. Don't do it. Don't. Don't. Aww fuck, she is. The stick thing glides over her bottom lip, layering her lip in a thick, wet shine. Holy shit. I can think of quite few other things that I'd want to trail over those sexy lips.

"Hey Dre, cat got your tongue?" Kathryn asks, winking at me. Well, well, well, what do we have here? Kathryn Howell is flirting with me. This is a strange turn of events.

"No Ma'am, the cat most certainly does not have my tongue. I can do anything you'd like me to with my tongue … anything," I say, seeing her sexual innuendo, and doubling and raising anything she may add.

Fanning herself, she says, "It's getting too hot for my blood; I fold," she announces, walking to the office door. "Seriously though, what brings ya back to the Agency?" she asks coyly.

"I wanted to see if a certain literary agent wanted to have dinner tonight," I admit.

"If she's an agent, then she's probably 'booked' for the night," she says, cracking herself up. I groan at her cheesy joke. "Ba-dump-ba! I'm here all night, folks."

Kathryn Howell is adorable. She's corny, quirky, and sexy too. I can't take my eyes off of her. Smiling, Kathryn says, "Well, what's her name? I'll ask her when I get inside."

"Katie something or other. Just tell her I'll be out here tonight at 5:30," I say, starting to walk away. I stop, turn around, and add, "If she's not here by 5:45, then I'm hitting up that waitress, 'Allie with i.' I hear she's got crabs, but I'll take my chances."

Laughing, she says, "I'll let her know. Wouldn't want those all-you-can-eat-crabs spreading all over town." Kathryn waves, turns to leave, but stops, and then looks back at me to add, "Oh … and Dre, please don't call me 'Katie.' I hate it."

"Then you'll never hear me say it again," I promise her. A grin travels all the way across her face; you can even see the smile in her eyes. I thought she might be a little hard to get, but this was going smoothly—very smoothly.

Kathryn exits the Seaside Literary Agency, earlier than expected, 5:21 p.m. to be exact. She's laughing with a male co-worker as they approach me on the sidewalk. When Kathryn sees me, her face falls immediately, a frown forming on her face.

"Dre! Oh God, I totally forgot," she says, dropping her head and lowering her shoulders. "Theodore, Dre, Dre, Theodore," she nods, batting our names back and forth, introducing us as we stare at her in confusion.

"Dre, I completely forgot that Theodore was coming into town for the night. We made plans for dinner and drinks," Kathryn explains. "I'm so sorry."

I nod, not knowing what I'm supposed to say here. She forgot? No woman has ever forgotten she had plans with me before. I'm shocked. No, not shocked. I'm … I'm … shit … I'm hurt.

Realizing I need to say something, I say, "Oh yeah, no problem, some other time." I shove my hands in my damn pockets, because, well, because I have no idea what else to do.

Then Theodore offers, "Hey man, it's cool. Why don't you come with Katie and me?" Theodore, fucking Theodore, thinks he's doing me a favor, throwing me a bone? Uh, no thanks, Teddy. Fucking Theodore. What kind of goddamn name is that?

"No, no, you two have fun. I'll catch ya later, Katie. Maybe some time next week or something," I say as aloof as I can. Ha! Take that, Katie!

As soon as I say it, and I see the reaction on her face, I realize I've hurt her and wish so badly I could retract it. That's the thing about pain, you only realize how bad it is when you actually see the hurt it's caused. Man, I'm a prick. I knew I should've stayed away from her—and we haven't even really gotten started.

"Yeah sure, Dre," she says. "Some other time."

Kathryn half-heartedly waves at me, and loops her arm through the crook in his. As they walk away, I can't take my eyes off of them. Who is this guy? Just as I begin to leave, Kathryn turns back to look at me and whispers something to him, motioning for him to wait. Then, she walks back to me.

"Dre, I'm sorry that I forgot about my plans with Theodore; I really am," she says. "I forgot about my plans with him—not with you."

I shrug, not knowing what else to say. Admittedly, I'm slightly relieved that she hadn't forgotten about me. It still sucks that Kathryn's going out with him though. This is a first for me. I've never been turned down, stood up, or picked last.

"And, I told you not to call me, 'Katie.' Don't do it again … I also told you that I don't play games," Kathryn reiterates.

"I said it's no big—"

"It is a big deal. It's a big deal to me, because I wanted to see you tonight," she affirms. Kathryn is so straightforward, so honest. I'm not used to this from a woman, from anyone for that matter. "Dre, are you free tomorrow night?"

"Are you asking me out?" I ask, grinning.

"Do you need a handwritten invitation or will an oral—I mean—verbal do?" Kathryn asks, chuckling at her innuendo.

"Nah, I think I'm good—verbal or oral—it's all good. Tomorrow works," I laugh.

39

"Oh it does, does it?" she jokes, shaking her head. "Same time. Right after work."

I nod. I can't wait. Shit. I like this girl. As she starts to walk away, I lightly touch her arm and turn her back toward me. "I know I shouldn't ask this, but ... but ... fuck it ... who is he? Theodore?"

I hate showing envy, but damn it, I'm jealous. I cannot believe we haven't gone on a real date, kissed, touched, or anything, and I'm jealous of some douchebag in pastel yellow shorts and boat shoes.

Frowning, she nods her head, and says, "My ex."

"Oh that's just—"

"Stop," she says. "It's over. We're friends. Just friends. Read. My. Lips. I don't play games, Dre," she confirms.

Kathryn Howell winks at me and begins walking backward toward Teddy, not taking her eyes off of me. This woman is something else. Then, she yells, "Oh Thee-adorable, are you ready for some grub? I've got the grumbellies."

Thee-adorable? There goes that green-eyed monster yet again. I haven't even as much as brushed up against Kathryn, touched her hand, or kissed her ... her ... cheek, and already I'm as jealous as fuck over a guy, referred to as "Thee-adorable?" He's the epitome of someone I'd beat the fuck out of in high school or college—in my past. A long time ago. But seriously, the dude's wearing yellow shorts. Come on.

~ Kathryn ~

I can't believe it. I cannot even begin to believe it. I actually forgot that I had plans with Theodore Baker. My Teddy Baker. There was a time when I never thought that I'd be able to forget him, never be able to move on, and most certainly never be able to love anyone else.

Theodore and I were the perfect couple; "were" being the operative word. I met him when I went to college orientation at Georgetown University. He was one of the tour guides. Upon sight, I was smitten and convinced there was no other college—or college guy for me. I kind of have a thing for the nerdy type. A 4.0 grade point average is an aphrodisiac for me. I love a man with a mind. My friends used to gag and groan whenever I said some chemistry genius or marching band boy was hot. I always laughed it off, pretending that I was only kidding. Truth was, I have a type, a type that was social suicide to pursue.

Finally, the summer after senior year, at college orientation, I decided that high school Katie and college Katie were going to be two different people. If I wanted something, then I was going to get it. I was going to stop caring what everyone else thought, and I was going to do what I wanted to do without fear of ridicule. I remember telling Sydney that I was crushing on Theodore, and she started in on me with the teasing and eye rolling. When she realized that I was serious and that he'd really gotten to me, Syd helped me get his attention.

Truthfully, it didn't take much. Theodore wasn't really in high demand, so the competition wasn't too steep. Basically, on the second day of orientation, I wore a tight-fitting tank top, short shorts, and flip-flops. Since I hadn't found my "Freshman Thirty" yet, I was rocking that tank top. I told Theodore that I couldn't understand the online tutorial for scheduling and asked if he'd come back to the computer lab during lunch to help me. I was armed; he had no defense. Within ten minutes of being in the computer lab alone, we had plans to meet up that night. By the time I moved into my dorm room that Fall, we'd been dating for six weeks.

Theodore was my first real love (and only thus far). As far as anyone else knows, he was my first sexual experience too. As long as we can keep this under wraps, I may or may not have given my virginity to Sydney's older brother, Kyle, when I went on vacation with them during Spring Break of my senior year. I'll never admit anything; I really want to keep my breasts in tact. Sydney always told us that if any of us ever touched her brother, then she'd rip our tits off and feed them to us for breakfast. I'm all for trying new delicatessens, but I'm not too interested in consuming my own body parts. Don't judge me, Kyle Rogers was the hottest guy in a 60-mile radius. It was unfair of her to make us vow such a ridiculous thing, especially since Sydney is the very definition of a promiscuous rule-breaker.

Anyway, Theodore and I were the most balanced couple. We weren't inseparable, like most college couples. We saw each other quite regularly, but we had our own lives. I had my friends; he had his "Physics Phun." He went to all of my events with me (reluctantly). I went to all of his events with him (reluctantly). We supported each other in any endeavor we chose to embark upon. Theodore even spent the summer before his senior year in Japan for an internship. When he returned, he was more worldly, more adventurous, and just all-around more fun. My junior year (his senior year) was by far the greatest year of my life. We talked incessantly about what was going to happen after our graduations, making plans for the future. We had it all figured out.

Theodore was going to get a job as a physicist in a "big small town" or in a "small big town." I would finish my English degree and join him. We'd get an apartment, get engaged, and eventually get married, buy a house, trade in our 2-door cars for a mini van, and have six kids. It was the best laid-out plan. Perfectly devised and meticulously created.

But it wasn't. My senior year of college was the worst year of my life. Suddenly, Theodore and I couldn't agree on anything. Everything was a fight; everything was a battle. Who was coming to visit whom? Who was going to pay? Our fights even escalated into the bedroom. Who was going to be on top? Who initiated sex the last time?

We couldn't get along to save our lives—or to save our relationship. I spent the first semester crying, because I either missed him or because I was sick of fighting with him. It was awful. I knew it was over, but I couldn't accept that fate. People always do that—hold on when they should really be letting go. That's exactly what I was doing. I wasn't ready to end it, and neither was he. Until he was.

It was one of those unseasonably hot days in early November. It was beautiful. Theodore planned the most romantic date for us, a picnic in this small clearing in the woods, the same place he and I first made love. Theodore brought wine and a fluffy blanket, creating a romantic setting. It was at that moment when I realized that I really did want to spend the rest of my life with him. I wanted to make it work, needed to make it work. By God, we were going to make it work. We made love. (Incidentally, much better than that first time around years ago.) It was poetic and passionate, perfection.

Cuddling on his chest afterward, he leaned up on his arm, and stared at me, tucking my hair behind my ear. "Katie, I want you to remember this moment forever."

My breath caught, certain I knew what was coming. "I will Theodore; I promise I will," I vowed. He was right. It was a moment I'll never forget.

"You'll always have a piece of me. Always," he said, his eyes tearing up. Wiping his eyes, he shook his head, and said, "I wanted us to have one last day together, making love and trying to hold on to what we no longer have."

"What we—huh?" Confusion set in.

"I wanted to give you one last day of wonderful," he admitted. "You deserve an eternity more. But ... but ... I'm not the one to

give them to you. I don't **want** to be the one to give them to you."
I sat up, covering myself with the blanket, suddenly feeling overly exposed and vulnerable. Dropping his gaze from my face, he continued, "I'm just not into this anymore … into us."

"Theodore, are you … are we …?"

"It's over, Katie. I'm just not in love with you anymore. We have no future."

Theodore was right. We didn't have a future. After flooding my campus in my tears and eating my weight in ice cream for months, I finally pulled myself together and started getting on with my life. I finished school, stopped burying my sorrows in food, got my English degree, and moved out of state to start anew, landing a job at the Seaside Literary Agency. And finally, I stopped being "Katie" Howell, the girl everyone walked all over and felt sorry for.

Theodore and I remained amicable, because he "couldn't imagine me ever becoming someone he once knew." Theodore is always very sentimental, beautifully romantic, and aggravatingly practical. There was no reason to fight and battle our way into mutual hatred and detestation. Just because we once loved each other, didn't mean that we needed to switch gears and start to despise one another. We held special, intimate places in each other's hearts.

Sadly, people spend entirely too much time on fueling fires and burning bridges, when in reality, they should marvel at those magical moments they were able to cherish and experience. Theodore's wise, I'll give him that. As always, he was right; we have the nicest, most pleasant ex-relationship in the world.

After Dre showed up at Seaside during my lunch break, I didn't stop thinking about him all day. I wanted to spend the evening with him—getting to know him better. I mean, the man is beautiful, perfectly crafted for the visual pleasure of any woman (or man) on the planet. How could I not want to spend the evening— and possibly the night—with him? I may have a "type." I may be drawn to the intellectual, be attracted to ambition and education, but I'm not an idiot. When someone as sexy as Dre Donley enters the picture, I'm certainly going to zoom in and take the shot. It's not like I've been inundated with dates and offers since Theodore and I broke up either.

Anyway, I spent the majority of my dinner with Theodore thinking about Dre, and the way his muscles looked in his tight, gray t-shirt and the way his jeans hung loosely on his hips. It was the first time that I was ever in Theodore's presence that I was not captivated by his words, his intelligence, his … everything. However, last night, Theodore, my Teddy Baker, couldn't hold my attention. I was focused on someone, something entirely different, right up until Theodore dropped the bomb.

I was swirling my finger around the top of my wine glass, absently thinking about what it would be like to trace my finger around Dre's bellybutton. (Give me a break; it's been a while, a long, lonely while.) Theodore was rambling on about his girlfriend, Melody. Six months ago, Theodore called me and told me he'd met someone. I only felt mildly upset, and that was only because her name was "Melody." I didn't care (too much) that he'd moved on.

Actually, every time that he's mentioned her name since then in our phone calls or text messages, I giggle. Melody. If he and I didn't end up together, I wanted him to marry an "Eleanor," like from the *Chipmunks*—not of the Roosevelt variety. I was convinced that he was destined to be with an "Eleanor." All Teddies end up with Eleanors, right?

After the first time Theodore told me about Melody, I called him later that night (drunk) and said, "You should hold out for an 'Eleanor,' get married, make beautiful music together, and name her 'Melody,' it seems like the right thing to do." I stated, laughing hysterically, while Sydney shook her head in disbelief at my immature and childish behavior. Break ups are hard. I say deal with them whatever way you want, just as long as you deal with them, and then finally get over them.

Anyway, so during dinner, while I was fingering my glass, for lack of a better word, Theodore turned to me and said, "I couldn't do it; I just couldn't do it."

I nodded sympathetically at him, deciding to take a sip of my drink.

"So, what do you think?" he asked, staring intently at me.

Since I had no idea what he was talking about, I said, "If you couldn't do it, you couldn't do it."

"So you think we have a shot, then?" he asked, reaching for my hand. Panic set in as his hand covered mine.

"A shot? At what?" I asked, nearly choking on my drink.

"A future. You and me … sorry … you and I." he answered.

Apparently, Dre's chest was extremely riveting, because I missed the part in Theodore's story where he told me that he'd bought Melody a ring, booked a room at the most expensive hotel in Richmond, took her to a romantic dinner, and then couldn't, could not, get himself to propose. Why? Why couldn't he pop the question, you ask? Because it wasn't me on the other side of the table. Holy Life Twist! I did not see that coming. Dang wine. Dang Dre in a tight t-shirt.

Since Theodore is forever the intelligent man that I give him credit for being, he said that he knew he unloaded a lot on me (darn straight) and that I needed time to mull it over (his exact words). He didn't want to pressure me, so whenever I had an answer for him, then I was to give him a call. He hoped "sooner, rather than later." Theodore wanted to give us another shot, a more adult and more mature effort toward a future together.

But that was last night. Right now, I am sitting on my balcony, nearly three hours late for work, drinking my third glass of wine. I'm probably going to call off; there is no way I can concentrate on some author's fictitious story when my reality just blew whatever dumbass story that author wrote out of the water. A part of me wanted to grab and hold on to Theodore for the security he's always given me. The other part, well, the other part has already moved on. Theodore was my past. I'd finally accepted that. But the safety and security of the past was so familiar and extremely tempting.

When I woke up this morning, I immediately wanted to call Dre. I wanted to talk to him. I knew that he wasn't the one to confide in, but I wanted to know if I'd get that breathless feeling talking to him, even knowing that Theodore was waiting in the wings. Did I only want Dre, because I had nobody else? Did I only want Theodore back, because I know deep down that Dre Donley is the unattainable, mysterious heartthrob who will never be mine?

I didn't know any of the answers to the million questions that were bombarding my mind. I couldn't call Dre. I didn't know his number, nor did I know where he lived. He was a drifter of sorts, so I knew I had to wait until he drifted back to the agency tonight at 5:30 p.m. Therefore, I'm drinking and thinking—in the embarrassingly late morning hours of the day.

Just as I decide to bite the bullet and actually start getting ready for work, my cell phone rings. I don't recognize the number on caller I.D. "Hello," I say, hoping to avoid a lengthy phone conversation with my student loan bill collectors. I needed to dodge them for a few more months.

"So should I hit up 'Allie with an i,' or are we still on for tonight, Kathryn?" he asks, emphasizing my full name.

"Dre, I was just thinking about you. How'd you get my number?" I ask, genuinely curious.

"I've got your receptionist wrapped around my little finger. She's option #3," he jokes. (At least, I hope he's joking.)

"It's probably smart to keep your options open," I agree, without meaning a word I say.

"So, are you telling me that things went well with my bro, Theo, last night?" he fishes.

"Not taking the bait Buddy, you can fish all you want," I say. "But no, don't get any crabs tonight. The plan's still the same. Meet me after work."

"Oh great, so you are going to roll out of bed and go to work some time today?" he asks.

"I'm out of bed, thank you very much," I say. "I'm even dressed and showered," I lie.

"I'd almost believe you if you weren't slurring your words," he says. "You either just got up or you're already drunk … And since I doubt you're pounding back a few at 11:30 in the morning, I'm gonna go with you just woke up."

Slurring my words? Crap. I can't go to work like this. "You're right, I just woke up … and I'm still pretty tired," I lie. I can't believe I'm lying like this to him. I don't lie. "Actually, I'm gonna call off and sleep for a few more hours. Why don't you meet me at the marina at 5:30 instead?" I ask.

"No chance," he says. "You can't call the shots. You blew me off last night … for your ex. That gives you no control," he states. I start to protest, but he cuts me off and says, "Go back to sleep. I'll see you outside of your apartment at 4:00 p.m. Not a second later. Sweet dreams, Kathryn."

- Dre -

Son of a bitch! Who the fuck ripped off my dick and gave me a vagina? I didn't sign up for this shit. How did I get myself into this? I had crazy-ass, hot plans to bring one Kathryn Howell to the brink of climax over and over again, withholding her pleasure until I finally drilled into her, making her orgasm harder than she ever has in her life. God knows, douchebag Theo couldn't pull off mind-numbing pleasure like that. Could he? Nah, no way.

It was the perfect agenda for a night of hot passion and pleasure. Instead, instead, I spent the night drinking beer and throwing darts with Rory, whining about how I watched her walk away with her ex-boyfriend, arm-in-arm. Rory, of course, laughed his ass off all night, pissing me off.

So what am I doing right now? I can't even bear to admit it. I'm reading a book. A book! Rory decided to stalk Kathryn's Facebook page last night at the bar, so we could find some shit on Theodore Baker. First of all, he's a freaking physicist. I mean, what is that? He makes potions or some shit like that. What a douche. Secondly, there was actually a picture of him sitting on a Jag with some chick. What the fuck? He couldn't be cool if he stood in a fucking freezer. Look at me; I'm getting all pissed off again. Who the fuck am I?

Anyway, since Kathryn's Facebook page is public, I also saw everything she's interested in. I stayed at Rory's last night, watching shows she loves on Netflix, hoping to find something to connect with her on. I also went and got her favorite book at the library (the library!) to read it—well skim it actually. I hate competition, mostly because I've really never had to compete before. I usually just get what I want. This is all too new and strange for me.

To think, I'm doing all this work to bang and bail. That's it. One bang and one bail. Nothing more! It's absurd. I just can't pretend anymore. I want this woman. I want this woman badly. Tonight. No more Mr. Nice Guy. I'm taking what I should've gotten a month ago. Christ. This waiting game is over.

Or maybe not. Kathryn has me. It's basically whatever she wants when she wants it. I can kid myself as much as I'd like, but the truth is blinding the second she exits her apartment building.

Now, I've only ever seen Kathryn in her afternoon work clothes. Apparently, she's got a Dr. Jekyll and Mr. Hyde wardrobe thing going on, because her getup is nothing close to professional or intellectual, like you'd naturally assume a literary agent would wear. Remember when I said that the first time I saw her that she wasn't drop-dead gorgeous, but was adorably cute and quirky? Well, cute and quirky are all hung up primly and properly in her closet. Smoking hot and sexy-as-Hell have come out to play. Thank God! I sort of thought she was a little frumpy before, but now that I can see every curve and every contour of her body, I see that I was wrong, dead wrong.

I'd never even seen Kathryn's hair straightened out. She typically wears it curly, or I guess it would be called wavy. But tonight, it's poker straight, and long as shit. I didn't realize it was that long. I retract my earlier thoughts. She should cut all her hair off—if and only if—Hell decides to freeze over. Holy shit, it's fucking gorgeous.

Kathryn's got on a light purple see-through shirt with one of those tank top deals underneath. Man, I wish she'd have left that tank top in her top drawer. Her tiny silver skirt is so short that I doubt she could bend over without people slipping dollar bills into her panties. God, I want to slip things into her panties. Kathryn's dressed to kill … to kill me. Christ. At least now, I know we're on the same page. It looks like Kathryn wants me as much as I want her.

My jaw drops; she winks at me, and says, "Where to Dre?"

Shaking my head clear of all sexual thoughts, I finally respond. "Well Pebbles, dressed like that, it looks like we're off to Bedrock," I groan, raking my hands through my hair.

Kathryn shoves me and says, "What? Too much to handle, Bam-Bam?" Damn, I dig her spunk.

"Not at all. Not. At. All." I say, appraising every inch of her voluptuous and dangerous body. "I just think that the daddies and kiddies at the fair might think you're the amusement for the night."

"The what?" she asks, bewildered.

"We're going to the Ladson Fair. Ya know, rides, games, funnel cakes, the works," I say. "Ya might want to put on something a little … a little … well more." I tease. "I wouldn't want any family men leaving their kids and wives to ride the Skyline with you in that skirt."

"You're serious? You want me to go change?" she asks, looking at me shocked. Nice. Looks like I got my upper hand back. Relenting, she looks at me in defeat with an impressed look on her face. "Alright, wait right here then," she instructs and walks back toward her apartment.

"Let me know if you need any help getting those clothes off," I offer. "I'm kind of a savant at undressing people."

Turning around to look at me, she nods, and says, "Oh I know. You sure are a savant … an **idiot** savant." Then she hops up the front steps and walks back into the building.

As I'm waiting for her to come back out, I start thinking about how the score's tied for the night. This is like a personal tennis match, back and forth, back and forth, a battle to the death. So far, it's one point awarded to me for making her change; one point to her for calling me an "idiot." Sometimes, I think when it comes to her, I've definitely met my match. Then, she walks victoriously out of her building. Screw it, I'm definitely outmatched. Another point for Kathryn Howell.

"Well Pebbles, you definitely changed," I say, shaking my head at her.

Kathryn's now wearing track shorts, an old high school football t-shirt, knee socks (knee socks!), tennis shoes, and pigtails.

Frigging pigtails! I'm not talking about those sexy kinds that models in magazines wear that are low on their heads. I'm talking about those kinds that are really high on a chick's head that stick out like ears. Not only that, she's got big, white ribbons tied around them. And, she no longer has on one bit of makeup. She looks like she's 12-years-old, making me look like some creepy-ass pedophile. But here's the biggest problem: she's still goddamn irresistible. What the Hell is going on?

"What? Did I not get this right either, Dre?" she asks, feigning innocence and ignorance. There was no way in fucking Hell that Kathryn was innocent or ignorant.

"I thought you didn't play games?" I asked.

"Katniss didn't either, but when she was thrown into the arena, she had to play or die," she said, matter-of-factly.

Damn, three to one.

"So, are you really not going to tell me how it went with your ex, last night?" I ask, while we're sitting on a grassy area stuffing our faces with French fries, funnel cakes, and cheese-on-a-stick.

"Before you do though. Who knew this cheese shit tasted this good?" I'd never tried it before; she insisted we get two of them.

"I knew. Actually, everyone does. It's cheese. It's fried. Duh," she laughs, stretching her cheese from the stick and dangling it above her mouth. She glances over at me, smirks when she sees that I'm watching her every move, and then sticks her tongue out to wrangle the cheese into her mouth. Really Dre? Watching some chick you barely know eat cheese (cheese!) is turning you on?

Continuing she says, "Honestly though, growing up, I'd only tried a fried food once. Fried cauliflower. It was despicable," she grimaces. "I had my first French fry in college."

"No way, that's a lie," I argue. Laughing and shaking her head, she goes into the craziest story I've ever heard. Don't get me wrong, I know firsthand that parents do some messed up stuff, but Kathryn's mom sounded insane—and delusional if she thought there was one thing wrong with Kathryn's body.

"Unfortunately now though, I just love anything fried. Heck, I'd fry my toothpaste if I could," she adds. "But I'd have to add up the Weight Watcher points every time I brushed my teeth. Heck, after this meal, I'm probably over my points for the whole dang month.

"You're cute, Pebbles," I say, staring at her. I blurted it out before I could stop myself.

"Well thanks, that's the adjective girls just die to hear," she says, flipping her head back and forth, making her pigtails bounce around.

"I don't think you get it. You're sexy as shit, but your personality is just cute, fun … and … and refreshing." I admit.

"Refreshing. You just called me cute and refreshing. Wow. I'm like the perfect date … for the Kool-Aid man," she says.

Kathryn makes me laugh. Everything she does; everything she says. "How about I just say this then, I haven't seen a girl that I wanted to sleep with, much less talk to in over a year, and I gotta say, just this past hour with you has been … well worth the wait."

And make that three to two. Kathryn's eyes widen and her mouth clamps shut quickly. I don't know what she's thinking, but she's obviously thinking something. Her eyes narrow and then widen and then narrow again, like she's trying to figure out if she wants to say something to me.

"Theodore told me that he didn't propose to his girlfriend, because he'd rather be proposing to me," she blurts out. Then her eyes really widen at the same time she covers her mouth with her hand. Just as I'm about to respond, she says, "I have no filter. It's my biggest flaw. I say what's on my mind. I never hold back."

"That's a good thing, right?"

She continues, "No, not really. Everyone knows that girls are supposed to play it cool, be coy, and challenge men. I'm not like that."

"Kathryn, believe me, you are very challenging," I admit. "I've never worked this hard in my life to get a girl interested in me. It's usually dinner, maybe some slow dancing, and then … well, you get the idea."

"Dinner? Dancing? I get fried, processed food on a wooden stick, and you think you're working hard?" she asks.

"I am; I've never talked this much in my life. Typically, I just feed a girl a bunch of lines, and I'm golden," I admit. "With you … I … I … have to think," I whine, rubbing my head, faking pain and turmoil. "This is like a serious game of strategy and skill."

Staring at me intently, she takes a deep breath, and then says, "So, I told Theodore that for months I dreamed of the day he'd come back to me and say those exact words." I feel my shoulders fall, but I keep my eyes on her, not wanting her to see right through me, and register how disappointed every ounce of my body is.

Smiling, she says, "Then I told him that I've moved on, and although he'll always be special to me, he's my past."

I can't help the smile that is betraying me and splaying itself ridiculously across my face. She's right; she doesn't hold anything back. God, I don't want to hurt her. But I have no idea how I can possibly walk away like I should. I should finish this date, take her home, and forget I ever met her. Utterly impossible. I could never forget the honesty of her words, the sincerity of her voice, the beauty of her presence … all things I'm not used to. I'm definitely not used to spending so much time trying to get a girl interested in me. But the truth is Kathryn Howell is too wonderful to be crushed by the weight of my lies and deceit.

As much as I don't want to believe it, I like working this hard. People should have to work hard for what they want, what they get out of life. People shouldn't be handed every little thing they want on a silver platter, like it's hors d'oeuvres at a fancy country club dinner party. If you want something, then you have to go get it, not just wait until someone gives it to you. That's not the way life works.

I have no idea what to say to her; I'm not even sure that a response is necessary. She just gave me the green light, when I know damn well I should hit the brakes and come to a screeching halt.

"If you're done gorging yourself, I'm ready to ride some rides," I say, pulling her up to her feet.

"Dre, I'm not really a thrill ride kind of girl," she confesses.

"They have like five rides here. You can at least ride the merry-go-round with me," I say.

Walking up to the ticket booth, I yell, "Hey Dave, two tickets please."

Dave hands me a bunch of tickets, a lot more than two, and says, "Hey buddy, thanks for coming by earlier and—"

"No problem, anytime," I say, cutting him off.

Nothing Dave says in front of Kathryn right now will be a good thing for her to hear. I have to remind myself of the goal: Bang and Bail. I have no intentions of getting serious with a woman right now—not even Kathryn Howell. Not even Kathryn Howell. Damn, it's nuts how much I have to remind myself.

Dave nods and turns to the next customer. "Looking back and forth between Dave and me, Kathryn inquires, "What was that all about? Did you do some stuff for the Fair earlier today or something?"

"Or something," I say, handing her some tickets.

"Dre, ummm, do you know everyone around here?" Kathryn asks.

"Nobody could possibly know everyone," I say, blowing off her question. "That would be hyperbole—right? People don't like exaggeration, do they, Agent of the Literary World?"

"No, no, they definitely don't. Nobody wants to hear that he was the smartest, hottest man in the entire galaxy, and he took me to the edge a thousand times before—"

"Easy Pebbles, Bam-Bam might whip out his brontosaurus burger right here and—"

"Oh for God's sake, are you ever going to let that go? The outfit wasn't that slutty, geez. I'm sure you've seen much worse," she argues.

"First of all, not from someone like you. Secondly, I like 'Pebbles.' It's perfect for you," I admit.

"What does that even mean, Dre, 'someone like me,' huh?"

"It means, good girls, classy girls, girls worth working for, don't need to work so hard," I explain. "What you already have works; you don't need to try to make it work."

"I don't get you," Kathryn says, staring at me like I'm a math problem with no solution. "One minute you're kind and sensitive, the next minute, you're chauvinistic, vague, and arrogant."

"That's me, a man of many faces—a mystery, an anomaly, a puzzle—"

"A walking thesaurus," she laughs. "Easy there, your head might explode.

As we get in line for the carousel, I watch her as she watches the ride. Her eyes light up at an adorable little blonde girl, who's squealing each time the horse rises and falls. Kathryn's smile is infectious; I have this undeniable urge to make her smile like that— at me.

I feel a switch; I'm fighting something more than the urge to Bang and Bail. I feel like I could watch her all day long. I want to know what she thinks about, what her dreams are, what her childhood was like …

Son-of-a-bitch, I do not need this right now. There is no place in my life for feelings like this. Shit, I was doing so well, until she floated into my life, like an angel out of nowhere. Really? Am I about to bust out in tune, serenade her at the fair? God, get ahold of yourself, man.

Kathryn seriously takes forever choosing "the perfect horse." She circles the carousel four times, before deciding on a white horse with a pink mane and golden reigns. "I couldn't decide between this one and that yellow one," she points, frowning between the two. "I want to ride both of them," she says, climbing up on the white horse.

"Then we'll ride it twice," I offer, solving her dilemma. Kathryn smiles and kicks her feet back and forth. She's so tiny; her feet don't even hit the leather stirrups or the metals ones. It's the cutest thing I've ever seen.

"Let's play a game," I say. "This time, this ride, count how many times your horse goes up and down."

"Okay … but why?" she asks.

"You'll see … just wait," I instruct. "Next time, count how many times the yellow horse goes around in circles." She nods, and the ride slowly begins to move. Kathryn's horse starts easing its way up and further away from me as my horse remains in place.

Smiling, she waves, and says, "three … four …" I can't take my eyes off of her. She's beautiful, but adorable, sexy, but sophisticated, smart, but yet fun. I'm treading on very dangerous ground here, but have no intentions of trying to get out. Not one part of me wants to bail—bang yeah—bail, no. My purpose has switched; the change is in motion. Shit that was fast. All I want, all I can see is Kathryn Howell.

The ride comes to a stop, and she giggles and says, "26 times. It went up and down 26 times." Quickly, she runs to the yellow horse and jumps on.

I walk over to the yellow horse, and swing my leg up on the back of the horse, sliding down into the seat against her back. Slowly, I wrap my arms around her, trying to gauge her comfort-level. I don't want to do anything she doesn't want me to do.

I lean forward and whisper in her ear, "This is the horse I wanted."

Kathryn turns around, grins, and says, "Then hold on tight … it's going to be an incredible ride."

Every time I think I'm going to weaken her knees and make her melt, she counters with something more knee-weakening and melting. I spend the entire ride trying to control the big-guy-in-my-pants. What? Like I'm going to refer to him as "little man" or "baby Dre." Not going to happen.

With my arms around her and Kathryn sitting snugly between my legs, I feel like that adorable little blonde girl, like I'm on the greatest ride of my life. I'm pretty sure I am. Although Kathryn's petite, it's almost as if she was made to fit perfectly within my arms and legs. I can hear her counting, taking my game seriously. My thoughts are too heavy; I've got to lighten things up.

Suddenly, I jump up, standing on the back of the horse and start singing, "You spin me right round, baby, right round" as everyone stares and laughs. I'm horribly off key and loud as hell, but surprisingly not feeling the rush of embarrassment at all. This is who I want to be now.

Kathryn flips a leg around, sitting sidesaddle, and belts out, "Like a record baby ..." We continue singing, destroying Dead or Alive's hit, until the merry-go-round attendant comes over the speaker, admonishing us, instructing us to remain seated.

Once the carousel comes to a "complete and final stop," I help Kathryn down off of her yellow horse, and she says, "Redundant much? 'Complete and final stop.' That's stupid."

As we step down off the platform, I take her hand in mine, interlocking her tiny fingers with mine. Kathryn doesn't protest, but says, "Dead or Alive's got nothing on us."

"Hell no they don't! We can sing about spinning while spinning," I proclaim.

Sitting on a bench near the kiddie rides, Kathryn asks me, "So what's the game?" She pulls her knees up and tucks them under her chin. She's so small, I wonder if she'd fit in my pocket.

"Easy game, your horse went up and down 26 times; you have to tell me 26 things about yourself," I announce.

"Oohh ... I love it. Love talking about myself," she giggles, adjusting her body to face me. "Hey wait, **that's** why you sat on one of those stationary horses! No fair!"

"I can't help it if you aren't any good at this game," I say, smirking at her.

"Whatever. Fine. Number one, my favorite color is yellow," she states.

"Boring! I want good stuff. Not favorites," I complain.

"Two. I hate coffee. Three. I don't use profanity," she reveals.

"Wait? What? You don't cuss?" I ask, realizing that she must think I have the most vulgar mouth in the world.

"Not really. When it's a **must**, I do. But normally, I just try not to," she explains.

"But why?" This bit of information is crazy to me.

"I had a college professor who said that swearing breeds ignorance and lack of class. I thought about it for a while, and decided he was probably right. So, I've tried to quit," she says, shrugging her shoulders. "I do 'think cuss' though … a lot. I've got a potty brain."

"Think cuss? What the fu—what the heck does 'think cuss' even mean?" I ask, correcting my language.

"Just because I don't verbalize it, doesn't mean I don't think it," she elaborates. "Four. My middle name is Denise."

"Come on, Kathryn, give me the good stuff, not the stuff I can read on your Facebook page," I pry. "Don't be a coward."

"Me? The coward? You sat on an invalid horse," she points out.

"Touché. touché"

"Five. I've been in love once, maybe one and half times." My eyebrows rise, questioning her on the half, but she doesn't reveal anything further. "Six. I haven't had sex in over 14 months—not that I'm counting."

"Fourteen—"

Cutting me off, she continues, "Seven. My middle toes are my longest toes."

I glance down, laughing that she has those silly knee socks and tennis shoes on. I reach down, grab her foot, and take off her shoes and socks. She's right; her middle toes are her longest toes. I've never seen that before. I have to admit; it's pretty ridiculous.

Absent-mindedly, I start massaging her feet. Kathryn's eyes widen in surprise, but she makes no effort to remove her foot from my lap.

Winking at me, she says, "Eight. I have two tattoos." I eye her carefully, looking for visible ink. Not finding any, my penis hardens. Shit.

"Nine. I want to write a book someday about my parents' marriage."

A book? Now that's interesting. About her parents? That's something I could never do—nor want to do. I sit listening to her continue to pepper me with little facts and tidbits about her life. With each number, I get more and more intrigued and interested in her. I listen intently to her likes, dislikes, funny idiosyncrasies, and I cannot get enough.

"And finally, number 26 ... um ... um ... you're the hottest guy who's ever spoken to me," she confesses, looking away from me.

"That doesn't count! It's about me," I say, wiping my shoulder, feigning arrogance until she looks at me again. "That does not say one thing about you," I argue.

"Actually Dre, you're wrong. It says a lot about me," Kathryn says sadly, dropping her eyes from my gaze.

At that point, my body takes over; I have no control over my actions. Pulling Kathryn closer to me, wrapping her one foot around me, I lean over and lift her chin, forcing her to look me in the eyes. When she does, my stomach flutters. Her eyes are stunning, dark and full of mystery, but also full of worry and hope.

I take a deep breath, and say, "Then those other guys don't know what they're missing."

Kathryn smiles and closes her eyes. It's beautiful the way she looks, almost as if she's absorbing the compliment, letting it wash over her. When she opens her eyes again, I pull her close to me, and kiss her, lightly on the lips, praying for an invitation to deepen the kiss. Kathryn's mouth opens more as my tongue finds hers. Pure bliss. I could never touch her again and know that I just experienced Heaven.

Kathryn wraps her arms around my neck, and teases the hair at the nape of my neck, sending chills down my spine and fire to my groin. I begin to kiss her jawline, working my way down her neck. She gasps as my tongue flicks the flesh behind her ear.

"And now, we're done," Kathryn says, standing abruptly. "Number 27. I'm not a big fan of public displays of affection."

Kathryn bobs up and down on her toes, shaking her hands and arms back and forth. She looks like she's warming up for a race. "I gotta hand it to you, Dre, that was one pretty good kiss," she compliments. Kathryn bends over to put her shoe and sock on, and I'm awarded with an excellent view of her ass.

I stand up, wrap an arm around her waist, pulling her entire body back against mine, and whisper, "You ain't seen nothing yet."

Kathryn's breath catches. Then shoves back against me, and says, "Whatever Mick Jagger."

"Mick—" I release her immediately, stepping back in astonishment. "Mick Jagger? Did you just confuse B.T.O. with Mick Jagger?" I turn from her, pretending to be disappointed.

Realizing her mistake, she says, "Oh my God, you're right. B.T.O! How could I forget?"

"Seriously, you do something like that again, and you won't 'get no satisfaction,' Miss Howell," I threaten.

Laughing, Kathryn nods and says, "I'm terribly sorry ... I've ... I've seen the errors of my ways."

"By the way, I've been meaning to ask you. Who's Jose?" I ask.

"Jose? How do you know—"

"The day your battery died, you were leaving him a message," I remind her.

"Oh, he's a high school boy, who wants to be a writer. I've been helping him with his writing for about a year now. It's kind of fun," she explains with a glint in her eyes.

Kathryn and I start walking to the exit of the fair, when she says, "So what was the deal with counting the times the horse went around the merry-go-round? What does the six mean?"

"Oh yeah, I forgot! You get to ask me six questions," I declare. "Go easy on me."

Kathryn smiles and says, "Ooooh this game just got a lot better. Alright, what's 'Dre' short for?"

"What a waste of a question!" I respond. "It's not short for anything. My name's just Dre." I lie. "Wow that sucks for you— wasting a question like that. Next question."

"Have you ever been in love?" she asks, looking away from me as she does so.

"Seriously, I'm almost 28-years-old. What? You think I'm a loser, that nobody'd ever love someone like me?" I joke.

"No, I didn't say that. I was just checking. So, with whom?" she probes.

"Really? You're gonna waste question number three on her name?" I ask.

Waverly Harrington was my first love, but lately I've come to realize that maybe it wasn't love at all—more like convenience. I thought that since everyone in the world wanted her that she must be worth all the time, effort, and love I could muster up. I was wrong. So wrong. Unfortunately, it took three years to figure it out.

When I finally ended it, Waverly looked at me said, "You have no idea how sorry you're going to be." Waverly turned on her heels and walked out of my life. I haven't seen or heard from her since. Thank God.

"No! You're right. Hold on … Let me think. Okay, number three, what was the best day of your life?"

"Now that's a good question. Now you're thinking," I compliment. This game will go much better with questions of opinion rather than questions of factual material. "Well … truthfully … I haven't had it yet."

I eye her carefully to see if my answer is going to fly. It does. I'm impressed with her willingness and restraint to not pry into my personal life. Most girls jump at the opportunity to delve into a man's privacy. Kathryn respects my boundaries. I like that. No, I love that.

"I hope I haven't had mine either," she admits, nodding in agreement. "If so, the rest of my life is really gonna suck."

We both laugh, and she bumps into me, like we're old middle school friends. If Kathryn and I had been friends since high school, then I could pretty much guarantee that my life would have turned out differently.

"Number four. Did you grow up in Charleston?" she asks.

"Nope," I say, hoping to avoid any further questions of where I'm from.

"I knew it! You're some paranormal angel or alien put here to help people in Charleston with their groceries and broken door hinges," she says, excitedly.

"Holy crap! It was a secret. Please don't tell anyone, okay, Pebbles?" I laugh, shaking my head at how goofy and carefree she is. Kathryn Howell doesn't try to be the most beautiful, perfect woman I've ever known; she just is.

"Number five. Where do you see yourself in ten years?" she asks.

"Hmmmm … another good question … well … I really don't know. I want to be alive. Maybe married," I speculate. "But above all that stuff, I just want to be happy." I cannot believe I just said that. How could I just admit such personal thoughts and feelings to her?

"Me too, Dre, me too," Kathryn agrees. "Number six. Hmmmm … I'm gonna need some time to think about the last question. Let me think for awhile."

Kathryn and I drive back to her apartment. The car ride is quiet. She stares out the window for a long time. Breaking the silence, she says, "Can you please drop me off at my friend's house?"

"What? Why?" I ask.

"Well, remember the rules … numbers two and five from that first dinner we had?" she asks. I laugh, remembering them vividly. Kathryn put a strict rule out in the open that she was not sleeping with me.

Continuing, she says, "Well, I don't trust myself—and I don't trust you. Something tells me that if you take me to my apartment that those rules will be null and void."

"Pebbles, are you thinking about sleeping with me?" I ask, feeling every inch of my body rise up and pay attention.

"Dre, I haven't stopped thinking about it since I came out of work, and you were lounging on the hood of my car in those tattered jeans and t-shirt, Kathryn admits, bluntly.

"Let's just get that straight right now," she states. "But just because I'm thinking about it … a lot … doesn't mean that it's happening … yet."

"Yet? You said, 'yet.' Damn, I knew I should've worn those jeans tonight," I joke. I would never tell her this, but I actually have two pairs of jeans. I thought the ones I had on were the nicer ones.

"Probably should've worn them, might've made all the difference," Kathryn says, laughing.

"So you want me to take you to your friend's? What if I just promise to not touch you?" I offer.

"Right, almost believable … Anyway, I'm not worried about you, Dre. I'm worried about me jumping you as soon as we get to my apartment," she clarifies. Son-of-a-bitch, I'm going to need more than a cold shower when I get home; I'm going to need an ice bath.

"Plus, I'm going to end up over there tonight anyway. A girl doesn't go on a date like the one we just had without dissecting every word that was said, every touch of the hand, and every kiss," Kathryn explains. "Sydney and I have a lot to analyze."

"You really don't have much of a filter, do you?" I ask, chuckling at her straightforwardness.

"What's the point? Playing games doesn't get anyone anywhere," she says.

As I put the car into park, I turn to look at her. Kathryn unbuckles her seatbelt and turns toward me. I don't have to slide toward her or pull her to me, because she leans over the counsel and kisses me. Kathryn starts slowly and softly, but begins to hungrily explore my mouth with her tongue. Her scent and taste are intoxicating; I adjust in my seat, relieving some of the pressure of the growing strain against the zipper of my pants. We stay entwined in each other's arms, kissing, tasting, and savoring each other. It feels like high school, nah like middle school, making out like this, knowing it's going no further, but wishing with every fiber in my being that it will.

Finally, Kathryn releases herself from my embrace and leans back against the car door. Breathing heavily with a flush on her face, she says, "I know number six."

"What?" I ask, not following her.

"I saved question number six. I know it now," she clarifies.

"Alright, hit me," I say, hoping that it's not something I'm going to have to lie about.

"Are you going to break my heart?"

~ Kathryn ~

"Shut up! You did **not** fucking ask him that? No way!" Sydney screams.

I love that I can knock on her door at 8:00 p.m., unannounced, tell her that I'll need a ride home, and that we need to talk, and all she does is step aside and says, "I'll get the corkscrew." Better than that even, Syd looks at the half-naked guy on her couch and says, "Dude, the bestie's here; hit the road."

I tried to apologize and get a cab, but she wouldn't hear of it. She scurried the Orlando Bloom-look-alike out the door and grabbed a bottle of wine and a bag of chips, while I started recapping every single detail of my night, ending with question number six.

"Yes, I did," I admit. "I've gotta know where I stand."

"Well, what the fuck did he say?" she asks, bouncing on the couch, spilling red wine in the process. "Fuck! Hold on." Syd rubs the wine into her couch cushion with one of her throw pillows, and then flips the cushion over. "Perfect, good as new, now what'd he say?"

"Ummmm," I stall, not wanting to repeat it; hearing it the first time hurt enough already.

"Fucking tell me," she orders.

"Alright. Fine. He said, 'Fuck Kathryn, I wanna say no way, but I can't. I don't want to hurt you; I don't want to at all." I relay, remembering the agonized look on his face as he answered my sixth question. "Then he shook his head, kissed me again, and said, 'I'm gonna try like Hell not to."

"Holy shit. That's like ... raw ... honest ... and hot as fuck," she exclaims. "Why the fuck are you here and not on your knees in your apartment?"

"Sydney!" I scold, hating when she talks like that. "I don't know ... I'm kind of scared."

"Scared of what? How fucking hot he is?" she asks.

"Of getting hurt! Syd, he can crush me," I whine. "It's so different than it ever was with Theodore."

"Well no shit! Have you ever actually seen Theodore?" Sydney asks, rolling her eyes at the thought of comparing Theodore and Dre.

It was true though. I've spent a grand total of five, maybe six hours with Dre now, and I already know there's something there, something incredible. Every time any part of his body as much as brushes up against mine, I can feel it from my toes to my neck. I just want to bust out in song, singing, "I've got chills; they're multiplying."

Honestly, I used to get butterflies and goose bumps when Theodore touched me the right way or whispered in my ear with the right amount of breath and heat. But with Dre, even when he just puts his hand on the small of my back to guide me through a gate, my knees get wobbly, my breath catches and quickens, and my heart skips multiple beats.

When Dre slid behind me on the carousel, I knew for certain that I was getting in over my head, but I wasn't about to pull back on the reins and make it stop. I've reluctantly ridden roller coasters at nosebleed heights and at break-neck speeds, but yet, one kiddie carousel proved to be the most thrilling ride of my life. Everything changed the minute I felt his arms envelope me. I knew then that I would take this until the "complete and final stop."

I can't figure him out though and that's the problem. One minute, he's romantic and sensitive, and the next minute, he's crass and cocky. I'm not going to lie; I like the complexity and mystery that he brings to the table. However, he scares me, because this feels like the calm before the storm, the bliss before the heartache. But the bottom line is, nobody ever gets what she wants without going for it. I want Dre Donley. I'm going for it.

"So who was the barely dressed man on your couch?" I ask, changing the subject.

"Ahhh, just a new guy on the set. He's my co-star," she answers. "He needs work, but too much for me to handle on my own. You wanna give it a shot?" she asks.

"Are you serious? How could he need work? He's beautiful," I wonder. The man was perfect; he was no "Dre Donley," but was damn good-looking.

"He's got a two-pump peter; ain't nobody got time for that," Syd says, waving him off. "I'm supposed to see if he's got something, anything, we can work with."

Sydney Rogers dropped out of college after her sophomore year of school. Syd likes to say that she "dropped out," but that's debatable. Academic probation and her 1.9 grade point average could have a little to do with it as well. It was mind-blowing that she scored high enough on the SAT to actually attend Georgetown, but she did. I'm still not sure how that was possible. Our high school was a joke, so her grades were high enough, I guess.

But anyway, Syd is not the most academic person around. Shortly after she dropped out, she started waiting tables at a local bar in D.C. When she realized that her tips were not paying the bills, she began stripping at one of the upscale joints in D.C., a place frequented by Senators and Congressmen. It wasn't long before Sydney made a name for herself, bringing in the big bucks.

Sydney's too pretty to be a stripper, even if she was making over a grand a week in tips. She knew she should be taking her talents elsewhere. Where she took them wasn't exactly what I had in mind. Sydney quickly became Ivy Sterling, adult movie star. Ivy is in high demand, because she does it all and takes it all on. I tried repeatedly to talk her out of these decisions, but the more I pressed, the more she was certain that "acting" was the career she wanted to pursue. Kyle, her brother, came to D.C. to help me talk her out of it, but she wouldn't budge. Sydney loved the limelight, even if it only shined a dim, gray light on her.

When I got the job in Charleston at the Seaside Literary Agency, I convinced Sydney to become a "remote" actress and move to Charleston with me, so I could keep an eye on her. Whenever Syd's director needs her, she flies to location and films. Sometimes, the film crew even comes to her in Charleston, which I prefer the most. I hate that she chose this avenue, but I can't judge her for the choices she makes. I just have to be the friend she deserves and pray like crazy that she's happy and safe.

I do have to admit; she's pretty good. Sydney actually made me sit down and watch her movies, all 17 of them. It was the most uncomfortable I've ever been in my life, but she said that if I were a true friend, then I'd watch them and not look away. I'm scarred for life and may remain celibate for eternity, but at least I have the title "true friend." When she is recognized in public, Sydney's usually mortified—if I'm with her. When she's recognized without me around, Sydney disappears, and Ivy becomes the life of the party or the restaurant or the gas station, wherever she happens to be.

Overall, Syd's a pretty good actress with a killer body. If she were more ambitious, then she could've been a real model or a real actress, but she's not. I've accepted it—for the most part. I just pray that someday soon some rich mogul will snatch her up, marry her, and take her out of this lifestyle. I don't want this to be her forever; Syd deserves way more than that. Plus, I don't know how long the career of a porn star can really last.

- Dre -

"Good morning, Pebbles. I'd have brought you a coffee, but I know you don't like it," I say, leaning against the building as Kathryn gets out of her car.

"Hmmm … I've nothing clever to say," Kathryn responds, frowning. "I'm exhausted; I was up all night talking about this guy I went out with last night." My heart rate quickens, which pisses me off, because I don't want to be that guy, that whipped douchebag, that I could so easily turn into in her presence.

"Yeah, I heard you were with a pretty irresistible guy last night," I brag.

"Really? You heard that? Hmmmm … that's interesting. He was actually very resistible. I spent the evening at my girlfriend's house," she counters.

"Ouch," I say, grabbing my heart. "I guess I'll just drink this extra-sweet sweet tea myself then." I start to bring the straw to my lips.

"Man, I'd do anything for that sweet tea and caffeine," she teases, eyeing the drink in my hand.

"Anything?" I say, grinning. "Have lunch with me today, then."

"Done! Now hand over the tea," she says, greedily. I hand her the cup, but leave my hand on it. Our fingers overlap, and all of my senses kick into gear, revving up. Goddamn, I'm losing it.

"So Dre, did ya roll out of bed and sprint over here to see me this morning? I wouldn't have minded if you showered and changed," she asks, pointing out that I'm sporting the same outfit that I wore last night—and to bed.

"You could say that," I admit sheepishly. "Or you could say that I'm about to go work out with my buddy at his hotel and plan to shower and shave after the workout … to take you to lunch."

"Sounds like an excellent plan," Kathryn smiles as she turns to enter the building. "However, if I were you, I'd leave out that silly shaving part. Some girls like a little scruff. I know one in particular who does."

"*Duck Dynasty* here I come," I threaten.

"I wouldn't go that far," she says before entering the building.

After Rory and I worked out, I head over to Ariss' Oyster Oasis to help Lanette Ariss with a few odds and ends around the restaurant before it opens. When I first got to Charleston about a year ago, I stumbled into the Oasis for a drink, just as they were closing for the night. Lanette was the only "front of the house" person working since it was so near closing time. A couple that occupied the booth in the back got into a pretty heated argument. The guy started roughing up his girlfriend, and Lanette tried to break it up. The bastard pushed Lanette back, and she fell backward, hitting her head on the bar. I'd had a pretty fucking bad day already, so I welcomed the outlet for my rage and pent up anger.

Immediately, I checked on Lanette, making sure she wasn't hurt. Being in her early 60s, she was pretty shaken up, but relatively uninjured. The girlfriend was sobbing when the thug turned back on her. I punched him in the face, tackled him to the ground, pinned him easily, and called the cops. He was a total drugged-out loser.

The son-of-a-bitch had a domestic violence charge already. The police cuffed him and brought him down to the station. Lanette let the girlfriend take a few minutes to calm down. Lanette gave her a piece of pie and milk, and offered her a place to stay for the night. Probably not having anything else to do or anywhere else to go, the girlfriend accepted the offer. However, some time in the middle-of-the-night, the girlfriend snuck away, bailed her boyfriend out of jail, and accepted what I'm sure where heartfelt apologies and promises to never strike her again.

I've seen them around downtown from time-to-time, and I always have an overwhelming sense of anger to pummel the bastard and shake some sense into the girl. However, the bruises and marks on the girl remind me that people have to find their own sense of self-worth before they can better their own lives. You can't force people to see what you see and do what you want them to do.

"Dre Donley! Thank God, you're here, Sugar," Lanette rushes toward me, embracing me in a bear hug. "The kegs came in a day early, and I can't get 'em back to the cooler alone. You know these puny busboys can't carry them."

"Glad to help, Lanette," I say, smiling at her. In the past year, she's become my confidante, a go-to person when I need a little motherly advice.

"What's with that shit-eating grin, Doll? You holdin' out on me with somethin'?" she asks, eyeing me suspiciously.

"Nah, I 'd never hold out on my number one gal … But I did just want to make sure you had a table available for lunch today … out on the patio?" I question.

I hate outdoor seating, but Kathryn seems to love it. I guess I can sweat my balls off to make her happy. But really, nobody should sit outside to eat in the middle of the afternoon in South Carolina.

"Dre baby, you knows I's always gots room for you … Wait just a second. Hold on one minute. Why you checking with me first?" she asks, putting her hands on her hips and tapping her toe.

"I just wanted to make sure, that's all Lanette," I say.

"How many people gonna be at this table, Dre?"

"Two," I reply

"Rory comin' wit ya?" she asks.

"Nope, he's gotta work."

"Spill it! You ain't brought one person here before today. Now tell me what's going on," she orders.

After Lanette hears about my month-long stalking saga of Kathryn, she's as giddy as a schoolgirl, making plans for my lunch date. Lanette's more excited for my date than I am. Well, maybe. She even makes one of the bussers go steal some camellias in the gardens from some of the neighboring houses, so she can put a special bouquet on the table she's planning to reserve for us. Lanette loves flowers and greenery, but she'd never cut down any of her own.

"Dre, I just can't wait to meet her. I've been wondering about you," she admits. "All pretty boy and never bringing any young women around. It's good to know my instincts were right. You's just a picky one—not a prissy one," she says, laughing loudly.

"Lanette! You didn't really think I was gay, did you?" I ask, somewhat offended.

"I hoped not, but ya never know in this day in age. Everyone always experimentin' with something … or someone," she says, shaking her head.

Kathryn and I are laughing hysterically as we enter the Ariss' Oyster Oasis, which visibly thrills Lanette. On the way over, I attempted to woo Kathryn and make her swoon, but I inevitably made myself look like a total douchebag instead. I mentioned how I loved a certain book (the book I saw that she was raving about on Facebook). I'd picked it up at the library and tried to get through it, but it was a snooze fest.

Seriously, it's amazing what people find entertaining. I tried to "wing" it, but she caught on immediately, and asked me about what I thought about so and so and this and that. I answered like the scholar I was pretending to be. However, the events and people she mentioned weren't actually in the book. Kathryn had caught me, and instead of making it a big deal, she was actually flattered by my effort. I do however have to finish it before she'll see me again. Kathryn drives a hard bargain, which means I'm going to be doing some serious speed-reading when I get home today, because I plan to see her tonight. I'm going to need a good six hours or so of uninterrupted reading time if I plan to get through it.

"Dre baby, you didn't tell me that she's as pretty as the sunset over the marina … and oh honey, you're just a tiny little thing," Lanette oozes, staring at Kathryn. "Come on over here and give me a big old hug. Any girl that's got Dre in a trance is number one in my book." Great. Perfect. At no point did I ever claim to be in a trance.

"Lanette," I say through gritted teeth. "She's on a short lunch break," I warn, eyeing the table out on the patio.

"I know; I know, Sugar. I've got ya all set up. I even have your favorites all ready to go," Lanette says, leading us through the door to the patio. The patio is the best thing about Ariss' Oyster Oasis. Lanette and her late husband really did turn the place into an oasis, complete with beautiful gardens, ponds, and waterfalls.

Lanette and her husband wanted to buy a little restaurant on the marina or right on the beach, knowing how well waterfront businesses do. However, the real estate for such places was entirely out of their price range. So the two of them created a "waterfront" establishment on their own. The place is gorgeous, putting all those other restaurants to shame.

"Oh Mrs. Ariss, Dre told me about this place on our way over, but nothing in my wildest dreams could prepare me for this," Kathryn swooned.

"There ain't no 'Mrs. Ariss' here, young lady. You walk in here with Dre, and we're instant family. I'm 'Lanette' to you," Lanette says, beaming at Kathryn. "And thank you dear, my husband Roland, bless his soul, and I built this from the ground up."

Lanette steals Kathryn for longer than I'd have liked, showing her the many different flowers, ponds, wishing wells, and waterfalls. Kathryn doesn't seem like she's "being polite" for the sake of good manners. Kathryn is clearly impressed and smitten with the beauty and magic of the oasis, just as all customers are. It's easy to fall in love with the place and with Lanette as well. She's the mother people wish their mother could've been like.

"And this one right here," Lanette points, "is the waterfall of everlasting love and passion." What? I'd never heard her say that before. What the Hell? "Legend has it, if you kiss your lover under this waterfall, then you're guaranteed an eternity of passionate love and happiness."

"Whose legend? Yours?" I ask embarrassed.

"Of course mine," she says, matter-of-factly. "The day we finished this patio area, Roland kissed me under that waterfall. We weren't in the water, but a mist of water sprinkled on us from the side. And I'll tell you what, I loved that man passionately our entire lives together ... still do." Lanette recalls, getting misty-eyed.

Wrapping her arm around Lanette, Kathryn says, "That's the kind of magic everyone dreams about." Lanette beams at Kathryn again, and in that moment, their friendship is sealed.

Kathryn strolls over to the wishing well, retrieving a penny from her purse. Lanette pulls me aside and whispers, "Ya done good, young man." I smile, knowing full well that Lanette's seal of approval means everything to me. "I can already tell she has what you need … be honest with her, Dre."

"What?"

"About your situation," Lanette states.

"I wish I could, Lanette. I wish I could."

"Honey, I gots me feelings about things and this one … this one's a keeper." Lanette says, nodding toward Kathryn. "She's got beauty and heart. Hard things to find these days."

Feeling nervous and like I'm about to suffocate, I walk over to Kathryn, and say, "Pebbles, I'm starving. Are ya done ogling everything, so we can eat?"

Kathryn and I had an incredible lunch, too quick, but wonderful. She was reluctant to try the oysters, claiming that I was just trying to get her turned on and ready for anything. I'm not going to lie; I know that oysters are an aphrodisiac, but they're also delicious and light, exactly what you should want for lunch. The aphrodisiac part is just an added bonus.

Throughout lunch, Kathryn relayed stories to me about her middle school and high school antics with her friend, Sydney. For the first time in my life, I was interested in the storytelling of a woman without feigning intrigue just to get her in bed. Albeit, I definitely still want to get her into bed—the plan has not changed. Christ, do I.

As we walk out of the restaurant, I stop at the waterfall. I grab Kathryn's hand and urging her back to me, feeling my body heat up as hers presses against mine.

"So Pebbles, whattya think about this legend?" I ask, staring at her lips.

"I think it's a ploy to get people in the mood and feeling romantic," Kathryn admits. "I also think it's a great way get people wet." Kathryn slowly licks the corner of her upper lip.

"Get people ... w-w-w—" My voice betrays me. Son-of-a-bitch, I'm stammering. The girl's got me stammering.

Before I can collect myself and say "wet," Kathryn beats me to it and says, "Yeah wet." Then, she splashes the water from the waterfall all over me, giggling and running away as she does so. It's on.

Not caring about the spectacle, we're making of ourselves, I grab her around the waist and take her back to the waterfall. I stand her up, turn her toward me, and say, "Since you have to go back to work, I'm gonna go easy on you."

"Why? I'm not going easy on you, Dre," she admits, and splashes me again.

Then, taking me by surprise, Kathryn kisses me in front of the entire restaurant, wrapping both her arms around me as mist from the waterfall sprinkles us lightly. Getting lost in the moment, I deepen the kiss, tangling my hands in her hair. I could've stayed there all day, all week, forever. I would've too if the erupted applause from the patio patrons didn't break us from our trance. Damn, I am in a trance.

Panting and reluctantly breaking away from her lips, I put my forehead against hers and stare into her eyes. "So much for your aversion to public displays of affection."

"I wouldn't call it 'affection,' per se," she smiles, grabbing my hand and turning toward the door. "I'd say it was more an aversion to public submersion," she laughs, pointing to the waterfall.

At that moment her face gets contemplative, entirely full of thought. Her eyes light up as a genuine smile splays across her face. Nodding, Kathryn looks at me, and says, "Nah, I think I'm submerged, completely submerged, almost drowning if I'm gonna be honest."

"Can I see you tonight?" I ask, standing on the sidewalk outside Seaside.

"I'm counting on it," she admits, "as long as you're finished with *Cider House Rules*."

"Oh my God, Pebbles, it's so long. Can't you give me a week ... or two?" I beg.

"Nope. If you wanna see me tonight, then you'll have the book done," she says, shrugging her shoulders. "It's just a matter of how much you want it, Dre."

"Woman, you're killing me," I groan. "You're really gonna make me read it ... before ... before I take you out tonight?"

"Nobody said anything about going out tonight," Kathryn states. "I thought we'd stay in … maybe I could cook for you at my place." I can see the uncertainty on her face, but can also make out the hope in her eyes. She's gorgeous, the sexiest amount of confidence coupled with insecurity that I've ever seen.

"I gotta go," I say, turning abruptly from her. "I've got over 500 pages or some shit like that left. I've got to go read."

~ Kathryn ~

"It's black, mom! You said it would be fine," I yell into the phone, before hanging up on her.

Granted, it wasn't her fault. I'll call her tomorrow and send her a cookie-gram to make up for how volatilely I just treated her. How in the world did I get myself into this? I can't cook. I've never even attempted to cook anything in my life. What was I thinking? I wasn't thinking—that's what. I was still reeling with weak knees from having the most sensual tongue in the world exploring my mouth.

I got home from work and decided to make lasagna, since I knew I wouldn't see Dre until later tonight. *Cider House Rules* is a pretty tough book to get through. Anyway, I figured that I could put some noodles in a pan, throw on some cheese, and drown the thing in marinara sauce and call it a day. Wrong. It's hard. Really freaking hard. I also thought it'd be easy to whip up a fancy salad and put some garlic bread in the oven. My lettuce was brown, and the tomatoes turned to mush when I tried to slice them. Who knew lettuce could go bad within in a month? That's just stupid. People can't possibly eat a whole bag of lettuce in a month. I really should eat at home and cook more often, if this wasn't proof of that, then I didn't know what was.

The garlic bread turned out wonderfully. It was delicious. Was. After seeing my black, crunchy, lasagna, I buried my sorrows in the cheesy, buttery, deliciousness of that perfectly warm and soft garlic bread (exceeding my points value for the day). I'm now scouring my apartment for menus of delivery places that can deliver something more than just pizza and fried chicken. I'm so screwed. I don't even think I have time to run somewhere and get a fancy takeaway meal.

Of course, there's knock at my door. Of course. As I open the door, I realize that I'm still in pajama bottoms and a t-shirt. I threw them on quickly when I got home, as not to spill sauce all over my work clothes. My plan was to change and freshen up before Dre got here. I'm beginning to learn the hard way that planning doesn't necessarily guarantee how everything is going to turn out. I planned to look sexy. I planned to cook an incredible meal. I planned to knock Dre's socks off. None of that planning was panning out. Looking down, I giggle. He's in flip-flops. No socks. Finally, something that went my way.

As I start to apologize and explain, Dre says, "I'm not done with the book. I had to put it down for a bit." Dre hands me a bottle of wine and brushes past me and slumps down on my couch. He hasn't even really noticed me yet. Truly, he hasn't even glanced my way or greeted me.

Continuing he says, "I thought I knew exactly how I felt about abortion and everything. This book is totally fucking with me." He props his feet up on my coffee table and leans his head against the couch. "I mean, I keep questioning everything. And Homer ... my God ... what more does he have to endure?"

I sit down on the coffee table and take his legs into my lap. "Dre, when was the last time you read a book?"

Finally noticing me, he says, "Well ... ummm ... I'm not sure. High school?" Dre's eyeing me carefully now, taking in my spaghetti sauce-stained shirt and Spongebob pajama pants. "Uhhh ... Kathryn? I'm supposed to be here, right?"

I launch into my disastrous attempt at culinary cuisine and multiple failures, apologizing profusely at my ineptness. Laughing, he takes my face in his hands, pulls me toward him, and kisses the tip of my nose. "You are irrefutably the most adorable woman in the world." He stands up and pulls me up with him.

"So then, will you help me decide which pizza joint we order from?" I ask.

"Pizza? No way! You promised me a home-cooked meal; we're home cooking tonight, Pebbles." Dre says making a beeline for my kitchen.

"Oh Dre, thank God. I didn't know what we were going to do. So, you can cook?" I ask.

"Fuck no. Do I look like I can cook?" he questions, looking shocked. "I guess we're just gonna have to figure it out together."

Dre and I ate a culinary feast of shrimp-flavored Ramen Noodles and pretzels. He even decided to "kick it up a notch" and put slices of hot dogs in our noodles. Although it looked like the most disgusting meal ever created, it wasn't too bad. There wasn't a bite left of anything on either one of our plates, so we can therefore call it a success. Or so he claims.

"Alright woman, get this place cleaned up, while I watch *Sportscenter*," Dre says, flopping down onto my couch.

"Yeah, I'll get right on that, Your Highness, just as soon as I massage your feet and finish your sponge bath," I reply, throwing a dishtowel at him.

"Just the words 'sponge' and 'bath' coming out of your sexy little lips is enough to send me over the edge," Dre whines, shaking his head at me as he removes the towel from his head. Standing up, he takes my plate from the coffee table and says, "You grab the glasses."

"Don't you want more wine?" I ask.

"Nah, I don't really like wine," Dre admits. "I'd just rather have soda."

"Then why'd you bring it?" I ask, rinsing out the glasses."

"My buddy, Rory, sent it over with me. Said it was a surefire way to get your panties to drop," he boldly admits. I look at him, shocked that he would admit that and not care about offending me. We've definitely hit a new place of comfort with one another. And in such short time.

I pull out the waistband of my jammies and look down. "Nope, panties are still there ... haven't dropped yet," I joke, grinning at him. Dre laughs and smacks my butt. It's fun being with him, playful and sexy at the same time.

Dre and I load the dishwasher talking about my job and the few odds and ends that he does around town. "So that's it?" I ask. "You just do work for people here and there, and it's enough for you?" I know I'm prying, but he seems too smart to waste his time fixing people's chairs and swinging doors.

"I guess I haven't decided what I want to be when I grow up," Dre says, smirking at me, like a schoolboy.

"Well then, tell me about your family? About where you're from? Tell me anything … ya know … that I can make fun of you about." I say, hoping to erase the scowl forming on his brow.

"Well, are you sure? 'People only ask questions when they're ready to hear the answers.' At least, that's what I always say." Dre grins.

"Oh for God's sake. I've created a monster … Irving would be so proud that you're quoting him … good quote by the way. But seriously, dish some goods," I joke. "Tell me something good."

"Not much to tell. I didn't have much of a childhood. I turned eighteen, packed up, moved out, and haven't talked to anyone in quite a while," he admits, averting my gaze. "I grew up further north … on the east coast."

Apparently, tonight was not the night that Dre Donley was going to open up and share his innermost secrets with me. I can catch on pretty easily. I know better than to try to pry things out of a man, who's nowhere near ready to part with certain secrets. I can wait; I'll wait until he's ready.

Patience is a virtue that I was given an abundance of. Most people, men especially, are not like me. Men are private and impatient. I'm patient and an open book; I'll share all and tell all.

Dre obviously isn't an open book; he's private and reserved about intimate and personal topics. It's strange not knowing anything about the man that I plan to sleep with tonight. Yes, tonight. I can't wait one more day; he's got me all tingly and ready. Heck, when I was talking to Sydney today, she said that even **she** felt sexually frustrated and jumpy, all because of me—that's a lot coming from a porn star. My sexual tension is becoming contagious.

I can't figure it out. I made Theodore wait five months before I slept with him. I knew Kyle for almost 10 years before I had sex with him. And now, with Dre, I've basically been on three dates with him, and I'm crawling out of my skin just waiting for him to touch me, taste me, ravage me. Whatever. Anything. I'm game for anything at this point.

Once the kitchen is cleaned, Dre walks back into my living room, and says, "So, are you gonna give me a tour?"

"A tour? It's a one-bedroom, one-bathroom apartment. You've seen it all," I say, facetiously. "Unless you have to use the bathroom. It's down the hall to the right."

"Well, mathematically speaking, that would leave one other room I haven't seen," he says, grinning, pretending to count on his fingers.

"Really? That's seriously the best you've got, Donley?" I ask, rolling my eyes and shaking my head. "I'd have pegged you for better game than the old 'can I have a tour' pickup line."

93

"No really; it's the best I've got. I told ya, I've never worked this hard, Pebbles. I wasn't kidding." Dre groans.

"So what? You buy a chick a meal, and she basically seduces you, comes on to you … just like that?" I ask, snapping my fingers.

"Pretty much, yeah," he admits, as he puts his head in his hands. "This shit's crazy. If I had to do this all the time, I'd probably still be a virgin."

"Doubtful," I laugh.

"I'm serious. This shit's hard."

"So ultimately, what you're saying is that some bimbo would come up behind you … and just start rubbing the back of your neck … and running her fingers through the back of your hair?" I ask, making my way across the living room toward the couch.

Still not looking at me, he says, "Yeah, I guess."

I sit on the arm of the couch, wanting so badly to reach out and touch him. I really want the courage, the chutzpah, to initiate this. I thought I could do it. But I can't. I'm actually afraid he'll turn me down. I know it's a ridiculous notion; Dre's been one giant flashing green light since the day I met him. I just can't let go of my insecurities, no matter how hard I try to convince myself that I'm no longer pathetic Katie Howell, shy, backward, little girl. That girl still lives inside of me. She totally needs an eviction notice. I fricking hate her.

Still trying to will myself to run my fingers through his hair, I say, "So ummm, then what?"

Laughing, he turns to face me, and says, "Really? That's all **you've** got Pebbles? I thought for sure you were going to be running this show tonight."

"I wanted to," I admit. We both laugh, shaking our heads. "I chickened out. I guess my sexy courage went right in the trash with that blackened lasagna."

"Well now, we've got a problem here, then, don't we?" he asks. "We've got one douchebag whose game is so rusty that it's embarrassingly cliché. We've got a blind brunette who can't see how incredibly sexy she is. Looks like it's either not going to work out," he explains, as he inches closer to me. "Or … or … someone needs to grow a pair and make his move."

Just as he moves in to kiss me, I shove him back on the couch, and straddle his legs. Willingly, he lies back as I crawl up the length of his body until our mouths are inches apart. "You're right," I say, winking at him. "Someone needed to make her move."

I lean down and kiss him delicately, barely touching his lips, but lingering softly and as excruciatingly long as possible. I'm breathing his air; he's breathing mine. Every one of his exhales fills me as I inhale. Our eyes are locked on each other, staring intently, waiting for the next move to be made. Dre's eyes are mesmerizing with every last hint of sexual desire and want. They're saying exactly what I'm screaming.

"Thank God," he mutters, breathlessly, and in one motion, Dre flips me over. He's lying atop of me, our legs entwined around each other's. I can feel every part of his body pressed against mine. The sculpted muscles of his thighs and chest are hard against my legs and breasts. It's almost as if every inch of my body wants contact with his, begging for a connection.

Dre tangles his hands in my hair and kisses me hungrily. His mouth drowns out my moans as I allow his tongue to guide mine around. He's in control, knowing exactly what to do to make me yearn for him. Pulling back, but not breaking contact, Dre eases our tongues out of our mouths. Kissing him in the open, feeling the cool air around our mouths, with the warmth from our kiss, sends a burning heat throughout my entire body. When he sucks my tongue all the way into his mouth, my pulse quickens. I've never felt such arousal in my life.

Slowly, we separate, and Dre lightly trails his tongue along my lower lip, and whispers, "Delicious." My body ignites. I want him. I need him.

Dre kisses his way down, gliding his tongue along my jaw, working his way slowly toward my ear. Once he reaches my ear, he breathes softly against my neck, sending chills down my spine, and quietly says, "You're so beautiful, Kathryn," just as he sucks my earlobe into his mouth. I respond with a moan, wrapping my legs around his waist.

Kissing his way down my neck and over my collarbone, his hand finds the swell of my breast, while his fingers circle the hardened bud of my nipple. Dre delicately teases it through my shirt and bra.

"Oh God, Dre," I say, encouraging him to continue.

Dre rubs his hands along my side, running his fingers over my ribs, toward the bottom of my shirt. He slowly eases my shirt up, kissing my stomach as he does so. I shift my body to help him remove my t-shirt. Dre leans back on his knees, staring at me hungrily, his breathing labored.

"Found the first tattoo," he says proudly, tracing his finger over the tattoo surrounding my navel. "Ying-Yang? It's so sexy. So hot."

"How about I give you that tour now?" I ask sitting up. Dre just nods and backs up off the couch. As I stand, he pulls me against him and kisses me again. Dre returns to my ears, kissing and licking them teasingly, as I lead us back toward the bedroom.

Wrapping only his one arm around me, he sweeps his other hand under my knees, lifting me off the floor and carrying me down the hallway. "Where to, Kathryn?" Dre murmurs into my mouth.

I jerk my head to the side, indicating to the left. Dre walks into my bedroom, as his hand searches for the light switch. Pulling back from his lips, I say, "Just leave it off."

"Not gonna happen, Sweetheart," he says, still reaching for the switch. "I wanna look at you. I don't want to miss one second of this," he whispers. Dre kisses me softly, and says, "I've never seen anything more beautiful than you."

Once he turns on the light, Dre walks over to my bed and lies me down. I slide over to the middle, watching him as I do so. Dre whips his shirt off and drops it to the floor, staring at me.

Dre walks over, and I shake my head. "No?" he asks, looking hurt and bewildered.

Smiling, I say, "Your pants too."

His face lights up, and he unbuttons his jeans. They fall to the floor. God, I love boxer briefs, almost as much as I love his body. It's titillating how beautiful he is. His body is perfection, each muscle chiseled and defined. I can't wait to taste every part of his body, every groove of his muscles. Dre's messy hair looks like it's begging to be pulled and knotted in my fists. I can't wait to let my hands get lost in his overgrown locks.

Dre crawls onto the bed, sidling up next to me. Kissing my shoulder, he takes down my bra strap, trailing his tongue along my shoulder. Leaning up on his arm, he stares down at me and smiles. Then says, "I love the guy who made the front-snap bra." I giggle at his appraisal.

Then, he unhooks my bra, easing the material away from my breasts. My nipples feel like they're going to pop off my body if he doesn't greet them soon. "Fuck, you're perfect," he groans, taking one of my nipples into his mouth. I grab a handful of his hair, pressing him harder against me, urging him to increase his pressure.

Oh my, it has been entirely too long. Holy Hell, he knows what he's doing. As he licks and lightly bites my nipple, his hand explores and tweaks my other breast, sending a burning fire straight through me.

"Dre … Oh …" I whisper. "I can't believe it can feel this good. This is … God … so good."

Dre pauses and glances up at me. "Pebbles, I haven't even started yet," he says, grinning proudly.

"Don't stop," I beg as he rolls his tongue around my nipple, and his hand slips into my pajama bottoms.

"Damn woman, no underwear?" he asks, biting on my nipple. I chuckle, running my foot up his leg.

"It was Rory's wine. They must've dropped right off," I giggle.

Dre's finger slips inside of me. Slowly, he begins a soft rhythmic motion, in and out, in and out, sending shivers through my body. Leaving my breasts, his mouth finds mine, and he kisses me deeply, passionately, just as his finger finds that special sensitive spot. Dre circles his finger, around, and over, and around, and around, applying more pressure each time he touches me. My hips begin to move with the rhythm of his fingers as they glide over me.

"You're so wet," Dre whispers breathlessly into my ear.

Quickly I feel my release approaching, building and growing from deep within, I open my eyes. Dre's eyes lock with mine, just as I cry out in pleasure. His smile fades, and he kisses me again. Holding me close to him, I feel his heart pounding against mine while I try to calm my breathing. I run my finger along his chest, circling my finger around his nipples and through a tiny patch of hair.

"Wow, all that, and I'm still wearing my pajama pants. Nice work," I joke.

Dre's smiles, but his body tenses. He kisses the top of my head. "You are so sexy, ya know that, don't you?"

Grinning, I say, "Oh God, not again. I hear that like 500 times a day." I kiss his chest, darting my tongue out to tease the tip of his nipple. Dre shifts his body, moving away from me. My hand runs down along his stomach.

Dre's hand interlocks with mine, stopping it from reaching the waistband of his underwear. He pulls my hand to his lips and kisses each knuckle softly. Taking a deep breath, coupled with a small groan, he says, "Thank you so much for dinner. No woman has ever cooked—or tried to cook for me before."

"Ummm … you're welcome?" I reply, making it sound more like a question than a response.

"You're incredible … flawless really," he compliments, nodding his head, staring directly into my eyes. There's a sadness in his eyes that certainly wasn't there a half an hour ago.

"Thanks. Ummm … Dre—"

"I had fun tonight … truly. I've … I've got an early day tomorrow," he explains.

He's leaving. He's leaving now? My breath catches; I can feel the tears filling the corners of my eyes. What happened? What did I do? Or not do? I sit up, grabbing a throw pillow to cover my chest as I reach for my t-shirt. Standing, with my back toward him, I throw my shirt on, covering my body. My flawed and unattractive body. Of course, the shirt's backwards and inside out. Nothing can turn out right tonight.

"Oh yeah, sure," I say, not really knowing how to respond. Feeling like I need answers and feeling more than a little confused, I say, "Is everything okay?"

"Oh no … I mean … yeah … everything's great. Wonderful," he says, hugging me awkwardly. Just five minutes ago, I was in his arms, experiencing the greatest pleasure I've ever known. And now, now, it's awkward and uncomfortable? What just happened?

Continuing, he says, "I just didn't want this to go any further … especially since I know that I can't hold you all night … and wake up with you in my arms." It's a beautiful sentiment, romantic as heck, but I can tell beyond a shadow of doubt that Dre Donley is lying to me. Lying through his perfectly straight white teeth.

- Dre -

"You're fucking with me! Ain't no way you up and left a sexy piece of ass half naked in bed," Rory groans, starting his second set of reps on the bicep curl machine. "Dude, what the fuck?"

"I'm telling ya I don't know. I don't fucking know," I admit, wiping off my face and sitting down on the bench. "I couldn't do it. I just couldn't."

"Ya mean, 'little D' didn't wanna get up on it?" Rory asks, and loses count.

"No, he did—he really did. I just … I just couldn't imagine … ya know … putting it …"

"You couldn't fuck her, because you're not telling her the whole story," Rory states. Rory sits up and looks at me, shaking his head. "Fucking tell her dude. If she's as incredible as you say—"

"Oh she is," I confirm. "It's just … it's … it's gonna hurt her. She's gonna feel betrayed … and … and then she's gonna know I'm a total fucking asshole."

"Dammit Dre, you're not an asshole. You're just **being** an asshole," Rory says, before taking a long drink out of his water bottle. "If you're into her—just tell her the truth." Rory stretches for a bit, silently, which is a first for him.

I just can't believe I screwed up like this. I should've fucking stayed away from her. Now, I feel all guilty. And sad. Guilty and sad. And horny. Guilty, sad, and horny. Guilty, sad, horny, and fucking sad. I know I'm not going to be able to walk away, to forget that I ever met her. Why'd I have to meet her now? Now of all times? Fuck!

"Alright, hear me out, first of all, you need to admit that you have real feelings for this chick," Rory says, waiting for my response. Staring at him, I know he's right. I shrug my shoulders and reluctantly nod my head.

"Look ahead a few months, a year maybe … maybe next Christmas … think about Christmas, do you see her opening a gift you got her?"

"What the fuck? What are you, Dr. Phil?" I ask, avoiding his question.

"Fuck Dre, you need to learn your daytime TV. This is Oprah shit," he admits, admonishing me. He shoots me a look of total disgust and disappointment. "Do you? Can you see yourself with her a few months down the road? Like … is she better than Waverly?"

"First of all, your mom is better than Waverly," I joke.

"Don't ya even disrespect my momma. Ya damn right she's better than Waverly-fucking-Harrington," Rory says. "That bitch is whack." Rory shivers and says, "Just thinking about her gives me the goddamn heebie-jeebies."

Rory's right; Waverly was a mistake. A mistake that took a long time to correct. Once I got in, it was nearly impossible to get out. Rory only met Waverly a few times, but those few times were enough for him to decide that the chick was as "crazy as a crack whore on ferris wheel." (I never really understood what he meant by that.)

"So Dre, what's the answer?" Rory probes again.

"I don't fucking know," I admit. "I do know that as soon as you mentioned 'Christmas,' I got all worried about being able to find her the right gift."

"Well what do we have here? Dre Donley's thinking about the future," Rory laughs, smiling smugly.

Rory comes over and sit on the bench next to me. "Now seriously, get her to forgive your ass for last night," he plans. "Turn on the old Donley charm and get her to go out with you tonight," he says. Rory's face lights up, and he says, "Bring her here, let me do my magic ... and I'll even give you the honeymoon suite. You can make up for those pussy-balls you had last night."

"Pussy-balls? That's just fucking foul, dude, fucking foul," I cringe, shaking my head at him. What the Hell is a "pussy-ball" anyway? Dude just makes shit up.

As I sit at the hotel bar waiting for Kathryn to show, I'm still reeling with disbelief that she actually agreed to see me again tonight. After talking to Rory, I stopped by the Oasis to see

Lanette. Within 10 minutes, she had a bouquet of her prize-winning flowers and a box of her most decadent chocolate cheesecake to take with me for my groveling session. Lanette was pissed that I was so quickly able to fuck this up. In 10 minutes' time, she must've whacked me upside the head over a dozen times. Lanette went over all the important steps to "winning Kathryn back," starting with something sweet, something beautiful, a look of total regret, and a whole lot of apologetic groveling.

It took no groveling at all. Kathryn was surprised to see me, but pleased nonetheless. When she opened the door, her face lit up, and she stepped aside, inviting me in. When she saw the offerings, she kissed me lightly on the cheek, thanking me. The cheesecake and flowers were a good touch, but she saw right through it, making me promise to also thank Lanette the next time I saw her.

Kathryn and I sat on her balcony, sharing the cheesecake and talking about *Cider House Rules*. (I finished it last night—since falling asleep wasn't a probable option. It's a fucking phenomenal book.) While feasting on the cheesecake, neither of us brought up last night; I never even apologized. Kathryn didn't seem pissed or hurt. I must've misread the entire situation. The whole way there, I felt like I could shit myself from being so scared that I'd blown it with her. On the way home, I felt like—like a grinning-ass douchebag, who couldn't believe his luck.

Kathryn had a hair appointment and facial scheduled with one of her co-workers, so she said that she'd meet me at the hotel for dinner and drinks later. I waited while she finished getting ready and walked her to the spa. The place was one of Charleston's upscale spas. When we arrived, she looked at the building, frowned, and said, "Thank God Sydney buys me gift cards all the time for places like this." I laughed, knowing exactly how she felt—not that I'd ever gotten a spa gift card before. I watched her walk in and went down to the marina to help my buddy, Dale, with the incoming shrimp boats. I needed something to distract me for the remainder of the afternoon.

"Barkeep, a dirty martini, extra dirty ... with four olives," a familiar voice says on the other side of me. I turn to see Kathryn standing next to me in a long, red, skin-tight dress; her hair piled up on her head.

"You're exquisite," I say, running my hand along her bare back, stopping at the top of her ass.

The bartender hands her the martini; she giggles, and says, "Can I please have a glass of Riesling, too?" He looks at her, then at me, shrugs his shoulders and walks away, returning with her wine.

"Fourteen," he says, staring down her dress, as she pulls a twenty out of her wallet. I want to gouge out his fucking eyes and put them on the swizzle stick in her martini glass.

"I got this," I say, trying to stop her from paying the bartender.

Kathryn slips her hand under my arm. "Keep the change," she coos, scooting the twenty toward him, never taking her eyes off of me. "Don't you know, it's dangerous letting men buy you drinks in bars," she explains, smiling at me. I laugh, loving her sense of humor.

Once he's out of earshot, I ask, "What's with the martini?"

Laughing, she says, "I've just always wanted to say that. I hate martinis ... and olives. God, they're awful."

"Well, he was impressed ... really impressed. Dude was looking straight down your dress. I wanted to throw a cape over you," I confess, seething.

"I know, right? Total bonus," she said, nodding.

"Bonus?"

"Every girl wants her date's jaw to drop when he sees her, but if **another** guy is checking out the merchandise too, then you know you've got it," she explains, smile growing, eyes sparkling.

"You want me to see if I can get his number for you," I ask, sarcastically.

"Heck yeah, we can double. You and 'Allie with an i" and me and ... ummm ..." she says, pausing and thinking for a bit. Then a wicked little grin crosses her lips and she says, "Me and Olive-r."

"Olive-r! Awesome," I laugh. As she sits up on the barstool, I swivel mine, so she's directly between my legs. When she crosses her legs, the slit of her dress reveals a dangerous amount of thigh—sexy, toned, tanned thigh. I can't help but stare down at her legs, and when I do, I get hard immediately. I place my hand on her thigh, gliding my fingers over the silky skin of her upper thigh. I'm internally kicking the mother-fucking shit out of myself right now. I can't believe I left her in ... bed ... alone ... last night.

"By the way," I say, barely audible. "Olive-r can look and dream all he wants, but he isn't getting anywhere near you." Her cheeks redden, and her eyes drop. Kathryn is one of those rare gorgeous women who have no idea how truly stunning she is.

Clearing her throat and taking a deep breath, she asks, "Did you help your friend down at the docks?"

"Yeah, I'm sore as shit now too," I say. Realizing how crass I must sound to her, I say, "I mean, my body aches now."

"Dre, you don't have to watch your language around me. That's just silly," she says, shaking her head. "You don't have to change for me."

"Pebbles, I'm not trying to change for you," I admit. "I just wanna show you that I respect you … you deserve my respect."

"Well that was nice. Thank you," she says. "But truthfully, sometimes, at the right time, it's fucking hot."

Kathryn fans herself, cracking up. I laugh, grabbing her hand. I drag her close to me, kissing her softly. She wraps her arms around my neck, tickling my skin lightly. It's amazing how something so new can feel so familiar. She backs away, breathlessly, running her tongue along her top lip. "See, hot."

"Yeah, really fucking hot," I agree, taking a long drink of my beer.

Staring at her, I smile and recite, "There was a young lady named Brent/With a cunt of enormous extent/And so deep and so wide,/The acoustics inside/Were so good you could hear when you spent."

"Oh my God, seriously Dre, John Irving's going to think you're stalking him," Kathryn jokes, shaking her head at me, but smiling widely. "But … it is kind of hot, I gotta admit."

"The girl's cunt?" I ask, laughing. "Or me reciting great British literature to you."

"First of all," she says, counting on her fingers, "Ewww, don't use that C-word around me again. Bleh," she cringes and shivers.

"Secondly, it's American literature, Einstein … and third … yes, you reciting any literature … or poetry to me … is in fact very hot."

Running my hand down her arm, I lace my fingers through hers, bringing her hand to my lips. I kiss the back of her hand, staring in her gorgeous, dark bedroom eyes. "I'll never use that word again," I say. Opening her fingers, I slip her pinkie into my mouth, swirling it around my tongue. Kathryn's breath catches; her lashes flutter. Kathryn bites on the corner of her lower lip as her chest rises and falls.

"Alright … alright … you two. Get a room," comes an all-too-familiar voice from behind Kathryn. Her eyes widen and jaw drops as she sits up straighter, retracting her hands, and folding them primly in her lap.

Laughing, I start to explain, and Rory says, "Good thing it's a hotel … and oh wait … you two are already booked here for the night."

Rory walks around to put his arm around me and says, "Reginald Carlson, general manager of this here joint." Kathryn extends her hand to shake his, but Rory takes it and kisses it. Then, he pulls her into his arms and says, "Damn Dre, you're right. She's gorgeous."

"That's enough buddy, back up," I say, yanking him off of her. "Rory, Kathryn; Kathryn, Rory. He's currently in grave danger of losing his 'best friend' title though," I say through gritted teeth.

"Rory, this hotel is magnificent. I heard the food here is sensational," Kathryn compliments.

"You're still going with the dinner plan then, eh?" Rory asks. "I thought that once you saw how well my man, Dre, cleans up that you'd be high-tailing it to the honeymoon suite with a 'Privacy Please' hanger on the door until sunrise."

Laughing, Kathryn says, "Well Rory, Dre here, never told me we were spending the night. I didn't even pack my pajamas." She winks at him.

Rory turns to me and says, "Fuck man, why do you always find them first?"

"Sorry buddy," I say, pounding him on the back. "This one's taken. Eyes, hands … and … and your dirty gutter mind … off."

"Dude, ain't no way you can control what's on my mind," Rory says, shaking his head, smiling at Kathryn.

Kathryn smiles, grabs Rory's hand, and says, "Here's the deal, Rory, if Dre leaves me high and dry … well, not dry … not dry at all … again tonight, you better believe I'm coming to find you." Rory whines, banging his head on my shoulder.

Growling and locking eyes with Kathryn, I say, "Not gonna happen, mark my words. Not gonna happen, Pebbles."

"Better not," she says, sipping her wine.

After a frustratingly painful, but delicious dinner, Kathryn and I make our way to the elevator. Just as we're about to enter, Rory runs in and leans on the door. "Dre, I almost forgot. Ya got another letter from Piper," he says, handing me an envelope.

"Uhhh ... thanks," I mutter, shooting daggers at him. What a fucking dick! He knows not to mention her in front of Kathryn. Fucking asshole.

Realizing his mistake, he says, "Uhhh yeah, sure, anytime."

As the elevator door closes, I make my move, hoping to distract Kathryn from the obvious question coming my way. I turn her around, wrapping my arm around her waist, pulling her back against my body. As my hand rubs the front of her thigh, my other hand holds her against me while I kiss the back of her neck and down her bare back.

Kathryn's breath catches as she lets out a small moan. "Who's 'Piper,' Dre?" she asks, offering more of her neck to me. I love that she questions me while still urging me to continue. Nobody is getting between us tonight.

"Nobody ... just someone from my past," I reply, not at all truthfully. Piper is most definitely somebody—somebody significant.

Apparently, the answer appeases her; Kathryn turns around and kisses me deeply. I spin her, backing her up against the wall, hiking her leg up around my waist. "Oh God," she moans, feeling my erection through the thin material of her dress.

The elevator dings, indicating our arrival, I groan, separating from her. "You can just call me, 'Dre,' tonight," I joke. I grab her hand and lead her out of the elevator. I fumble with the keycard, dropping it. My attempts at cool, collected, and suave are failing miserably.

"If you're so 'Godlike,' then just open the door, for Dre's sake," Kathryn kids, easing my nerves. Dre's sake? That's pretty funny. I've got to give her that one. I'm not sure why I'm so fucking nervous. What the fuck? It's not like I haven't done this before—a couple hundred times. There's just something about being with her that has my head all in jumbles, and my hands in fumbles. And I'm turning into Dr. Fucking Seuss.

Finally, we walk into our room, and Rory's got it all sexed out. There are probably five-dozen roses all around the room, a bottle of champagne chilling in a bedside bucket, and chocolate covered strawberries and a box of condoms on a silver platter on the nightstand.

"Fucking Rory! Kathryn, I'm sorry. I didn't mean—"

"Sorry for what? Looks like it's all covered here," she says, walking over to me. "Listen Dre, I don't know what happened last night, but I've … I've … been on fire since you left," she admits. She begins unbuttoning my shirt, and says, "If you're ready to finish what we started last night, then I'm game."

She stops midway down my shirt, leaving the rest of the buttons fastened, and holds both of my hands. "But if you want to drink champagne, eat strawberries, and just hang out, then I'm game for that, too."

I'm speechless. Kathryn thinks I don't want her. She thinks that I'm not into this. Holy fuck, those thoughts have got to end now, right fucking now. I grab her forcefully around the waist, yanking her against my body. Her eyes widen, and her breath catches.

"Listen to me, last night was … was … a fluke. Nobody's leaving this room tonight. This room, that bed, my body … everything in here tonight will be for your pleasure … tonight you're going to learn the real meaning of pleasure," I state, taking back my authority, knowing exactly what I'm about to do to her.

I lean in to kiss her, purposefully missing her lips and connecting with her neck. I suck the skin of her neck into my mouth, using just enough pressure for her to feel it, to ignite her inside, but not enough to leave a mark on her gorgeous, flawless skin. I continue to kiss her neck, working my way around to the back of her. When I'm completely behind her, I kiss and bite her shoulders, easing the red straps down off of her shoulders and arms, finding her second tattoo, a small four-leaf clover on her right shoulder blade. Talk about getting lucky.

The dress slides down her body, pooling around her feet. There is nothing sexier than a braless, confident woman. I continue kissing her bare back, wrapping my arm around the front of her to cup her breast in my hand. Her nipple is hard against my palm. I watch as tiny goose bumps cover her arms; I trail a finger along her arms, knowing the effect it's having on her.

I back away, "Turn around, Kathryn … slowly. I want to see you." Kathryn spins agonizingly slow, wearing nothing but a black lace thong and black heels. "Stunning."

Without any prompt from me, Kathryn steps over the dress, and shimmies her underwear down, standing naked and self-assured in front me. She walks over to me and finishes unfastening the buttons on my shirt. With my shirt open, she slides the material off of me. I step back and take my t-shirt off immediately, dying to feel her bare breasts against my skin.

As I reach for her, she holds her hand out, stopping me from coming any closer. "Not just my pleasure tonight, Dre," she says, running her hand down my chest to the waistband of my pants. "Our pleasure."

I nod, knowing that there's no going back. Kathryn Howell has possessed me. She's so much a part of me that I don't know how I've even survived this long without her. I spent the last month worrying that I was going to break her, destroy her. But, I now know how wrong I was. Only one woman in my entire life has ever had the power to crush me, and she's standing right in front me.

"Kathryn, there's something that I need to tell—"

"Not now Dre," she says, covering my lips. "Confessions later. Pleasure now."

Kathryn runs her nails up my chest, sending the heat to my groin. She bites on my lower lip, guiding me back toward the bed. Just as I'm about to lay her back on the bed, she shifts, pushing me down on the bed. I sit with Kathryn standing between my legs; we're nearly eye-to-eye, chest-to-chest. I wrap my arm around her while my other hand finds her breast. I roll her nipple between my fingers, tugging on it while it hardens in my hand.

I'm staring at her as she's watching me touch her. Kathryn hasn't taken her eyes from my hands. She licks her lips and chews lightly on her bottom lip. She likes watching me. "Do you like that?" I ask, wanting to hear her voice.

"Don't stop, Dre. It feels so good," her voice is raspy, full of excitement.

"I wouldn't dream of it," I respond, pushing her breasts together, tonguing and tasting her nipples alternately. Kathryn wraps her hands in my hair, pressing me against her.

Abruptly, she pushes me, forcing me to lie back. As she crawls up the length of my body, she pauses at the button of my pants before undoing them. I help her get them off, taking my underwear right along with them. Kathryn stares at my face and looks down at my naked body, grinning wickedly. I can't imagine anyone being more beautiful, more confident, and more tempting than she is right now.

Kathryn kisses my chest, circling my nipple with her tongue, working her way down my body. She pauses at my bellybutton, teasing me with her tongue and fingernails. I'm fighting the urge to flip her over, when she continues to go further south. When she skips my erection, kissing and licking my thighs, I punch the bed, groaning in frustration and want. Kathryn massages my legs, pushing them further apart. My body is on fire; I don't know how much longer I'm going to be able to stand this incredible torture. Kathryn sits up on her knees and grins as she reaches for the champagne.

"Rory's gonna regret giving us this," she says, smiling mischievously. Kathryn shakes the bottle and pops the top, showering the bed and me in champagne and bubbles. "Awww … what a mess!" she says, displaying the most pouty-mouth I've ever seen.

"I guess I should start cleaning it up," she says, leaning over my body. Pausing, she sits back up and says, "But before I do ..." Kathryn doesn't finish her statement. She reaches up and pulls a pin from her hair as it all cascades down around her.

"Fuck," I mutter, gripping the sheet. Kathryn looks magnificent astride me with her hair falling all around her, wearing nothing but black high-heels and a sexy smile. I want to impale her, be deep inside her, and wrap my hands in that hair, pulling it back hard as she screams my name.

As Kathryn licks the champagne from every inch of my body, I keep trying to reach for her, to touch her, to kiss her, but she just bats my hand away when I do. Finally, Kathryn's lips engulf me, taking me in to the back of her throat.

"Yeah, that's it," I say, hating the way it sounds. I want so much to be able to tell her how incredible her mouth feels on me. I want to explain it in every detail. Kathryn needs to know that what she's doing is beyond any gift, any winning ballgame, and beyond anything I've ever experienced. It's not just the act of what she's doing; it's that it's Kathryn who's doing it. I'm captivated by her beauty, entranced by her intelligence, and mesmerized by her confidence. And goddamn do I need to fuck the Hell out of her.

When I know that I can't hold out any longer, I tangle my hands in her long hair, easing her head back. "Hold on, Pebbles," I say, running my fingers through her hair. Looking back up at me with a gleam in her eye, she trails her tongue up my body, licking my chest and neck.

Kathryn whispers in my ear, "You taste so good, Dre."

Fuck. I can't take much more; I'm about to explode. I roll her over, pinning her beneath me. "I haven't had my dessert," I say, kissing her neck and working my way down her body. The curves of her body are tantalizing; I want to touch, taste, and tickle every peak and valley of her entire body. Kathryn's eyes are glued to me, watching my every move. "You like watching, don't you Kathryn?" I ask, praying that I'm not pushing her too far.

"God yes, Dre. It's … you're … you're so sexy. It's so hot," she says, through shallow breaths.

"Then keep watching, Darling. It's all about your pleasure now," I say, wanting to satisfy her more than she's ever been before. Kathryn nods, touching her breasts as she does so.

"Mmmm," I groan, dipping my tongue into her bellybutton. Kathryn's legs open further, inviting me in. I'm craving her taste, her scent, and her surrender. I want to bring her to the brink and watch in awe as she soars over the edge.

As my tongue finds her innermost sexuality, I glance up, staring into her eyes. Her chest is heaving, her breathing erratic. She's still touching and tugging on her nipples, not taking her eyes off of me. As I continue to taste and lick her, her eyelids begin to flutter, while her hips begin to circle.

Kathryn's getting close to release; so I continue to bathe her in my tongue, using my fingers to enter her and leave her. I go faster, applying more pressure, slowing down and easing off, continuing a steady rhythm of denial and acquiescence. Suddenly, Kathryn's legs tighten; her eyes close. She's got a handful of my hair and a handful of the pillow as her toes curl along my back.

"Oooh Dre, yes, Dre!" she calls, panting heavily. Kathryn's body trembles as she catches her breath and sighs.

Looking down at me, she casts a mysterious smile on me, and says, "Wow, That was Won-DRE-ful."

Fuck yeah! Take that "Thee-adorable!" I'm 'Won-DRE-ful," and don't you ever forget it, I think to myself.

Joining her on the pillow, I say, "That was the sexiest thing I've ever seen."

"Kiss me," she says. "I need to taste you, taste us."

Us? Holy shit, she's so fucking hot. I devour her mouth, kissing her hungrily. We moan against each other's tongues. "I want you … God, Kathryn, I want you so bad," I say, her tongue circling mine, drawing it further into my mouth.

"Now, Dre," she says. "Please, now." I reach over, grab a condom, and try to rip it open. It flies out of my hand. "Fuck."

"Easy boy," she says. "I got this."

Taking another condom from the box, she opens it deftly, removing it carefully from the wrapper. "Lie back," she commands, coming over to me. I do as I'm told. "Hands behind your head."

I relax, putting my hands behind my head, smirking at her as I do so. Kathryn strokes me a few times; I groan in the process. Easily and seductively, she slides the condom down over me.

"Ready?" she questions, glancing down at my erection and back into my eyes. I nod, and she straddles me, easing herself down onto me. I watch in awe as her eyes widen and slowly close. Kathryn's tongue trails along her upper lip as she begins to rock slowly on me. I unclasp my hands from behind my head and slide them up her smooth thigh.

"Damn, you're amazing," I say, beginning to rock with her. Eyes closed, she smiles, increasing her speed, sliding up and down, up and down. I reach up with one hand and caress her breast, taking her nipple between my fingers.

"Oh yeah, harder Dre," she begs. I buck my hips faster and squeeze her nipple. "God … yeah … please," she moans, rolling her hips around. Kathryn is completely in control. I watch as she gets lost in the moment. Her hips are increasing their motion; her moans are breathy. Another release is approaching. Fuck yeah! Round two, Darling.

I grip her hips, moving her up and down, faster and harder. Kathryn calls my name when she finally lets go, falling limply onto my chest. I run my fingers along the length of her back, pushing her hair aside to unveil the satisfied smile on her face.

I kiss the top of her head. Kathryn looks up at me, kissing me lightly. She rolls off to the side, pulling me on top of her. "Your turn," she says, easing her body under mine. Kissing her breast and rolling it around my tongue, I slide back into her. Kathryn wraps her legs around my waist, urging me further into her. I thrust against her; she meets me, pressing against me. I quicken my pace, deeper, harder, faster. I'm climbing, reaching, almost … almost. I call her name softly as I let go, knowing the importance of this encounter. I know with every fiber of my being that I will never have sex with another woman again. I just have to tell Kathryn the truth first.

~ Kathryn ~

Best sex of my entire life. The very best freaking sex I've ever had. And just because I've only slept with two people, now three, doesn't mean that I don't know what I'm talking about. I slept with Kyle twice. Oh yeah, I only mentioned that one time on Spring Break. There may have been a drunken Fourth of July rendez-vous in the bathroom of a bar. I'll neither confirm, nor deny. And, I guess there was that other time in the front seat of his car when we volunteered to pick up pizza. But again, I want to keep my breasts, so Sydney can never find out that I slept with her brother—many, many times—the entire summer before I met Theodore at orientation at Georgetown. I still stand by the fact that Kyle's hot; Sydney wasn't being a true friend asking me to stay away from him in the first place. I'd never do something like that to her—if I had a brother.

Anyway, Theodore and I had a healthy and "sexperimental" relationship, but nothing, absolutely nothing, could ever compare to what I experienced last night in this hotel with Dre "God" ley, I mean Donley. I didn't know it could be like that. I wasn't just being complimentary when I called him "won-DRE-ful." It was extraordinary. I tend to be open to anything, but am usually pretty timid when it comes to initiating and asking for what I want. With Dre, I felt myself letting go, ignoring my inhibitions and reveling in the pleasure. I just hope he didn't think I was too timid, too reserved.

Apparently sexual attraction and desire play much bigger roles in one's overall satisfaction than I actually knew. I'd never felt like that before. I was so turned on; I wanted him so badly that I truly felt like I was going explode, that my skin was just going to burst into a million pieces right off my sexually frustrated and overly turned on body. It was the craziest thing I've ever felt. There were times when I thought I might reach climax without him even touching those certain particular parts of my body.

And then this morning, Holy St. Sebastian, he woke up early for two more rounds of sexcapades and fantasy-fulfillment. Watching him eat strawberries off of my stomach and breasts was thrilling, but having him wash the melted chocolate off my body in the shower was erotic and sensual. This man knows what he's doing.

However, I need to keep my focus on track, and not lose sight of the facts. It's a serious red flag that (1.) Dre will not open up to me about anything. (2.) He avoids all personal questions that I ask him. (3.) I have no idea where he lives, where he's from, what he actually does for a living, or even his phone number. (4.) Some girl named "Piper" sends him big yellow envelopes.

I'm not dumb; I recognize these giant, flowing, soaring red flags. But, I'm also smart enough to take this slow and possibly get these answers gradually. If I start harping on the questions, prying into Dre's life, he's going to pull back. I definitely don't want that. I'm not saying that I want to spend the rest of my life with this guy, especially not knowing a thing about him. I'm just saying that my attraction to him, my piqued curiosity, and my overall sense of intrigue are all heightened enough to stay in this until I get the answers I need—even if I may not necessarily want them.

Here's the thing: Dre's into me, or we wouldn't be in his best friend's hotel room. I'd be an utter psychopath if I weren't into him. I know this isn't an ideal situation, seeing as how I'm being blinded by the red flags flying in my face every time I open my eyes. I don't look at Dre and think that he's the future father of my children or the man who's going to be sitting next to me when we're 80-years-old, rocking in our rocking chairs on the front porch. I'm not naïve.

Right now, I'm looking at him as the man who's going to take me to paramount levels of ecstasy for the time being, entertaining me all winter long if I can help it. Now don't get me wrong, I could easily fall for Dre Donley, easy-peasy. Like, I'm reminding myself at every interval, every turn that Dre isn't in this for the long haul. This is just his way of having some fun. I get that.

Like I said last night, "I'm game." I could use a little entertainment and sexual gratification. Who couldn't? So sue me if you think I'm being a whore or whatever. Sometimes a girl needs a little something-something. And I have definitely been "jonesing" for a lot of something-something. I'm just going to keep reminding myself of what this is: hot sex for the sake of hot sex. Nothing more. Nothing less. I get that.

There are so many girls, even extremely intelligent girls, who just don't get it. These clueless girls seem to think that if a guy takes them home, then those same guys are thinking wedding bells in the morning as they search under their beds for misplaced thongs. Just not the case. Sydney used to be one of those girls. She unfortunately learned the hard way. It took her so long to learn the rules, that she'd already formed a thick exterior of male-bashing hatred—trusting none of them—screwing many of them.

If a guy is into a girl, then he's into her, full speed ahead. It's not like the movies; he's not going to "play it cool" or "play hard to get." Guys see what they want, and if they really want it, they make sure they get it. Girls need to learn how to read—read the situation. If a guy sleeps with a girl and he's looking for something more, he ensures there's something more. He doesn't just wait around until the next time he's free or the next time he runs into her. A guy makes the time to see her or plans to see her. It's not rocket-science.

Syd used to hook up with guys for a night of fun-filled mediocre passion. Those same guys would promise to call her later. And guess what? Those calls never came. She'd sit around and think that he was going to "come to his senses" or "realize what he's missing." Men do not miss what they never really wanted in the first place. I better repeat that one: Men do not miss what they never really wanted in the first place. (With Dre in the picture, it'll do me some good to keep reminding myself.)

Wise up, ladies. Make him want you. If he doesn't want you, enjoy what you got to experience and move on. Move on. Don't just hang around for the sake of "what if" or "might be." People can't just keep a box of "what ifs" and "might bes" piling up in their closets, clouding and crippling their lives. Screw "what if" and "might be." There's no time for all that nonsense. People need to live their lives, while there's still a life worth living. And right now, I'm going to live a little—with Dre Donley in my bed.

For some odd reason, Dre's drawn to me; I think he likes my no-crap attitude. I'm sure we'll go out a few more times, and then that'll be it. I knew going into this that I needed to leave my heart in my apartment; otherwise the fragile little thing was going to be severed and demolished.

Sydney thinks there's something "real" going on here, because Dre brought me a cheesecake and stolen flowers. But like I said, Sydney isn't really the one to ask. Dre had typical "panty-dropping" ammunition with him, things I don't usually fall for. I can't even say that I "fell for" them, because I wanted to sleep with him probably a lot more than he wanted to be with me.

However, there is one little prop or detail that still has me second-guessing his motives. The book. I can't believe he'd read an entire book for me. That one has me stumped. Why would he do that? Seems like a lot of work just to get laid. I'm still dissecting that one. I'm going to ruminate on that one for a bit before I decide what I think about it.

"What in the world are you thinking about?" Dre asks, standing in front of me. He's been searching for my left shoe for over 10 minutes. I'm not exactly sure how I could've lost a shoe that I wore pretty much the entire night in a tiny hotel room. "I've been watching you for a few minutes. Are you having a conversation with yourself?"

I can feel my face redden. I have a tendency to have full-out conversations in my head, but they show up quite visibly on my face. The more intense the thoughts are the more animated my face becomes. My family and good friends have made fun of me about it for ages. It's always mortifying when I launch into a cranial tirade in public with strangers gawking at the crazy woman with the dramatic facial expressions. I don't go as far as actually "talking" to myself. Although, according to Syd, talking to myself would look and seem a lot less bizarre.

"Just thinking about where my shoe could be," I flat out lie to him, wishing I could just tell him everything I was thinking. Honestly, I just really, **really**, want another round of bedtime fun with him again. So, I'm going to hold back for the time being right now.

"I found it," he gloats, smirking.

"Where?" I question, knowing that we turned this entire place upside down looking for it.

"Hanging off the balcony," he answers, wiggling his eyebrows at me.

"The balcony. Right. That was a good time," I laugh, grabbing my shoe from him.

After our first round of fun, we heard laughter outside, so Dre went out on the balcony to see what was going on. A few people were having fun in the pool below. Clothes were flying; alcohol was flowing. Dre called me out to enjoy the view. Grabbing a blanket and wrapping myself in it, but still only wearing my heels, I walked out onto the balcony. Things in the pool got pretty heated up—as we watched in awe and arousal. Once security stopped what was going on down in the pool, nobody could stop what started on the chaise lounge chair on the honeymoon suite's balcony. Good times. Great times. Indescribable, losing-my-shoe times.

"Wanna have lunch?" Dre asks, staring at me expectantly.

"With you? Like you and I—together?" I ask stupidly.

"Well, maybe, but if you'd rather sit at separate tables, that'd be cool too," Dre jokes, shaking his head at me. "Of course with me."

"I'm sorry. I'm supposed to meet Syd for lunch today," I say, eyeing him suspiciously.

I can't do it. I can't be carefree and "C'est la vie." It's not me. I need answers. Taking a deep breath, "Alright, what's going on?" I blurt. "Shouldn't you be trying to duck out of here, getting away as soon as possible? What gives, Dre?"

Walking toward me, he says, "When are ya gonna get this? I'm interested Kathryn—very interested. If I leave right now, then I won't be able to talk to you ... to look at you ... to do this—"

Dre grabs me and kisses me, taking my breath away. He runs his hand down my back, pulling me harder against him. The kiss deepens as his tongue dances with mine hungrily.

Feeling the tingle and want on my lips after he backs away, I trace my finger along my lip, grinning. "Rory really should stash some extra toothbrushes in this place."

Laughing, Dre comes closer again and says, "Oh really? Really Pebbles? Take that," and breathes into my face. Oddly his breath isn't bad at all—not minty and fresh—but manly and hot. I push him away from me. Dre grabs my wrists in his hands and wraps his arms, along with my own, around me, trapping me against his body.

"And take this," he says, kissing my neck, nibbling on my ear, and heating me up all over again.

"If you're offering," I whisper, "then, I'm taking."

Lying in his arms, I say, "Aren't they going to need this room at some point?"

"Eventually," he jokes, "whenever we're through with it."

"If—we're ever through with it," I correct.

"Precisely," Dre grins at me, absently tracing circles on my back with his fingers.

"Seriously though, I'm supposed to meet Sydney for lunch in an hour. I gotta get home, do something with this just-showered, slept-on, and screwed hair, and change clothes, before I meet her." I say, getting up and looking for my clothes again.

"I wanna meet the infamous Syd," Dre admits. Holy crap! He wants to meet Sydney? I didn't see that coming. "Why don't we just tell her to meet us at the beach. Rory'll have the kitchen make us some sandwiches. We can eat on the beach," he plans. "Didn't you say she was hot?"

"Very. Remember? Blake Lively?" I say, wondering what he's up to. "I'm not into a three-way with Syd. Been there, done that. She's totally selfish—won't do that again." Dre's eyes widen, and his jaw drops. "Kidding Dre, totally kidding. About the three-way. Syd is selfish though. I'd get completely left out."

"Fuck that—I mean, 'screw that,' I be saying 'Sydney who' if you were there," he jokes.

"Try saying that **after** you see her," I explain. "But for real though, why do you care if she's hot?"

"If Rory finds out we're meeting your friend, then he's gonna want to come," Dre states, shrugging his shoulders.

"Fine by me, you set up your end; I'll get ready and handle Syd," I relent. "She's an eater, better make her two sandwiches."

After convincing me to tell Sydney to just meet us at the beach, Dre and I shower again and get ready in the bathroom together. Dre ran down to the front desk, requesting a crap load of toiletries. Rory hooked him up with more necessities than I'd ever need in a hotel room.

Looking presentable enough for a double-date afternoon lunch, I say, "Okay Dre, I do have to go home and change. I can't possibly wear that red dress to a picnic on the beach." He frowns, looking pensively at me. "Unless you think Rory's got a stash of women's clothes in his closet," I joke.

"Actually, yeah, come on," he says, his eyes lighting up with excitement and mischief.

"You will?" he asks, staring at me incredulously.

"Heck yeah!" I announce emphatically. "It's like playing dress up in my grandma's attic, but with cooler and more interesting finds. Like what the heck would someone bring this on vacation for?" I ask, holding up a life-sized cardboard cut out of Calvin and Hobbes from the comic strip.

"Weird sexual fetish," he figures, shrugging.

"Can you get your mind off of sex for one minute, while I look for something to wear?" I ask.

"Not with you parading around in a top hat and men's knickers, I can't," he says, laughing. "Now that's a strange fetish. Seriously though, we can go to your apartment … or shopping … or something."

"Nope, you brought it up. We're doing this—so start looking," I command.

Dre and I are rummaging through the lost and found at the hotel, searching for fun things to wear to lunch. Rory just guffawed and showed us the way when we asked about it. I think what's the most fun about wearing strange costumes to lunch is what it's going to do to Sydney. I can't wait. She's going to throttle me—or at least threaten to do so. Sydney would never do anything that would make her look badly in the eyes of a man, adult films notwithstanding.

I settle on God-awful yellow and brown paisley capris with a green t-shirt that says, "Golf: not that hole, **THAT** hole." I'm still sporting last night's underwear, because God knows I'm not wearing lost and found panties. (Yes, there are plenty of them to choose from in an old box, but no chance, no way, no how.) After using an aerosol disinfectant, I top the ensemble with a pink Polo baseball cap, pulling my hair through the loop in back. The capris and t-shirt will go in the trash when I get home, but the hat, I'm going to keep it. It's way too cute to trash.

After Dre finds plaid shorts and a "wife-beater" tank, he says, "Ready to go gorgeous," nodding at me like I'm a sexy piece of meat. It's hysterical really. We look hideous. Syd is going to freak.

"Yeah, but seriously though, I do have to stop at the gift shop and pick up some cheap flip-flops. I can't share shoes," I confess. "I draw the line at feet."

Nodding, Dre pulls me to him and says, "Every minute I spend with you, you're sexier than the minute before." He kisses my forehead, pausing while his lips linger on my head. "I can't believe I found someone like you."

I wish I could just relish how tender this moment is, but I just can't or I'll get sucked in and lose my senses. With someone like Dre, I can't get attached and hold on too tight. I know his kind. I typically steer clear of his kind.

Killing the moment, I joke, "If I get lice from this hat, you're shaving your head when I shave mine."

"You don't have to shave your head when you get lice," he counters, laughing. "But yeah, we'll shave our heads together anyway. It'll be hot."

I'm not going to lie; I'm confused as all get out. Dre's acting like this is a real thing—not a one-time fling. Every place we've walked or gone today, he's held my hand, or casually draped an arm around my shoulder. Even Rory seemed surprised by Dre's open affection. When we met Rory in his office to walk to the beach, Rory eyed us suspiciously, honing in on our interlocked fingers and high-class, semi-stolen attire.

It's all pretty surreal. I'm not so sure about this. Granted, Dre's the most beautiful male specimen I've ever laid—eyes on. It just doesn't make sense. According to the Charleston rumor mill, which is more active than the old paper mill, Dre is strictly "not into hooking up, hanging out, or fooling around" with women at this point in his life. Uh, yeah right! What does that make last night? What does that make me?

I want to be carefree and be able to just go-with-the-flow, but that isn't me. I so want it to be though, because last night was pretty climatic, in every sense of the word. However, I'm on the verge of a "middle-school-Katie-freak out." Those are not pretty. Not in the least. I'm going to need answers, and quickly. I'm also going to need to lower those flowing, blazing red flags flying over my head—at least lower them to half-mast. My God, they're blinding. I almost can't see how freaking spectacular Dre looks in the sunlight.

Dre's freaking hot, but he's not really my type if I'm being honest with myself. Like I said, I have a thing, a pretty strong thing, for the shy, quiet, ambitious intellectual. I love the studious, nerdy type. However, appearance, body type, devilishly sexy grins, and crazy amounts of confidence and sex appeal are all things that I appreciate, but never really value or covet, and certainly never drop my panties for. Until now. I just hope that now that I've experienced it first-hand … lips, tongue, and other things, that I can remember that I do in fact have a type, a strict type that I adhere to. But those hands, those lips, that tongue, and that …

that … gift to women may change my mind very quickly. It may have already changed my mind.

Walking across the parking lot toward the walkway down to the beach, Rory, Dre, and I get many stares and double takes. I'm not sure if it's the horrendous clothes we're sporting or if it's that I'm walking in between the hottest black man and most beautiful white man in all of South Carolina. Looking at Dre's chest in his wife-beater and at Rory's forearms make me believe that not one person within a gawking distance has noticed my cheesy t-shirt and repulsive, butt-cheek-squeezing capris. Nobody has yet to notice. Until she does.

"What the fuck? Did you go to goddamn hobos are us? What the hell are you wearing?" Sydney asks, grimacing at me. "I can't even look at that shit," she says, waving me off and looking away.

"What? This? Didn't ya hear? Hobos are the new rage. Totally chic," I say, spinning for effect.

"I wanna puke a little bit," Syd says, before actually looking at Rory and Dre. (Remember? Syd can be a total bitch.) Then she finally focuses on the guys, losing sight of my lost-and-found outfit.

"And holy fuck, now I **don't** wanna puke." Sydney pulls her sunglasses down slightly, eyeing Dre and Rory, equally. What she's doing to them with her eyes and mind could make anyone blush. Dre flashes her a crooked smile—the smile that most likely works on a vast portion of the female population.

Putting her sunglasses back into place, she coos, "Darling, if you would've told me we were lunching with gentlemen, I would've put on something a little more—more provocative."

We laugh at Syd's candor. Although she knew we were having a picnic lunch with Rory and Dre, Sydney's wearing the smallest bikini I've ever seen that could actually call itself a bikini.

"Honey, it doesn't get more provocative than that," I explain, pointing at her miniscule bikini top.

"This thing? This covers way too much. Doesn't it?" she asks, turning her head toward Rory. "What'd you say your name was, Handsome?"

"Sydney, this is Rory, and this is Dre," I introduce. "If you can keep it in your pants for a bit, we'd like to eat some lunch—while we're all still upright and clothed."

"Oh I can … if I must … I'm just hoping this one here can't keep it in **his** pants," she flirts, placing a hand on Rory's bicep. "And you, Dre, are you gonna keep it in your pants or put it right back in my best friend again … where it belongs," she asks, crassly. I gasp and redden, rolling my eyes in mortification.

Wrapping an arm around my waist, snuggling up to me, Dre whispers in my ear, "I'm gonna put it anywhere she asks—anytime she asks." My knees weaken, threatening to buckle.

Rory and Syd crane their necks to hear what he's saying, but Dre doesn't let them privy to those sexy and breathy words.

Then, Dre turns to them and says, "Now Syd, a guy like me doesn't kiss and tell." In front of both of them, he kisses my forehead, and says, "But I'm sure Pebbles will fill you in on anything she may want you to know."

"Pebbles?" Syd's brows rise.

"Don't ask," I say, walking down toward the beach.

"Dre calls her that, because he thinks she can make the 'bedrock.' Good one," Rory says, trying to high five Dre. Dre leaves him hanging, rolling his eyes at Rory.

"Don't kiss and tell, eh?" I joke.

"Well, not too much," Dre laughs.

"Dre, I'm surprised you're so pretty," Sydney announces nonchalantly. "Pebbles doesn't usually go for pretty boys with hot bodies like you."

Sydney emphasizes my nickname. I can tell she's mad that I never told her about it and that Rory already knew. Syd's kind of possessive and jealous like that, even with me, which is often why guys don't make the repeat booty call. Men fall for her sex appeal and beauty, but they run for the hills when they see her clinginess and envy.

"Oh really?" Dre says, taking an interest in Sydney's statement. "What's Kathryn's type."

"Watching *Big Bang Theory* is foreplay for her. Geeks make the bed squeak," Syd states. See! Total witch.

"Oh my God, Sydney! Do you have no filter?" I yell, shoving her with my shoulder. "Enough!"

"I'm serious, Dre. You better hit the books if you want her to stay at all interested … maybe get yourself a bow tie, some glasses, I don't know—whatever's popular in nerd world these days," Sydney says, shoving me back.

"Noted. Adding books and pocket protectors to my shopping list," Dre teases, grabbing my hand and kissing it as we find a secluded spot on the beach.

Rory brought a pile of blankets from the hotel's linen storage, so I grab a few of them and lay them out as Rory pulls food from the boxes he carted along with us.

"Croissants?" Syd squeals. "Sandwiches on croissants are my fave. Now this is a man after my own heart."

"That's not all I'm after, baby," he says, plopping down on the blanket right next to her.

"You're not gonna need to work too hard, Sweetheart, so save up your energy," Sydney states, smiling at Rory.

Dre and I roll our eyes at each other, knowing we only have ourselves to blame for this impending disaster. "Oh shut up McVay," Sydney warns. McVay? Crap, she really is mad at me for not disclosing things to her.

"McVay?" Dre says, looking at both of us, curiously.

"Oh, didn't Kathryn tell you that her last name used to be McVay?" Sydney laughs, smugly.

"Oh God, Syd, you didn't!" I exclaim, hating that I'm now going to be forced to divulge the craziness of my family.

"No, Kathryn most certainly did not tell me that her last name used to be 'McVay,' before," Dre said. "Like the Oklahoma bomber?"

Sydney lost it, cracking up. I just shook my head and said, "And there it is."

My father never got along with his father—at all. His father bailed early on him and his mother. My dad hated parading around with his deadbeat dad's last name, "McVay." Once Timothy McVeigh bombed the Murrah Building in Oklahoma City, our fate was sealed. Everywhere we went; everything we did was impacted by that event—even hundreds of miles away—not knowing anyone suffering from the tragedy. Anytime my parents had to say our last name, the follow up was "like the bomber?" It didn't even matter that the spellings were different; we still got those suspicious, accusatory glares. It sent my father over the edge.

My mother and father changed our last name to my mom's maiden name. My mom's parents are true grandparents and very close to us. It made the most sense for us to become the "Howells." I was only six at the time, so going from Kathryn McVay to Kathryn Howell was odd at first, but easy to adapt.

"That is a crazy-ass story," Dre said. "Can I call you Katie McVay?"

"Not if you want me to answer," I state.

"I'm actually glad they did it. Can you imagine being Kathryn McVay with Katharine McPhee being so popular?" I ask. "People would get us confused all the time."

"Yeah, until they heard you sing," Dre and Sydney say together. Laughing, they high-five each other, sealing their friendship. They both jump at the chance to start making fun of my singing ability. I hadn't realized I'd ever sung in front of Dre. Apparently, I have.

Rory's hands make it to Sydney's thighs; she's doing nothing to deter his soft strokes. "So Rory, what do you do?" Syd asks, directing all of her attention on him.

"I own a few hotels," he embellishes. Syd's hand quickly finds his arm. "So, you can use any room, any time you want?"

"Any time, any day, any minute, baby." Rory brags.

"Calm down you two; I'm trying to eat here," Dre scolds, taking a bite of his sandwich before sitting down.

"I'm not sure any part of me is staying … down … with her around," Rory admits, staring at Sydney. "Stop trying to cock block me anyway, Dude. I never did that to you in college," Rory whines.

Looking between them, my interest is piqued. "College?" Dre never mentioned college to me before.

"Yeah, at Brown. Dre used to get all the chicks, falling at his feet, but I never tried to make them back off—like he's doing now," Rory explains.

"You went to Brown?" I ask, surprised, shocked, and possibly a little hurt. Why was this the first I was hearing about it?

"That's like a good school, isn't it? Hard to get into?" Syd asks, looking bewildered.

"Uh yeah!" I exclaim, still reeling from this bit of information that was never bestowed upon me before.

"Yeah, it's not that big of a deal," Dre says, glaring at Rory.

"Fuck it ain't! Graduated top of his class. Fucking pre-Med," Rory discloses.

"Well there you go, Kathryn. He's a doctor; you can't get any geekier or smarter than that shit," Sydney states.

"You're a doctor?" I ask, feeling my Katie-freak-out coming on.

Hello? Dre Donley has a medical degree? What the Hell? I thought he fixed crap and helped fishermen. Okay, I kind of thought he was a drifter. Ya know, no ambition, no drive, no real future. A freaking doctor? Why wouldn't he tell me that? That's pretty big information to leave out.

Dre shakes his head. "Nah, haven't done my residency yet. Don't know if I ever will. That's not who I am anymore," he says, anger written all over his face.

Changing the subject, he says, "So Syd what do you do?"

"Oh ya know. A little of this, a little of that," she flirts, evading his question.

Sydney takes off her floppy hat and sunglasses, letting her long, blonde hair fall down all around her shoulders and back. She's perfected the flirtatious, "check-me-out" hair flip, and head cock.

Rory glances over at her, his jaw dropping. "Holy fucking dream come true!" Rory exclaims, jumping to his feet. "Fucking A. Oh fuck yeah."

Syd and I eye one another, all too sure of what's coming next. "You're Ivy Sterling. THE Ivy Sterling. Ivy 'Sure-I'll-Do-Anything-Sterling.'"

Rory is awestruck, star-struck, and pardon my language, but about to get Ivy-fucked. And me, I'm sitting here completely mind-fucked by this new bit of information about Dre.

"Oh? You've seen my work?" Sydney asks, feigning surprise and innocence. Seriously, how can she possibly pretend to be innocent when she's talking about her pornos? This girl is a piece of work.

"Seen your work? Baby, I **own** copies of your work," Rory swoons.

Sydney eats this crap up. Usually, when I'm around though, she tones it down a bit. I'm thinking she might seriously be digging Rory. Who wouldn't? Black, toned, bald businessmen are scrumptious. Rory has a "Taye Diggs" thing going on, and boy does he have it going on.

"What am I missing?" Dre asks, looking around at everyone.

"Dude, this is Ivy … Ivy Sterling." Rory says, casually placing his hand on Sydney's leg.

"I'm sorry. Should I know you?" Dre asks, looking apologetic and confused, but relieved that the subject was no longer centered around him. At least for now anyway. "Does anyone around here go by their God-given name?"

"Really? Have you been living under a rock Dre—well—scratch that," Rory says, shaking his head. "Your girl's best friend is Ivy Sterling, adult film star. She's known for—"

"I'm known for 'entertaining' Rory," Sydney interrupts. "Let's not give too much away. If Dre wants to see my work, then—"

"Over my dead body," I say, turning Dre's head to look at me. "I draw the line at you watching my friend perform." I glance over at Sydney and roll my eyes. Rory's hand is already travelling dangerously far up her thigh.

"So, let me get this straight," Dre says. "You're best friend, whom you hang out with and go places with is a porn star?"

"Yep," I answer, giggling.

"I'm assuming that people … men … everyone … flocks to her, to both of you, when you're out drinking and shit?" he asks, staring at me.

"Pretty much," I admit. "I haven't been out-out with Sydney in over a year and had to buy my own drink—unless you count lunches. But at bars and stuff, everything is bought by horny dudes or is suddenly 'on the house.' Can't complain. Saves me money."

"That's great. That's just fucking great," Dre says, throwing his half-eaten sandwich back into the box. "This day just couldn't get any better."

"Huh? Whattya mean?" I ask, having no idea what he's getting at.

"Oh nothing, Kathryn, not a thing," he states, blowing me off. "Ya have any other secrets you'd care to drop on me?"

"What? Me? Drop on you? Syd's career isn't my secret. What the heck, Dre? What about you? Doctor? Really? Like I wouldn't have been interested in knowing that" I argue, wondering where his anger and animosity are suddenly coming from, but feeling my own begin to escalate.

"Dude, let it go," Rory warns, eyeing him knowingly. "It's not that big of a deal. It's pretty hot if ya think about it."

"Sydney can do whatever she wants. More power to you, Hon. I just don't want ... want ... fuck it. Forget it." Dre waves us off, stands up, and starts picking up one of the blankets. "Ya know; I've got things to take care of today. I'll catch y'all later." And walks off. Yes, walks off. What in the world just happened?

"What the fuck is his deal?" Syd breaks the icy tension, as we all stare at him as he walks toward the parking lot.

"Uh Dre? Nah, nothing. He's just ... a little edgy at times," Rory says, scowling.

"Nothing? That was nothing?" I ask, shaking my head. "And forget that. He's not just walking away from me and 'calling it a day.' That's not how I roll, Buddy, not how I roll at all."

"Go get 'em, Tiger," Syd says, smirking. "Show 'em your fire."

I have no idea what just went on. We were all just laughing, eating, and enjoying ourselves. Dre just snapped. I can't figure him out. Cannot. He's sweet and tender one moment, volatile and dicky the next. He's a mystery. And a doctor. What in the world?

When I finally catch up to him, I'm breathing hard and sweating. Running along the beach in the middle of the afternoon, fully clothed, is not a good time to me, nor should it be for anyone else. People should not run. Life's too short to rush around all the time.

"Dre stop!" I yell. He doesn't. I run around to stand in front of him, splaying my hands across his chest, stopping him from moving forward, catching my breath as I do so. "What's … what's wrong with you? Why'd you get angry and walk off?"

"I … I don't know," he stammers, running his hand through his hair and looking away from me.

"You don't know?" I question again. "I'm gonna need a little more than that. You were rude and mean. I don't appreciate or tolerate being treated that way."

"Kathryn, listen to me; I don't know." Dre finally exhales loudly and looks me in the eyes. "I really don't know. I just … I just … I can't explain it."

"Dre, you're gonna have to try. From what I just saw back there, I'm pretty freaked out and … and really confused," I admit.

"Yeah, well, so am I," he says, sitting down in the sand.

"About what? What's going on?" I probe, softening as I sit down next to him. "Why don't you talk to me? Last night was amazing. We were so in sync, so in touch with … with everything. Why're you pulling back now?"

"I know. You're right. About everything. I'm sorry. I never should've—forget it," he says.

"Should've what?"

"Opened my mouth. I'm sorry. I was just sitting there hearing you talk about the crowd that surrounds you and Sydney when you're out, and I couldn't help it. I just … just … snapped, I guess," he explains.

"But why? Why would that even come close to upsetting you?" I ask, turning to face him, rubbing his forearm. "That doesn't make any sense."

"That's what I'm saying. I don't know. The thought of guys, lots of guys, buying you drinks and hanging all over you pissed me off—like a fucking lot," Dre admits, pulling my ball cap from my head, and then spinning it around his finger.

"Kathryn, I don't know what's going on … I know that this is fast—really fucking fast whatever's going on here. But, I just went a little ape shit thinking about you with someone else."

"Okay, so … what're you saying?" I ask.

Dre tucks my hair behind my ear, and then moves his hand to the back of my neck, pulling me in closer. Resting his forehead against mine, looking up into my eyes, he says, "I don't really know what I'm saying. I'm a goddamn nut case. I want to tell you to fucking run—run far the fuck away. But just thinking about you walking away makes me wanna kill someone."

"Dre, I don't know what this is. What we are or anything," I respond. "Right now, I don't really care either. I had fun last night—a lot of freaking fun. I'm fine with 'whatever' for a while." He smiles, closing his eyes, and sighing with relief.

"But listen to me, if this starts going somewhere—beyond the bedroom, I mean like between the two of us, then I won't stand around in the dark, not knowing who the person is that I'm making love to," I say, taking my hat back from him. "You're gonna have to start talking … like telling me you're almost a doctor, for starters." I explain.

"I know, Kathryn, I know," he agrees, nodding. Putting his head in his hands, with his elbows resting on his knees, Dre says, "I've done things, and I've been someone I'm not proud of—never really was. I'm just trying to sort all of it out." Dre stretches out his legs and stares out toward the ocean. "I wanted to fix my life. And I started to. I started becoming someone I can actually look at in the mirror."

"Dre," I say, making him look at me. "We all have pasts; we've all let ourselves down, disappointed the person we thought we'd become," I say. "Maybe more times than we'd like to even admit." Dre nods, his face pained.

Dre stares off, listening, but not looking at me. I continue, "The fact that you even recognize that there are parts of you that you want to change makes you worthy of your own reflection. You can look in that mirror, Dre. Seriously, you'll probably be proud of who you see. I know, I'm starting to like what I see," I joke, nudging against him.

I lean closer to him, putting my head on his shoulder, as he wraps an arm around me. I'm feeling all preachy, but there are things I feel like I can or should say to him. "Dre, listen, too many people make mistake after mistake, never learning anything. They refuse to recognize that their flaws and pains are self-inflicted and avoidable. You just have to figure it all out."

"I was counting on figuring it all out," Dre admits, kissing my hand and holding it against his cheek. "I just didn't count on meeting someone who makes it all worthwhile." I take the compliment, feel the compliment, and let it wash over me, feeling my body warm to the words. He's trying; he's feeling—something for me. I lean in, kissing him lightly on the lips.

"I think you're pretty worthwhile too," I grin, as I pull back.

"So now what? What do we do from here?" he asks.

"Well, based on what I see over there," I nod in the direction of Rory and Sydney. "We get back over there and cool them down before they both get arrested for indecent exposure." I stand, laughing, offering my hand to help him up. Dre yanks me abruptly back down onto the sand, swiftly maneuvering his body over mine, pinning me down.

"Or … we could just follow their lead," he says, nuzzling my ear and neck.

"Mmmmm, I would like that," I moan as his tongue trails along my lower lip. "But I told you how much I hate public—"

"Displays of affection, I know," Dre says, hiking my sandy leg up around his waist. "That doesn't stop me from wanting to please the fuck out of you right here on this very public beach."

Dre grinds into me. I can feel how hard he is. Even after his lie of omission, his crazy outburst, and tirade, I still want him; my body wants him. My body responds to his touch, his voice, his everything. There is no way my body will ever listen to my brain when it comes to Dre Donley. Kissing him, touching him, tasting him turns my brain to mush. I can't think straight when his hands are on me, his lips exploring mine.

"It doesn't stop me from **wanting** to … but it'll stop me from doing so," Dre explains, backing up off me, onto his knees. Dre leans in and kisses me softly on the lips. "For now, anyway."

As he helps me up, I say, "I hope there are more sandwiches; you sure know how to whet my appetite."

"Croissants aren't gonna cure that appetite," Dre states.

"Well, something better," I joke, looping my arm through the crook of his.

Closing in on Sydney and Rory, they cease their public exploration of one another's bodies long enough to tell us that they're leaving and going back to the hotel. Shocking news there.

Rory tosses his keys to Dre, "Drive this back for me, would ya buddy?" And Rory takes off with Sydney.

"Well that certainly didn't take long," I laugh. "I just hope 'Ivy' doesn't try to recruit Rory for her next film."

"Oh fuck, that's all I need. The guy's hung like a horse. Can you imagine what that thing would be like on the big screen? Christ, I don't even wanna think about it." Dre looks over at me as I'm pretending to stare off, thinking about Rory and licking my lips. "Oh Hell no, stop thinking about my boy's junk," he commands, picking me up, and throwing me over his shoulder.

"You're the one who brought up your brofriend's genitalia. It's obvious what **you** were thinking about," I tease. "Is there something I should know, Dre?"

"Yeah that I'm 100% straight and 110% into you ... and about five minutes from being **in** you," he explains, walking up to the dunes.

Still carrying me, Dre walks in the high grassy area in the dunes, throwing a blanket onto the ground. "Will this **do** for some **private** displays of affection?"

"I'm not sure. Will I do since I'm not 'hung like a horse?' We could call Rory back if you want," I joke, smirking at him, as he lays me down.

Lying down next to me, Dre trails his finger along the collar of my t-shirt and then glides it down over my breast. My nipple hardens at his touch. "No Pebbles, you are certainly all that I want ... and certainly all woman." Dre leans his head down and licks my nipple through my shirt, tugging it slightly with his teeth.

"I can't believe you just put your mouth on this used, dirty shirt," I remind him, giggling.

"You're not killing this mood," he scolds, continuing.

"Wouldn't dream of it," I say, staring at him.

"Nothing could keep my mouth and hands off of you, Pebbles," Dre says.

"I really like when you say stuff like that," I confess.

"What else do you like?" he questions, tugging gently on my nipple.

"Mmmmm, that," I say.

Dre glances up at me, smiling. "You really like watching, don't you, Baby?" I nod, feeling my face redden. "I love hearing what you like. It's so hot. Tell me more."

I shake my head, suddenly feeling nervous and vulnerable. "I just … I just like what you do to me."

I have fantasies, many of them unfulfilled. I like to hear a man talk dirty to me, using sexy and even raunchy words, but using them myself feels off, odd, out-of-place. Dre excites me so much, arouses the very center of my sexual being. I want to be able to say and do anything with him. I just feel "naked" saying them.

Tracing my nipple with his fingers, he whispers in my ear, "We'll do it together, watch together." Dre flicks his tongue in my ear. "Do you want to do this with me?"

I do. I want to do everything with him—even what embarrasses and inhibits me. I want him to open me, fulfill all of my fantasies, one-by-one. "Yes Dre," I moan.

"Keep watching and talking then, Kathryn," he says as he lifts my shirt over my head. "Watch my every move and tell me what you like and how you like it."

Dre kisses his way down my neck, while rubbing my nipple with the rough part of his palm. It ignites me, sending heat throughout my entire body. I can't take my eyes off of him.

"Are you watching?" Dre asks, staring at me through heavy, hooded eyes.

"Yes," I say, barely audible.

"Kathryn, talk to me," he commands. "Do you like it?"

"Mmmm, yes Dre."

"Yes, Dre what? What do you like?" he asks, taking my nipple into his mouth.

"I like it when you put your mouth on me," I moan. Dre tugs and nibbles more on my nipple. "God, yes."

"My mouth where?" Dre asks, while still pleasuring my nipple.

"I like when you lick and bite my nipples," I groan, feeling my body's heat skyrocket. The forbidden words feel freeing on my lips.

Dre moans against my breast, kneading and licking them together. "God, you're so sexy. Everything. Your body, your words, everything." Dre's breathing increases as he works his way further down my stomach. "Watch me Kathryn, don't take your eyes off me."

Unbuttoning my pants, he stares at my body, his eyes dark and hungry. After he takes off my pants, Dre takes my hand and kisses my palm and sucks each of my fingers into his mouth, his eyes never leaving mine. I've never felt this level of want before. I've surpassed desire; Dre has become a need. Dre places my hand on my breast. "Show me what you like."

I nod. "Don't stop," I say, spreading my legs further as I caress my own breast. "Keep going."

"You can count on it," Dre says, smiling as his fingers discover that the center of my arousal is ready for him. Beyond ready. He growls when his fingers enter me. My eyes flutter as his fingers flick over me. "Open your eyes, Pebbles. You don't want to miss this."

I lean up on my elbows, so I can stare into his eyes as he leans over and tastes me, using his tongue for my pleasure. It's erotic and sensual, liberating and hot. Dre increases his pace as I move my hips to meet his rhythm—never taking my eyes from his. It's perfect, purse bliss. Our connection is strong; my pleasure is building, yearning, needing. Abruptly, he stops, moving away from me.

"You're not talking," Dre says, grinning.

"Oh Dre ... no ... don't stop," I plead, rubbing my legs together.

"Kathryn, what do you want me to do?" he asks. I shake my head. Dre massages my legs, working his way back up my thighs. "You have to tell me what you want. I need to know what makes you ... you ... hot." Dre's fingers travel back into me. "Talk to me."

I whimper with pleasure, coupled with fear. "You. You make me hot Dre. Everything you do," I reply in sync to his finger's movements. "Every way you touch me. It ignites me," I say.

Dre stops, hands motionless, and says, "I only move when you talk."

I groan, and say, "You make me feel things I've never dreamed of feeling before," I admit, breathy and full of urgency. Dre's mouth replaces his fingers. His tongue is intense pleasure, intimate and pure. "Like right now, I hate that every part of you isn't touching me or inside of me," I plead. Dre increases his pace, sending my body to the edge. "So please, please Dre. I can't take anymore," I beg, as I finally cry out with release. My body convulses in spasms that want him, need him.

"Oh fuck, Baby; that was intense," Dre says, grabbing his shorts and rummaging through his pockets. Finding a condom in his wallet, he expertly rips it open and slides it down over himself.

"Well, you're certainly getting your game back," I tease.

"This game's win-win," he says, unbuttoning his pants. Dre's hard, ready and reaching for me. I pull him down onto me; I need to feel him inside of me. "God, you're so fucking sexy," he groans into my ear, as he enters me. My breath catches as he looks into my eyes. "So fucking incredible," he breathes, as we lie motionless, together, staring at one another.

Slowly, I begin to rock, while his eyes are still locked on mine. "Incredible," I echo, grabbing his arms, lifting up toward him. Dre's movements match and surpass my own. "Harder," I beg, thrusting against him, rocking to meet him. He wraps my legs around his waist and lifts his chest off of me. Staring down at me, his movements and speed increase; I meet him, push against him, rock harder, pulling him further into me until he cries out in pleasure, his body melding into mine.

I want to fucking destroy Rory. Mother fucker. First, he gives me Piper's letter in front of Kathryn. Then, he mentions Brown. Christ, I wanted to kill him, still do. He knows; he fucking knows how important Kathryn's becoming to me. I tell him everything— apparently too goddamn much. I can't believe she didn't try prying anything out of me. Kathryn was calm, collected, and patient. Man, I've never known a woman with those qualities before. Fucking A, she's perfect.

Kathryn – Katie – McVay – Howell – Nerd – Loving - Pebbles is perfection. Alert the presses, stamp and seal it, write it in the sky, I'm falling for her. I'm trying not to, but she's too damn irresistible. She's everything I've ever wanted in a woman, and she's everything I didn't know I wanted either. Hell, if I could tell her the truth and come clean about everything, and she still wanted me, then I'd marry her tomorrow. Women like Kathryn Howell don't come around very often and if they do, then you certainly don't let a gift like that slip through your fingers.

I'm going to tell her everything tonight; I have to. Otherwise, I'm going to get too far into this and pussy out. Right now, I know it's going to crush me if she can't handle the truth. If she wants out, wants to walk away, I'll be gut-fucked. But I suppose it's better to know now, than it would be to wait until I'm too far in over my head.

When I took Kathryn back to her apartment, she said that she'd love to see me tonight, and winked at me. I got hard just watching her do that, insinuate that there's more fun coming our way. Fuck man, I've never had it this bad before—ever. Just thinking about her makes me horny as hell. I think for a while I thought I was in love with Waverly. Holy shit was I wrong. Nothing's ever felt like this. Waverly's like cough syrup to Kathryn's fine wine.

As I approach her apartment door tonight, I can hear muffled voices inside. I knock, curious as to who is inside. Kathryn didn't mention having anyone over tonight. When she opens the door, she smiles, but her face doesn't light up. The smile looks forced, pained even.

"Hey Dre," Kathryn says, not opening the door the whole way. "I really need to get your number. There's been a slight change of plans."

"Is that him?" comes a dude's voice from inside. The door opens, and Theodore is staring at me. Oh Hell no. Not this guy again. Come on. "Sorry Dree, but Kathryn and I are kind of in the middle of something." Did this mother-fucker just call me Dree? What the fuck? Nobody's name is Dree.

"Theodore, don't. I told you I had plans with Dre," Kathryn says, emphasizing the correct pronunciation of my name.

"Kathryn, we need to talk. Make plans of our own," Theodore confirms. "Listen Dre, why don't you stop back some time tomorrow, and my girl here can fill ya in."

His girl? "Uh Kathryn, what's going on?" I say, looking away from Theodore, ignoring him completely.

"Theodore was on his way back from Atlanta and stopped here before going home … to Virginia," she explains.

"Okay. So … what? Do you want me to leave?" I want to punch this fucker until the pain I'm feeling goes away.

"Listen Dre," she says, pushing me out the door, closing it behind her. "You have to believe me; Theodore blindsided me. I had no idea he was coming."

"What the fuck is that?" I ask, grabbing her left hand, feeling like I was just beaten in the stomach with a two-by-four. "Don't answer that. I know goddamn well what that is. So that's it? You were just 'slumming' for a bit until he came back? That's just great. Fuck this." I punch the wall; my fist goes straight through the drywall. I feel nothing. Physical pain is for pussies. Emotional pain kicks physical pain's ass.

"Dre wait!" Kathryn yells. I don't even turn around. Fucking bullshit. I've seen and heard enough. "Stop! Please!" she screams as I go through the door into the stairwell.

"Come inside honey," Theodore says, "let him go." The door closes, and I don't hear her response—or fucking care.

Goddamn huge-ass diamond on her hand. Are you kidding me? What was I? Leverage to get the douchebag to finally fucking propose? Ammunition to fire at him to get him to do what she was waiting for all along? What-the-fuck-ever. I don't need this shit.

Out on the street, there's only one place that I can go, only person who I can talk to right now. I head over to the Oasis. Lanette will know what to say to make this feeling in my gut get the Hell out. I cannot believe I couldn't see this for what it was—a ploy to land the "nerdy" guy she wanted all along. Goddamn it. I shouldn't have gotten off course, changed paths, just because my dick wanted to come out and play. Christ. I knew better. Know better.

As soon as I walk in, Lanette says, "Oh no Sugar, what'd you do?"

I sit down at the bar, shake my head, and say, "Not until I've had a shot of Beam." Lanette goes behind the bar, pours me a shot, and hands it to me. I down the shot, tapping it twice on the bar. "One more," I nod toward the glass. She refills it.

"Start talking Dre," she says. I tell her the whole story.

When I finish, I tap the glass again, she grabs it, and says, "So what'd she say when she telled you to 'stop?' Did she 'splain everything?"

"I didn't stop. I fucking walked out the door and down the steps," I explain, reaching for the glass. Lanette jerks it out of my reach.

"Dre, yous as dumb as yous is pretty. How could you not listen to what that sweet thing wanted to say?" she asks, smacking me in the head. "I seen the way she looks at you. That ain't game-play. She's honey-suckered smitten with you, Sugar."

"Lanette, weren't you listening? She had a goddamn diamond on her finger. A fucking shiny-ass boulder," I said, pounding my head on the bar. "Just fill the shot glass … please."

"Yas need ta listen to her. Go back and hear her out," Lanette scolds.

"No, I'm done. I shouldn't have gotten started in the first place. I'm just gonna drown my pain. Hand me that bottle, please," I ask. "You know I love you. You're the only one I could come to for this. So give me the bottle."

"Ain't no amount of sweet-talking gonna get ya this bottle," Lanette says, moving it to the shelf above her head.

I feel a tap on my shoulder, turning around I recognize a busty redhead from being at the bar over the summer. "Dre?"

"Yeah?"

"I was listening to your story. That chick sounds like a total bitch. I'll buy you a shot. Miss Lanette, get my friend, Dre here a shot," she says, running her hand through the back of my hair.

"Sorry Darling, I'm not serving Dre anything more tonight," Lanette explains, glaring at me.

The girl scoffs, and whines, "Come on Dre, let's go somewhere else." As she's tugging my arm, I want to tell her to go away, that I'm not interested, and that I just want to be alone.

But more than I want to say those things; I want the pain in my chest to go away, so I can forget about Kathryn Howell. Releasing all rationality, I ask, "Sure Honey, where to?"

"My apartment is right around the corner," she coos, running her tongue along her top lip. And just like that, I'm back to being the asshole that I've been trying to overcome this past year. Goddamn Kathryn Howell.

As we get up to go, the redhead says, "By the way, I'm—"

"No. Don't go there. I don't even want to know," I say, cutting her off.

Shrugging, she giggles and says, "Whatever turns you on, handsome, and I mean whatever … you … want."

Man, I hope this helps. I need to shake this feeling. This kind of pain can't be natural. People can't possibly endure this sort of torture on a regular basis.

Walking to the door, she has her tongue in my ear and her hand on my ass just as the door opens and someone walks in. Kathryn. She rolls her eyes and shakes her head.

"Seriously?" Kathryn says, taking a deep breath. Kathryn walks right up to "whatever her name is" without as much as a second look at me.

"I'm sorry, Sweetie. Dre screwed up tonight and made some really really bad choices," she explains as if she's talking to a toddler about another petulant child, putting her arm around the girl and leading her toward the door.

Continuing, she says, "I'm gonna need to take him home. You need to run along now." Kathryn glares at me and rolls her eyes again.

"Oh I don't think so," the redhead says, crossing her arms over her chest like an obstinate preschooler, refusing to go any further.

"I found him first!" the redhead exclaims, stomping her foot for effect. Kathryn begins to laugh hysterically at her, covering her mouth in the process.

I glance down at Kathryn's hand; there's no ring on it. I look back at her, and she scowls at me, shaking her head. Needing to get to the bottom of this, I say, "Umm yeah, Kathryn's right, I really need to get home."

"I was going to do things to you that you wouldn't even comprehound?" she whines.

Still laughing in disbelief, Kathryn says, "Comprehound?"

"Yeah 'comprehound,' it means 'understand,' skank," the redhead says.

"Skank? Oh Honey, you have no idea," Kathryn says, patting her on the arm, condescendingly.

"Stop calling me 'Honey.' I'm not your honey. My name's Amber," she sulks, crossing her arms in a huff.

"I'm sure it is, Amber. I'm sure it is," Kathryn says. "Ya know, to this day, I've never met an Amber who wasn't slutty or stupid."

Amber's eyes light up, "So I'm the first one?"

Lanette walks over and hands the redhead a tall drink, and says, "A beautiful girl like you shouldn't be alone, I have someone you need to meet." As Lanette leads the girl away from us to "Levi the Lush," she looks at me and whispers, "Don't blow it."

"Kathryn, what're you—"

"Not here," she says, cutting me off. "Let's go outside, go for a walk."

Once we're outside and out of earshot from onlookers, Kathryn says, "All this storming off when things don't go the 'Dre-way' are gonna need to stop. I'm not gonna spend every minute running after you, Dre." I lean up against the wall, bracing my foot against it for balance.

"What're you doing here, Kathryn? Where's Theodore?" I ask, not looking at her.

"Finding you. And he's probably on 26 West heading home by now," Kathryn explains. I still can't look at her, because all I want to do is wrap her in my arms and kiss her until dawn. "Dre, what you think you saw and what was actually happening were two totally different things."

"So I didn't see your ex-boyfriend in your apartment, on the same day we had sex all day? And I didn't see nearly a 1-carat diamond on your hand? Oh yeah, you're right; I must be blind," I say, storming away.

"Holy shit, are you a fucking baby?" she screams after me.

I stop. Turn around, and say, "I thought you didn't swear Kathryn or is that just another one of your lies?" My hypocrisy is astounding.

"No, that is exactly what you **think** you saw. But that is not what happened, Dre," Kathryn said, grasping my shoulders. "Theodore came over. He delivered those same lines that he gave on his way down to Georgia. But this time, he knelt down, pulled out a ring, and then put it on my finger."

"Well congratulations, I'm sure you'll be fucking happy together," I growl, turning away from her.

"Damn it Dre, listen!" she yells. "The second he slipped it on my finger, the knock came. You got there. I didn't even have a chance to tell him 'No,' and take it off."

I'm staring at her, not knowing what to say or what to believe. "Theodore was on his way to the door to tell you that we just got engaged. It all happened so fast. I ran ahead of him to open it, forgetting that I still had the ring on."

I really want Kathryn to be telling me the truth, but it just doesn't add up. Why would she turn down someone like Theodore, someone who's apparently her type, for someone like me? I'm a dickhead. A lying loser dickhead—who has nothing to offer her.

"To tell him 'No?' You were going to turn him down?"

"How many times do I have to tell you this? I don't want Theodore, Dre. I don't want to marry him. I mean; we're not even together anymore. Who proposes to someone they're not even with? That's weird," she says, looking confused.

"What're you saying, Kathryn?" I ask, refusing to get my hopes up.

"I don't even know why he'd propose. It's so strange. He's my past." Kathryn walks over to me and clasps her hands together around my neck. "I was kind of hoping that you were my present— at least for a little while anyway."

"So, you're not engaged?" I ask, still not believing her.

"No! That's what I've been trying to tell you, " she yells, exasperatedly, hugging me, and putting her head on my chest. "What can't you 'comprehound?' My God, do you ever listen?"

I chuckle, not believing my luck or her patience. "Nah, not really," I admit, grinning, feeling my entire body relax and lighten. "So, you and me? Huh?"

"Yeah, you and me," she says, kissing me as I lean down. "But man, you need some serious tweaking if this is gonna work."

"Tweaking? Me?"

"Absolutely, this whole guy/girl thing's got you all kinds of messed up," Kathryn says, shaking her head. "You need to get it through your head that a girl like me is not gonna walk away from a guy like you."

"I think it's the other way around, Pebbles," I say, nuzzling her neck, suddenly feeling very aroused. "Does a girl like you want to take home a guy like me?"

"We can't get there soon enough."

I woke up early and watched her sleep for over an hour. Kathryn's even gorgeous when she's snoring softly and a small dribble of spit pools in the corners of her mouth. Watching her, I told myself, promised myself, that I would tell her everything today. I slipped out of bed to make her my specialty, peanut butter toast, for breakfast. Eh, so I can't cook.

Walking back into the room, Kathryn's sitting up, talking on her cell phone. "I know Mom, I'm just a little behind. I'll be there. I'll meet you at the church." She smiles at me, and scoots over on the bed, motioning for me to sit down. "I always do. Yes Mom, I always do. You too. Love you too." Kathryn hangs up the phone and groans, pounding her head back a few times on the headboard. Taking the toast from me, she says, "Thank you, but you didn't have to do that."

"Yes I did, we saw your cooking before," I tease, kissing her neck. "So, you're on your way to church with your mom?"

"Not really," Kathryn says. "I'm meeting her tonight at the church where I used to go … for a family picture. Our church has a family directory, complete with a family portrait in it."

Kathryn eats the last of her toast and starts to lick the peanut butter from her fingers. I stop her, finishing the job myself. Kathryn's breath catches as I slide my tongue over her fingers, dipping softly in the valleys between them.

Her voice quavering, Kathryn says, "Being away at school for the past several years, I couldn't come back for the picture. Now that my parents only live three hours away in Charlotte, I promised them that I'd make the drive to be in the family portrait with them this year."

"What time's the picture?" I ask, still bathing her hands and fingers with my tongue.

"Three-thirty," she says, breathlessly.

"Plenty of time," I reply, kissing the inside of her wrist.

"Yes, plenty of time. I'd told them earlier in the week that I'd come this afternoon for brunch, but we didn't get up and moving in time for me to be there by brunch. That's why my mom was yelling," she said, nibbling on my ear. "Now can we focus on other things now that everyone's all caught up?"

"Well how about this? How about we spend another hour having some fun in this bed, and then I go with you to Charlotte?" I offer, praying that she doesn't think I'm being too pushy.

I continue kissing my way down her stomach, so I don't appear too eager or hopeful. I figure I can tell her everything I need to tell her on the way home in the car, give her time to process it and think before we get back here, and she ditches me for good.

"You're offering to drive three hours with me to see my parents while I get my picture taken?" Kathryn asks, staring at me, shocked. It's so amazing to me still that she questions my feelings for her.

"Sure, it'll be fun. We'll load up on snacks, drinks, a little road head, what could be more fun?" I joke, winking at her. "Seriously though, let's do this."

~ Kathryn ~

I can't stop looking at him; I might drive right off the road. Last night was intense. Actually, everything has been intense since I met him, but yesterday was insane. I've learned more about Dre in the past 48 hours than I thought he'd ever let me in on. And another thing, I still can't believe that Theodore thought he could come to my apartment, get down on one knee, and propose, especially since he dumped me two years ago. Lately, it seems like everything I think I know; I'm wrong about. And the things that I think could never happen are happening. Too bad, I'm driving. I could totally use a drink right about now.

"Dre?" I take a deep breath, waiting for him to look over at me.

"Yeah Pebbles," he glances my way.

"Do you have a car?" I ask, feeling guilty, but it has been driving me crazy. Every time I see him; he's either walking or in Rory's car.

"Nope, not really," Dre admits.

"Not really? What does that even mean?"

"It means that I don't have a car, but if I ever need one, then I use Rory's."

"I mean doesn't everyone need a car?" I question.

"I don't. I either walk everywhere I go or borrow Rory's, but mostly I just walk," he confesses.

"What if you want to go somewhere far or travel or do **something** that involves a car?" I ask.

"Well, everything I need and want is right here—in Charleston. I can walk everywhere," Dre explains. "It's nice to not be tied down to all that."

"Tied down? To a car? Are you telling me you can't commit to a car?" I ask, incredulously.

"No Pebbles, I can commit to a car; what I can't commit to is the lifestyle that having a car entails," Dre answers, turning up the radio.

Turning it back down, I ask, "Do you have a phone?"

"Nope, don't need one. If I want to talk to someone, then I go talk to them," he says. "I'm not going to be tied down to gadgets that keep me from real conversations and real relationships," he states, turning to face me.

"I have no desire to tell the entire world what I ate for dinner or to text someone that 'I'm here' when they're sitting just inside the apartment," Dre argues. Feeling guilty, I can sense I've hit a nerve.

Dre continues, "I'll walk to the door, knock on it like a human being, and wait for whomever to open the damn door. Cell phones and this gadget-obsessive lifestyle everyone has is just ludicrous."

Now this is the stuff that I'm talking about. I don't get him. Dre comes across as a strong-willed, alpha male, going after and getting whatever he wants. The next second, he's running away, pouting, like a scolded puppy, because he didn't get his way. But saying crap like that makes me think he's some weird hippie or brainwashed cult member.

I cannot figure him out. Dre's like one of those people who's trapped in the wrong time period—like if Henry David Thoreau and Ralph Waldo Emerson were stuck in modern society. They'd freak if they saw what was going on nowadays.

"I know it must sound crazy to you," Dre says, looking worried. "But remember when I told you that I'm not happy with who I used to be? This is just a bit of what I'm trying to change."

"Is this a forever thing?" I ask, trying to understand him a little better.

"Are you asking if I'll ever have a phone or a car?" he says, staring at me quizzically. I nod. "I'm not sure. I guess it depends on if I ever end up needing them."

"Well, I think you should get them," I announce, positively.

"Oh, you do?"

"Yep, I like backseat sex, phone sex, and even sexting. And if you can't rise to the occasion with … with … the right equipment for my satisfaction, then maybe I'll have to look elsewhere," I tease, watching the visible tension lines on his forehead disappear.

Scooting closer to me, he whispers, "You have a car," as he begins nibbling on my ear and kissing my neck. "And a backseat."

"Dre, not while I'm driving!" I squeal.

"You keep your eyes on the road, I'll keep my eyes and hands on you," he announces, his hand rubbing my thigh. Man, I shouldn't have worn a skirt.

"I love that you're in an 'easy access' skirt," Dre groans in my ear, as his hands go under my skirt and trace the lace on the edge of my panties.

"I'm not gonna be able to drive if you keep that up," I warn.

"Trust me, Pebbles. I'm never gonna let anything happen to you, just relax and enjoy the drive," he commands, sucking my earlobe into his mouth while his fingers dip into my underwear.

"I can't believe that you agreed to spend the night here," I groan under my breath, leading Dre out onto my front porch. We walk the length of the white, wrap-around front porch to sit on the swing on the east side of the house.

"The thought of getting it on with you in your old high school bedroom got me all turned on," Dre admits. "I had no idea I was gonna get thrown into the spare bedroom-turned-sewing-room."

"They're my parents! That's what parents do—take the fun and excitement out of everything—no matter how old you are," I exclaim.

"I'm sneaking in that bedroom, Pebbles," Dre confirms, kissing my neck. I grip his hair, enjoying every second of this stolen, parent-free moment.

Ever since we arrived at the church, my parents have taken up residency in Dre's butt, grilling him with question after question. Not surprisingly, his answers have been vague, but that has not stopped my mother from eyeing me with pride as if I caught the biggest fish at the County Fair's fishing rodeo. I have one of those mothers who just wants to get her daughter married off, so she can brag to her church ladies about her ten grandkids and wonderful son-in-law.

My dad always wanted a son, so any boy who stepped over our property line immediately became the son my dad never had. My dad had Dre in the garage, showing him his prize-winning birdhouse. (I was in sixth grade when my dad won that contest, by the way.) Then, they went down to the creek, because my father insisted on showing Dre the clubhouse that he'd built for Sydney and me when I was in junior high. (The same fort that Sydney lost her virginity in three years later.)

Dre has been a trooper the entire time, going with the flow, and charming the pants off of my parents. He has a way of doing that with all the Howells, I guess. When my mom suggested we stay for dinner, Dre eagerly agreed and offered to set the table. When my father hinted around that we should stay the night and drive back in the morning for work, again, Dre was all over it.

"You better sneak in my room, because I need something to relieve me from all the stress of being here," I say, running my fingers through his hair.

"There you two are," my mom says. "The meatloaf's almost ready."

166

"Thank you, Mrs. Howell. We'll go wash up," Dre says, pulling me to my feet.

"Wash up? Seriously Dre? Do you think we're in Walnut Grove?" I joke, rolling my eyes.

"Nonsense Katie, leave him alone. Nothing wrong with a little manners, right young man?" my mom says, looping her arm through his.

"Absolutely, Mrs. Howell," Dre says, looking back at me with a wink and a grin.

"Call me 'Ruby,' I hope we'll be seeing more of you around here," my mom says, patting Dre's arm with her other hand.

"I'm sure you will, Ruby. I'm sure you will."

I need to freeze time and summon Sydney here. I can't believe what's going down here. So much has happened since Syd left the beach with Rory, and I've told her none of it. There is so much story piling up; we're going to need a two-hour lunch to get through it all. Before I sit down to dinner, I text Syd to tell her that we need to meet for lunch tomorrow. Immediately, she returns the text, stating that she has a ton to tell me. It's going to be a long lunch.

Dinner is meatloaf. Meatloaf is repulsive. Therefore, dinner is repulsive. It's logic 101. My mom had to have known that she and my father would convince me to stay for dinner. Couldn't she have drummed up a better idea for dinner than meatloaf? For God's sake, I want to bolt out the front door and hit a local drive-through. My father and Dre are eating it like it's the last meal on the planet before the apocalypse. In all actuality this could be our last meal, because I might die if I eat one more bite.

"You're picking at that food like you don't eat," my mom points out, scowling at me. "By the looks of your hips and butt in that skirt, you're getting plenty of food, Katie Dee."

"Oh, you noticed her butt and hips too?" Dre says, looking at my mom. "They're perfect, aren't they?" Dre leans over, kisses my cheek, and feeds me a bite of his potatoes. "Kathryn's the most beautiful woman I've ever seen, isn't she Mr. Howell?"

"Darn tootin!' They don't come prettier than my little Katie-kitten," my dad says, through a mouthful of meatloaf, spraying remnants of meat and sauce across the table.

I'd never seen my mother speechless, but Dre rendered her speechless. He is definitely sneaking in my room tonight; there is compensation to be paid for this little funfest.

"So Katie, did Theodore come see you?" my dad asks, with an all-knowing look in his eye, "because he came here to see me on his way down to Georgia."

"Yep, he sure did," I reply, curtly. Wow. Theodore talked to my father before proposing to me. I didn't see that coming at all. Theodore has always had the utmost respect and fondness for my parents. I'm impressed. I didn't make the wrong decision, did I?

"I take it he's back in Virginia now?" my dad questions, obviously knowing the answer.

"I guess; I haven't talked to him since he left," I respond, giving him the real answer to his question.

"Thomas, you never did tell me why Theodore stopped here," my mother pouts. "I was happy to give him a packed lunch for his long drive. Such a nice boy that Theodore."

"Dad didn't tell you?" I question, impressed with my dad's resolve.

"No, he wouldn't budge. Said it was a 'need to know' basis, and I would know when it was time," my mom whines.

"And apparently, you'll never need to know," my dad says, shoving green beans in his mouth.

Leaning over, Dre whispers in my ear, "Theodore's got class, impressive." I nod, agreeing with him. "Too bad he ain't got game." Laughing, I spit my iced tea out on the table, sending my mom in a frenzy to clean my mess.

Dre stands and says, "Ruby, you sit down. You made this delicious meal; you rest. Kathryn and I will do the dishes and clear this table." Dre grabs a handful of dishes and silverware, and says, "Let's go Pebbles, you wash; I'll dry."

"I told you; this isn't Walnut Grove. We've got a dishwasher," I argue as I grab more platters and bowls from the table.

While cleaning the kitchen, Dre and I get into a pretty wicked water fight with the sink sprayer, drenching the counters, floor, and each other. My mom and dad just laugh and head out onto the porch. It's been their after-dinner ritual for as long as I can remember.

Once we clean the entire kitchen, dry the floor, and pour ourselves some iced teas, we join my parents on the porch. We're still soaking wet, but still giggly from the childish fun. My skirt is sticking to my legs; my mascara's dripping down my cheeks. I'm a mess. Dre, on the other hand, has the sexy wet look nailed. Of course.

"Dre honey, you don't want to sit around in wet pants," my mom says. "Katie, you have old clothes upstairs to go put on yourself. Give Dre some old shorts or pants of your father's and put his pants and shirt in the dryer."

"Ruby, it's fine. They'll dry in no time in this heat," Dre argues.

"Nonsense! I'm a borderline hoarder. I've got pants from when Thomas was your age in the sewing room closet. Ya just never know when you're gonna need things," she states, looking at my father.

"See Thomas, I knew those pants would come in handy someday." My father rolls his eyes at my mother, continuing to read the local section of the newspaper. "Katie, take him upstairs to change."

"Sure thing, I'd love to get him out of those pants," I joke. My dad lowers the paper, glaring at me. "Kidding. Just kidding Dad!" I walk to the door and say, "Not borderline Mom, full-blown hoarder."

"Am not," my mother calls after us.

"Are, too," my father and I yell together.

Upstairs, I find a pair of pants for Dre and some clothes for me to change into. As he's changing, and I'm unabashedly staring at every ripple of his muscles, Dre says, "I don't know when I've had a better time, Pebbles."

"Being at my parents' house is a good time for you? Dude, you need to get out more," I laugh, throwing my pillow at him.

"I'm serious; lately I've been searching for what 'normal' is, and I've finally found it," Dre says, buttoning my dad's old pants. He looks ridiculous and sexy, all at the same time.

"Is that a compliment, because it certainly doesn't sound like it?" I ask.

"It's probably the highest compliment I could give you," Dre says, sitting down next to me.

"Nah, I'm thinking 'Kathryn, you are the sexiest, smartest, funniest, and most gorgeous woman on the planet' seems a little more flattering than 'hey I like you; you're normal," I say, grinning at him.

Dre grabs me and kisses me, hungrily. I marvel at how easily our tongues twirl around each other. His arms envelop me, holding me tightly and securely against him. Our hearts pound together, nearly beating the same rhythm and tempo.

After he breaks the kiss, he stares at me and says, "Kathryn, I ... I ..."

"What Dre? Tell me," I say, noticing how serious his eyes are.

"I want to tell you—" He looks down and then back up at me. "Ummm ... that ... why do ... yeah, why do girls bite their lower lips after a spectacular kiss like that?"

"That's your question?"

"Yeah, I've always ... ummm ... wondered that," he says, looking away from me. I know he's lying, but I promised myself that I wouldn't pry. I even promised him.

"I guess for me, it's because I can still taste you on my lips. I can lick and taste you all over again," I confess. "But that's just me, I can't speak for other girls."

"That's so fucking hot," he says, pinning me down on my bed, kissing me again. Things heat up pretty quickly as Dre tastes and nibbles on my neck and chest, working his way lower.

My mom calls from the steps, "Katie, bring down Dre's pants and shirt, I'll put them in the dryer."

"Sure thing, Mom!" I call, sitting up. "You stay here. I'll be back."

After quickly kissing him again, I grab his pants and shirt and head downstairs. I hand my mom his clothes and head for the steps.

"Katie! Here!" My mom hands me Dre's wallet and a folded paper. "I told you to always check the pockets before washing and drying anything."

"Right. Sorry Mom," I say, rolling my eyes, wishing we were heading back tonight. No matter how old you get, parents never stop treating you like a child.

When I get upstairs, Dre's in the bathroom. I plop down on my bed, staring at the paper in my hand. I want to be the type of girl who isn't even intrigued or curious by holding the folded paper in my hand. I want to be trusting in Dre and secure in myself. I want to recognize how defected it would make my character if I were to peek at the paper. I want to be all of those things, but I'm not.

I open the paper; seeing that it's a letter, my stomach falls. I know that I should fold it back up, not read it, and forget that I ever saw it, giving it back to Dre before I read one word of it. I should, but I don't. I read:

Dear Dre,

Please come home. My life without you is awful. If you won't come home, will you please just call me? I miss you. I love you so much.

Love you,

~ Piper

I can't catch my breath. My heart is racing. Who is Piper? Why is she saying that she wants him to come home? Home? She loves him. Does he love her? I can feel the tears pooling in my eyes. I don't want to cry. I won't cry. I knew I shouldn't let my heart play in this game. Every time I let it play, it always wants to win. It never does. My heart always loses in the end. I read the letter again, hoping that this time there are more answers in the five lines of tortuous betrayal. There are no answers—just lies, pain, and tears. Always left with pain and tears.

Dre walks in the room and stops abruptly when he sees the letter in my hand. I hand it to him and say, "My mom emptied your pockets before drying your pants."

Smiling painfully, he says, "Yeah, thanks." Taking the letter from me, I can hear his breathing quicken.

"Dre," I say, making him look at me. His eyes are pained; he's dreading the next question as much as I am. I take a deep breath, letting the tears fall, before saying, "Who's Piper?"

He looks away, shakes his head, and sighs. "Nobody Kathryn. Just someone from my past."

Dre looks into my eyes. I stare at him closely, watching the tears pool in the corners of his eyes. We both know he's lying.

In a movie or book, you're always aware of when the end is coming, but in real life, nobody ever gives you the hint, the foreshadowed event that the end is near. For the first time in my life, I can see Dre, recognize the look, and understand that this is it. This is the end; the lie is too big for both of us.

- Dre -

I wanted to tell her. Kathryn needed to know the truth, but everything was going so well, too well. I knew I wasn't destined for this kind of happiness, for this kind of bliss. When she told her parents that we decided to drive home tonight and not worry about the morning traffic, I knew it was over. You can only lie to someone for so long before it's been too long and too much.

I offered to drive, but she wouldn't let me. She said that she just wanted to get home and forget the entire day. It felt like someone was standing on my lungs; I couldn't breathe. Kathryn wanted to forget the same day that was one of the greatest days of my life. It was unfair. I hated being a coward; I'd planned to tell her everything. I just couldn't do it. I couldn't look at her, admit the truth, and watch her choose to leave me—not being able to handle the lies I've told. Not being able to stomach the truth of who I really am. Instead, I'm just letting her walk away, without the knowledge she deserves.

"Dre," she says, turning down her road, "where can I drop you off?"

Looking out the window, I just say, "I'll walk from your apartment—I need some air."

Kathryn parallel-parks in a spot a block from her apartment. Killing the eginge, she turns to look at me and says, "You can't be someone you want to be if you don't admit who you once were."

"Pebbles, I can't—"

"Don't call—"

Kathryn's phone alerts her to a text message, distracting her from her words. She looks down at her phone and shakes her head, frowning at the words she's reading. I don't even have to ask her what's wrong. Kathryn flicks her wrist at me, allowing me to read the words on her phone.

THEE-ADORABLE: (My gut-wrenches at the name and how it's programmed into her phone.) *I thought you'd like to know that there are no records anywhere of a Dre Donley attending Brown. Maybe you should reconsider your recent decisions.*

Kathryn must've told Theodore more about me the night he proposed. But she came to me, found me at The Oasis, and explained everything to me. Last night, she'd chosen me and right now, she can't even look at me. I did this. I knew I should've left her alone. She's too good for this, for me, for anything I could give her.

Kathryn throws her phone on the counsel, and looks away as the pain flashes in her eyes. "If you're not going to start talking, then just get out Dre," she says with her hands firmly gripping the steering wheel.

"I want to tell you," I say.

"But what?" she snaps. "There's a 'but', right Dre? God forbid you tell me the truth about anything. I'm not doing this. If you don't trust me, can't trust me, then there's no point," she says, shaking her head. "Just … just … go."

"I just want—"

"The truth Dre, that's all I want," Kathryn states. "If whatever you're about to say isn't true, then don't even bother."

Kathryn's right. I shouldn't bother. There's no way she'll look at me the same. Her eyes won't light up and crinkle in the corners when she laughs, or her hand won't casually caress my arm after I tell her everything, and she knows the truth—all of it. There's no way Kathryn'll ever see me the same again; nobody could look past who I am and the lies I've told. I don't deserve her, and she definitely doesn't deserve to be put through any more of my shit.

I put my one hand on the car door's handle and the other on her cheek. Kathryn doesn't flinch or move away. I trace her jaw with my thumb, and her eyes flutter, closing slowly. I want her to turn in to my hand, move closer to me. She takes a deep breath, frowns, and backs away from my hand. My heart falls.

Opening the door, I start to get out, but stop and turn. "Pebbles," she looks at me, "I fell in love with you and that's the only truth you should know."

I learned early on in my life that I couldn't always be who I wanted to be. Back when I was six or seven-years-old, I'm not sure which, I learned quickly that people's opinions and viewpoints of you mattered not only to you, but to your fucking family and friends as well. Although it was all very harmless, it was eye-opening and disappointing to say the least, teaching me the sad truths of growing up and being accepted.

We were at the Halloween costume store. I was always considered the "clown" of the family, making people laugh, doing things out of the ordinary. Picking out our Halloween costumes, I asked my parents many times if it mattered what I chose. Naturally, they told me that I could be whatever I wanted. Whatever I wanted, God damn it. They left out the "as long as we approve."

I remember being so excited about my choice, knowing how much it would make people laugh. All I wanted to do was make people fucking laugh, be the center of attention, and have a good time. That's it. That's all I wanted—back then. My parents were in the other aisle, looking at costumes for my older brother. Giggling, I chose my costume, put it on, looked in the mirror, and nearly died from laughter. It was hysterical; I loved it. I couldn't wait to show my parents.

I turned the corner in my shiny, sparkly mermaid costume, and my parents went fucking ballistic. My father started yelling obscenities about "not raising a goddamn fruit." My mother marched me to the back of the store, pulling each part of the costume off of me, bitching about how I'd upset my father and how awful it was to see me in such outlandish and embarrassing attire.

At home that night, my parents lectured me about appearances and public behavior, explaining that under no circumstances was I ever to do something so mortifying and damaging again. After my mother left the room, my father continued to tell me that he wasn't "raising a fucking fairy" and that he'd "beat that fucking fruity shit right out of me." At the time, I remembered thinking that I didn't want to be a fairy, but a mermaid instead. I knew better than to correct him.

It was years later when I finally understood what he meant. I was six-years-old, and only wanted to wear a costume for Halloween that made people laugh. I wasn't (nor am I now) gay, bi, or even a little curious. And who the Hell would care if I was? They were my parents. Weren't they supposed to love me for me, no matter what?

I was a goddamn little kid who wanted to dress up for Halloween, for mother fuck's sake. Incidentally, I went as a heavy-weight champion that year; it was the last year I ever participated in Halloween. Dressing up and being something other people wanted you to be never appealed to me after that—Hell, I did that every day.

Thankfully, I'm no longer doing that. I'm not going to be someone else's idea of me. I'm not living my life to someone's standards, especially if they can't accept it. It's ridiculous how intolerant people can be; I'm not adhering to what other people want. It's my life. It's what I want, and that's it.

Sadly though, what I want just walked away, leaving me alone on the sidewalk in the dark. I just wish I would've given Kathryn a chance to decide for herself; a part of me thinks she might've been able to accept the truth. Another part of me believes that all people are made from the same materialistic, money-grubbing, selfish, intolerant fucking cloth. Kathryn's gone. I'm alone. And that's the way fucking life goes, people.

~ Kathryn ~

"What? What the fuck? How in the goddamn world did you sit here and listen to me tell you fucking detail after detail about Rory fucking my brains out while all that shit with Dre went on?" Sydney hisses, trying to keep her voice low.

We're eating lunch in downtown Charleston on the patio of a swanky, upscale restaurant. "Ivy" just got this month's check, so Sydney wanted to splurge a little. However, we don't have to pay for our lunches. Apparently, the "fan in the corner" already paid for them. Sydney quickly morphed into "Ivy" and went and thanked him, signing his napkin with her signature and a lipstick kiss.

"And crabs? He gave you crabs?" she yelled, getting us a few nasty glares.

"Oh for God's sake! Would you keep it down," I whispered, trying to duck my head from the accusatory stares.

"I just think that's incredibly fucking romantic. I don't under-fucking-stand what went wrong," Sydney questions.

"Me neither," I confess. "Me neither."

This morning after a sleepless night, I went out early to get some doughnuts and milk. After what I'd been through the past few days, Weight Watchers could suck it, shove those points up their rear, and lick the glazed frosting straight from my fingers while they were at. There was no way I was going to get through this mess without a sugar-induced coma to calm me down.

Evidently, when I was gone, Dre must've stopped by with a gift for me. When I got to my apartment door, there was a box without a lid sitting in the hallway. I looked down and in the box was an aquarium, housing two hermit crabs with hand-painted shells. There was a note from Dre that said:

I wanted to make sure that I was the one who gave you crabs. Take care of 'Allie with an i' and 'Oliver.' See ya around,

— Dre

"You gotta make him tell you what he's hiding. Fuck, he might not even be hiding anything," Sydney says. "He might just be one of those chronic commitment-phobes who don't know how to be in a relationship."

"It's more than that. He doesn't tell me anything. Just keeps saying 'I can't.' Well, screw that. How long am I supposed to wait to know anything about the guy I'm sleeping with? That's just nuts," I argue, getting angry and hurt all over again.

A few days ago, I was perfectly fine with carefree and "just having fun." But then, things started moving really fast and getting pretty heavy. Dre and I connected, intimately, intellectually, and emotionally, whether he wants to accept that or not. I guess I can pretend all I want that I'm a "go with the flow" kind of girl, but the reality is; I'm insecure, romantic, and old-fashioned at heart. Trying to be someone or something you're not is just so freaking hard.

Continuing, I say, "And he didn't go to Brown! What the heck?"

"Yeah, what the fuck is that all about? Rory did. Rory even said that Dre did. Fuck that, if Rory wants to tap this again, he better start talking," Sydney threatens, grabbing her phone off the table and frantically tapping the keys. "I'll fuck him up if he lies to me."

"Theodore said there's no record of 'Dre Donley' at Brown," I reiterate. "I mean someone's obviously lying, and I doubt Theodore would make that up."

"Oh yeah right, why would Theodore lie? What does he have to gain?" Sydney says, rolling her eyes. "I can't believe that douchebag came here and proposed. I thought we were done with that piece of shit?" Sydney downs her mimosa, motioning for the server to bring her another one.

"I'm serious, don't even think about entertaining that thought. If you do, I would take you … along with the ring … and chuck you right in the fucking Cooper River."

"But Syd, what if Theodore's my only chance at the fairy tale?" I ask.

"What the fuck ever! You're not settling for Theo-dork as long as I'm around," she argues. "Snow White didn't fucking marry Dopey the Dwarf, and I'm not about to let you marry Theodore. Fuck that shit," she declares.

Syd's phone dings, alerting her to a new message. She reads it, nodding, biting on the corner of her lower lip. "Rory said that they both went to Brown. He also said that you shouldn't give up on Dre."

I gave him three weeks. Three long, lonely, and depressing weeks. Dre hasn't called me, stopped by, or done anything to make me think he's even thought about me once. Sydney saw him once at the hotel; she said he looked like shit and didn't talk to her. Apparently, Rory keeps trying to convince Sydney to use the "best friend card" to convince me to go see him or call him. Frankly, Dre's the one who screwed this up by not being upfront and open with me. Why should it be me who goes running back to him? Probably because I really can't eat, sleep, think, heck function, without him. When you experience a few seconds of bliss, a lifetime of mediocrity isn't going to cut it. Those dang "what ifs" can haunt you for a lifetime.

Leaving work, I have a plan; it's the worst plan I've ever had. However, it's a plan nonetheless, and I need to do something— anything. This whole thing with Dre has me so confused, so angry, and so utterly crushed.

You can tell yourself that you're not going to get caught up in someone, not going to get close, and heck, not fall in love, but damn it, sometimes your head and heart are at odds. There's nothing you can do to reconcile the war between the head and the heart. The heart always wins, and when it does get shattered, the smug little head, sits back, folds its arms, and says, "I told you so."

I traded cars with Warren for the night. It was pretty amusing watching a 55-year-old man drive off in my yellow Volkswagen Bug. I look pretty rugged in his black Ford F-150, if I do say so myself. My plan is basic, pretty silly and simple actually. I'm going to drive around this city in this man's car, searching for Dre, hoping to see him walking down the street. I just want to see him, see what he's doing. Not too complicated, but the slight complication is that I can't find him anywhere. I tried the Oasis, the marina, the docks, Battery Park, Meeting Street, and all the other scenic areas of historical Charleston. I've been driving around for over an hour when I decide that I just have to go see Rory. I'll be honest and tell him that I miss Dre and need to see him.

"It's about fucking time, woman," Rory says, smiling, when he sees me. He hugs me, and whispers in my ear, "He's wrecked without you."

"Sure doesn't show it," I say, releasing him. "I can't believe he hasn't stopped over, called, done anything to fix this. I left the ball in his court, hoping—"

"Have a seat," Rory instructs, directing me to a table. "Bring us a bottle of Pinot, would you?" The server heads off as if his butt is on fire.

"Niiiice," I respond, "Someone's got some pull around here."

Rory is an attractive man; Sydney really shouldn't blow this. His style is impressive. He's always dressed impeccably. Today, he's not wearing a jacket or tie, but is in his gray suit pants, a fitted, front-button gray vest, and a sharp light blue button-down with his sleeves rolled up. On three occasions, I've gotten to see his sleeves rolled up; his forearms are nicely chiseled and sculpted. I wish he would've been a bit more like Sydney at the beach and worn a little less. I'd be lying if I said I didn't want to see a little more of his physique. Sure, I'm into Dre and would never think of his friend that way, but I wouldn't mind a little peek. I am human.

"That's what they pay me the big bucks for," he replies, grinning. "Listen Kathryn, I know you're torn. He's been such a shit to you. But trust me, he's dealing with a lot. I wish I could tell you everything—"

"So do it. Anything, just tell me anything," I say, pleading with him. The server comes back with the wine, pours Rory a small amount, allowing Rory to smell, swirl, and swig it before pouring each of us a glass.

"I can't," he says, savoring his wine. "It's not my place or my story to tell."

"Rory, this is so messed up. How do I go back to him, trust him, when he's never given me anything to hold on to, to trust?" I ask, praying that Rory has the magic words to fix this. "I don't even know where to find him—how to find him."

"Do you care about him?" Rory asks, intently.

"How can I? He won't let me in," I ask, hoping for answers.

"It's a yes or no question, Kathryn," Rory states.

"Yes … yes … of course. I wouldn't be so hurt, so confused, and so freaking angry if I didn't care for him," I relent.

"What would your deal-breaker be?" Rory inquires; waiting for my answer, he drinks more of his wine.

"My deal-breaker? I don't know. How can I answer that?" I ask, sipping my wine thoughtfully. This is all just insane. Rory knows something and won't tell me. Dre's hiding something that he refuses to reveal and yet, I'm left alone in the dark, wondering everything.

"Think about it. What would make you lose all respect for him, stop caring, and walk away without ever looking back?" he repeats.

"I don't know. I guess … if he was … like … a … a pedophile … rapist … murderer. All deal-breakers," I state, gulping down my wine, praying that we're about to take all of those scenarios off the table.

Laughing, Rory says, "Dre's messed up, but Honey, I can promise you he's none of those things." He leans forward, puts his hand on mine and says, "Dre thinks you'd never forgive him or accept him if you knew the truth. I think he's wrong … if you ask me, you're the best thing that's ever happened to him … and he agrees."

"Good to know … but … but what's he keeping from me?" I plead, while Rory fills my glass again. "Why can't anyone tell me for God's sake?"

"I told you. It's not my story to tell. All you're gonna get out of me is that he's worth the fight. Fuck, if I were gay, I'd be all set with Dre. Wouldn't look any further," Rory states confidently. "Dre's the real deal. You'd be a fool to not go 'balls to the wall' to get him to wise up."

"But how? I can't even find him!" I exclaim.

"Finish another glass, relax a bit, let the wine do its trick," Rory soothes, standing up, straightening his vest. "Think it over. If you're sure you want the truth and you don't think that you'll go hightailing it out of town once you get it, then head over to Isle of Palms … check the beach." Rory leans over, kisses my cheek, and says, "He loves you, and I can see it in your eyes that you love him too. Isle of Palms."

I didn't finish the wine. I didn't mull anything over. Currently, I'm driving over the causeway to the island. I have to see him. I need to see him. The time I've spent without him has been unbearable, tortuous; I don't want to be without him. Whatever he's hiding, whatever it is, I think we should go through it together—he should let me go through it with him.

As I'm getting closer to the beach, I spot him immediately. He's walking out of one of the touristy beach shops, heading toward the beach. My first instinct is to honk and let him know I'm in Warren's pickup truck. But then my inquisitive, angry side kicks in, and I decide to let the anonymity of the truck keep me disguised. I want to know where he's going, who he's with, what he's hiding. Dre might still refuse to tell me even after I confront him. If I could just see and watch what he does, where he goes, then he wouldn't be able to lie to me or hide anything from me anymore. It can be all out in the open for us to deal with—together.

Dre turns down the street with the enormous beach houses, the ones that Sydney and I salivate over when we're "driving around" and fantasizing about our futures. Hollywood loves these beach houses for coastal Carolina movies. They're houses that normal people couldn't afford.

My curiosity is piqued when Dre stops at one of the mailboxes and gets the mail out. The tan-Lab-looking dog in the yard greets him, happily, as Dre pets him and roughhouses with him a bit. My stomach suddenly feels like it's going to come out of my mouth. Why is he here? Whose dog is that? My attention is averted when a gorgeous brunette, resembling a Hispanic goddess, appears on the front porch.

"You're back late tonight, Dre," she yells, walking to the edge of the steps.

"Just getting some stuff done," he replies, loudly, walking toward her. As Dre gets closer to her, I can no longer make out what they're saying. They're too far from me, and I can't pull closer to hear without being discovered. I watch as they have an amicable and intimate exchange. My stomach lurches when the brown-haired beauty runs her hand up and down his arm. She nods, and he starts walking to the back of the house.

I can't breathe. Who is that woman? Why is he giving her the mail? Why is she smiling at him like that? And why? Why is she touching him and looking at him so ... so ... lovingly?

I'm going to be sick. I'm going to puke right here in Warren's pride and joy truck. When I told Rory what my deal-breakers were, I never thought to include a wife or girlfriend. I never thought in a million years—never even considered it. Nobody in the entire town talks of Dre having a ... a ... whatever the heck she is. This is it; this is what he's been hiding. Dre Donley couldn't get serious with me, because he's with someone else. How could he?

I'll tell you how he could. I made it too easy for him. I never demanded answers. I never asked Dre anything, never pried into his life. The clues were there. He walked everywhere. Sneaky bastard, his car wouldn't be spotted around town if he stayed on foot. We only fooled around at my house, at the hotel, and in the freaking weeds.

Dre never gave me his number, never called me, or texted me, all because he didn't want to get caught. Lying and saying he didn't have a phone was pathetic, completely cowardice and ridiculous. How could I be so dumb, so naïve? I'm smarter than this. It was so obvious, but I refused to see the writing on the wall. Everything adds up now. Oh my God, I'm a mistress, the "other woman." I throw the car in reverse ready to hightail it back to my apartment and to leave Dre Donley in the dust of an afterthought, the bastard.

Suddenly, I slam on the brakes. No way. No way is he getting off the hook this easily. I'm not going to let him get away with treating me like this. I didn't do one thing to deserve this sort of betrayal. Dre Donley screwed with the wrong woman. I pull right into the drive, not caring if the woman accosts me. Let her find out that her boyfriend, fiancée, husband, or whatever the crap he is, that he's a cheating, lying snake.

Thankfully, I get out and walk around to the back toward the beach without that woman confronting me. I really didn't want that confrontation right now, despite my raging anger. I'll deal with all that later if I have to. Right now, Dre's number one on my hit list. I don't see Dre around their pool or deck area. I climb up the steps to the walkway down to the beach. The big dog is just sitting by the pool, watching me. Some guard dog. I walk down the steps, looking for Dre.

At first, I don't spot him. Then I see his silhouette a ways up the beach already, heading for the dunes. I run to catch up to him, wondering why I'm even bothering to chase after him again. Dre stops, looks at the sky, and then out at the ocean. I'm grateful that he stops, needing a break from running on the uneven sand. I stop to catch my breath, watching him closely. He's still staring at the water. Then, Dre turns around slowly and walks into the grassy part of the dunes. Dre must have a thing for those stupid weeds. Stupid stupid weeds.

I walk slower, knowing that I have time now to reach him. As I approach the dunes, I notice a small tent behind the dunes. It's not a camping tent, more like a tarp hung over some large sticks wedged into the sand. It's a shoddy, makeshift tent, resembling what people would construct if they were stranded on a deserted island.

Holy crap! It's a fort, a fort that a father would make with his kids. I know I'm going to hurl, right here, right now. What have I done? "I've gotta get out of here," I say, not realizing I've spoken audibly.

The flap on the tent opens and Dre comes out, staring at me. "Kathryn, what—what're you doing here?"

"I gotta go," I turn, starting to bolt.

Dre grabs my arm before I can leave, "I knew it would be too much for you. I'm sorry I couldn't tell you."

"Couldn't tell me? Are you kidding? You **chose** not to tell me," I yell, tears filling my eyes. "You knew I wouldn't come near you if I knew you had a wife … and … and kids," I scream, pointing to the fort. "Does she know, Dre? Does she know you've been … been … with me?"

Dre's eyeing me carefully, as his face falls. "Kathryn, I don't think you understand," he says, shaking his head. "I would … that's not …" He trails off, shaking his head. Dre runs his hands through his hair and sighs deeply.

"I'm not married. I don't have kids. I'd never do that … to you … to anyone."

"Right. Like I'd believe anything you say anymore," I snap, walking away. Suddenly, Dre grabs me around the waist and picks me up, carrying me toward his adorable little fort.

I kick and scream. "Put me down Dre, so help me … I swear to God—"

"Just listen, please," Dre pleads, pulling back the flap and putting me down in the tent. I try to break through, but he holds me back. "Stop. Listen to me. This … this is what I couldn't tell you," he states, motioning toward the tent.

"What? That you and your kids built a beach fort? Congratulations!" I grumble sarcastically, looking around, really noticing it for the first time. It's more than a tent, more than a beachside fort.

Dre's tent has bags of clothes, boxes of necessities from Rory's hotel, and piles of blankets. *Cider House Rules* is sitting on one of the boxes, opened, and face down, holding a spot in place. I glance at Dre. His shoulders are slumped, eyes staring at the sand.

"Dre, what is this place?" I ask, eyeing him carefully.

I watch as his eyes dart around, looking everywhere but at me. His lips form a pained smile, and he says, "Home."

"What? I don't get it. You're … you're—"

"Homeless."

PART TWO

Desolate Knowledge

I wait for it. It doesn't come. I wait longer; it still doesn't come. It's shocking really. I remember being terrified to tell my parents that I didn't want to go into the family business—in no way, shape, or form was I taking the business path in life. My parents fucking blew gaskets, screaming until they were blue in the face. I'd never heard the words "disappointment" and "disgrace" more in my entire life. My mother sobbed; my father basically disowned me, saying medicine was "for pussies." When I first told them, the look of total repulsion covered their faces. They've never accepted my choices, supported me in any of my endeavors. I walked across Brown's stage to receive my degree without anyone in the audience beaming with pride as I shook hands and was handed my diploma.

I'm waiting for disgust to overpower Kathryn's soft, beautiful, breath-capturing features. I'm waiting. All I see is confusion and curiosity. She's staring at me like one would gaze at a stray puppy or a bird with a broken wing, a look that clearly portrays her pity and sorrow. I don't want pity, sympathy, or sorrow. I don't want help or charity. I just want … want … her.

"Just go Kathryn," I say, sitting down on the bedroll that Rory insisted I have. Ever since I got to Charleston, twelve months ago, Rory's been trying to get me to stay with him, "bunk in swank," but that's not what I want. He and Lanette tried to get me to come work with them, make some money, and save a bit. But again, that's not what I'm looking for. What I'm looking for is answers, solutions, but mainly, I'm just looking for myself.

Kathryn turns and walks out, leaving me alone in the tent, in my world of fucked up Hell. I can hear her walking through the sand. Then, I hear the "Aggghhh" as she storms back.

Ducking her head back in she asks, "Why do you keep trying to get rid of me? Do you really not want me that much?" Coming through the opening she adds, "I thought we were really connecting. All you do is walk away and never—never once have you come back. And you've never come after me."

Holy fuck, she's right. Kathryn Howell is fucking right. For the first time, I can see this from her angle, her point of view. I keep running for the door, but she keeps closing it, keeping me in, holding me close. I thought all along that I was protecting her, but in reality, I've been hurting her, making her think that it was me who didn't want her. I've wanted her all along; I was terrified of her knowing the truth and not wanting me, which I couldn't bear.

"Kathryn," I say, standing up, going to her. "My God, you're right, you are so right." I take her hands in mine. "I fucked up. I've been fucking up for a long time now. I'm so sorry—so completely sorry," I explain. I stare into her beautiful eyes.

"Look at this. Look at me. I'm just so fucking ashamed. How could I ask you to accept this?" Kathryn's eyes pool with tears.

"I've been so caught up in how much it was going to hurt, break my heart to hear that you couldn't accept this ... accept me ... that I kept pushing you away, never believing that this ... that we ... could work."

Kathryn moves closer, putting her forehead against my chest; I wrap my arms around her, securing her close to me. I stroke her hair and can hear her small sobs.

"I don't understand any of this," she admits. "I just know that when I'm close to you, when your arms are around me, nothing's ever made me feel more certain or more clear about anything before."

Kathryn looks up at me, tears streaming down her face. "I don't want you to push me away anymore, Dre. I don't want to walk away either. But ... but ... I'm going to leave right now and forget about how incredible you make me feel if you don't start talking to me ... letting me in."

She's the most gorgeous, intelligent, accepting, and wonderful woman I've ever met. I put my hand on the back of her neck, urging her to me. Her eyes flutter; her tongue moistens her lips. I kiss her, softly, intimately, passionately, wanting her to feel just how much I feel for her, need her, want her. When her lips meet mine, the weeks we've been apart have disappeared, my struggles are gone, the fear dissipates; all that is left is warmth, desire, joy, and love.

"Dre?" Kathryn asks, pulling back. "I'm serious. I can't be shut out any longer."

"I know, Baby, I know." I kiss her neck, willing myself to stop, and respect her wishes. "I just love touching you, tasting you, smelling you. It's been too long."

"It won't be too long ever again if you just talk to me," she says, backing away, keeping my hand in hers. "We've got the physical and intimate connections nailed … we need to work on the emotional one too."

Kathryn's right. This isn't a fling. This isn't "for fun." I belong to Kathryn Howell—every part of me is hers and hers alone. Nobody will ever touch me, affect me, have a hold on me the way she does. I'm hers. And my God, do I want her to be mine.

"I really don't know where to start," I confess, sitting down on the blankets, pulling her toward me. She's sitting between my legs with her back against my chest. Kathryn tries to move her body to face me.

"Please, just lie like this, let me hold you against me. I can't bear to watch your face when I tell you the things that I'm going to tell you." She nods quietly, waiting for my story, the story I've been avoiding since the day I met her.

"Dre, I'm still here. Let that be your courage, your strength. The fact that I'm in your arms should be enough."

And it is. She's always right. "Maybe you could just start me off, ask me some questions."

Nodding, Kathryn laces her fingers in mine and says, "Who's your decorator? I love that lantern." Her giggle softens my mood. I missed hearing her laugh. Her laughter ignites my courage.

"Great. That's just great Pebbles, kick a man while he's down," I chuckle.

"God I missed that. I missed hearing you call me, 'Pebbles.' I almost went out and bought the box set collection of the *Flinstones*, because I missed you so much."

And that's it; her honesty compels me. Her total disregard of how her words, how the truth is going to make her look, is what's gotten to me all along. Kathryn Howell is exactly the change I've been searching for.

"I was sick of it. Sick of how everything in life revolves around who has what, how much he has, or who makes more," I start, feeling a small sense of relief as I finally open up to her. "I wanted to believe that I was better than that, better than getting all caught up in money and material things."

"Don't you think you took it to the extreme?" she asks, looking around.

"No, I don't. I wanted to prove … to prove to them … to myself … that money, prestige, and status don't fucking buy happiness," I explain. "My entire life it's always been about how things look on the outside. I've never gotten to really know how anything looks … or feels … on the inside." Until now. I know what it feels like now to know that your total reason for existence is in someone's else's hands. Kathryn is my everything.

"I understand that Dre. It's admirable really. It took me a long time to figure those things out too," she says, tracing small circles with her pinkie on the back of my hand. "But I still did it with a job … a car … somewhere to live."

"It's not that easy for me. If I didn't go 'cold turkey' or 'balls to the wall' with this plan, then it wasn't going to work out," I explain. I knew as soon as I made this decision that it had to be all or nothing. "I didn't want it to be too easy to go back to that lifestyle … and honestly, in the past year, I haven't wanted to at all."

"Then, you're growing as a person, Dre," Kathryn compliments.

"I was until you came along. Then, I started questioning everything. I spent one night with you and wanted to give you the world," I confess, remembering how I wanted to buy her anything that she ever wanted. "Your face lit up when we walked in to the honeymoon suite. I want it to light all the time up like that when I give you something, when you're with me."

"Dre, my God, don't you get it? It lit up like that, because I was there with you—experiencing it with you," she explains. "I'm not gonna lie. I enjoy ritzy, extravagant things on occasion. Really, who doesn't? You seemed to like that room, that champagne, and those strawberries—"

"Fuck woman, you can't bring those things up right now. I just got hard," I respond, pulling her against me so she could feel how hard she makes me.

"Really? Me mentioning strawberries got you hard? That's pathetic Dre," Kathryn giggles, turning her head to kiss my neck. "What would happen if I told you that I loved the taste of that champagne on your hard, big, di—"

"I'd fucking roll you over right now, fuck you so hard that you wouldn't be able to remember your name, Pebbles." I growl, fisting my hands in her hair.

"Mmmmm … looks like I better not finish that sentence then," she groans. "We still have more to talk about." Kathryn moves forward, turns around, and sits cross-legged staring at me. "So, you just packed up ... or actually didn't pack anything up, and started over?"

"Pretty much," I say, "I just needed to figure out how to exist without money, without materialistic things, and without power controlling who I am."

"So, do you plan to live here in this plush, quaint little tent forever?" Kathryn asks, running her fingers along my blankets.

"No Kathryn, I don't," I quip sarcastically, rolling my eyes at her.

"I do plan at some point to actually do my residency and use my medical degree," I explain. "I'm just not ready for all that. I've still got time to figure it all out." She sits, staring at me, wide-eyed and serious. I wish I knew what she was thinking, feeling.

"But ... but ... if this is too much for you ... too hard to accept, then I'll start my residency as soon as I can. I'm pretty sure I know what I want ... what I can be ... and who I want."

"Oh for God's sake! No, Dre," Kathryn exhales, "I'd never ask you to change or give up something that means a lot to you ... just to make me happy." She starts twirling her hair around her finger. "Granted, it's a lot to wrap my brain around. I mean, my boyfr— ... my ... my ... friend lives in a tent on the beach. It's not really something that ya hear all that often."

"Don't correct yourself, just hearing you insinuate that we have something ... something more here is enough to make me be a better man ... a man more worthy of you, Kathryn," I confess.

My heart lightens; the weight of the last few months is lessening. I feel fucking elated. Just being with her, hearing her talk, and watching her smile is reason enough to pack up and go the fuck to work.

Kathryn's face visibly softens when she smiles, blushing. "What I don't get though is if you wanted to change, become a better person, get away from modern luxuries, then why didn't you just go to some third world country, and help sick people, instead of setting up camp on the beach in South Carolina?"

"I thought of that—even considered it, I decided against it, because I wanted to be around the luxuries, the ostentation of modern society, and still be able to deny myself," I explain, hoping she understands. "Being in another country that doesn't offer up all of the hoopla would just mean that I **can't** get it—not that I'm resisting it."

Kathryn listens intently, taking it all in, nodding. "That actually does make sense. But why here? Why Charleston?"

"Rory," I reply easily. "When I told Rory my plan, he insisted I come here. I think he wants to keep an eye on me—he likes having me around ... I like being around," I admit. "He really is a great guy ... with a huge heart."

"So, ummm, you like have ... uhhh ... no money? Like none?" she asks as her cheeks redden.

"Now, I didn't say that," I chuckle. "I bought you a battery, remember?" Kathryn nods and smiles. I'm beginning to think that she may accept me for the freeloading, loser that I am.

"What money I do have, I keep in a safe at the hotel. Rory's under strict rules to only break into it for shit that I absolutely must have," I explain, hoping she understands me a little more.

"I usually get food and junk by working for it. I do odds and ends for Lanette, and she pays me in goddamn delicious-ass meals," Kathryn chuckles, probably remembering how incredible Lanette's food is or maybe even how perfect our kiss by the waterfall was.

"When I work down at the docks, I get paid in the daily catch," I explain. "I've realized that there's nothing more wonderful than cooking fish on an open flame on the beach ... it's so cool. Well, except when I get caught by the police. They're not too happy with open fires out on the beach." We both chuckle at the image of the police busting me for cooking seafood on the beach.

"So that's why you know everyone everywhere. I never could figure that out."

"Yep. I basically shower and shave at the hotel ... or at the McAllisters' when I don't feel like going all the way down to the hotel," I confirm. "I spend my days helping people, getting to know people, and just hanging out, taking it all in."

"McAllisters? Who are they?" she asks looking puzzled.

"They own that monstrosity down the beach. They called the cops on me a few times ... pissed that there was a homeless dude living on their beach," I reply, recalling how much Steve and Ava hated me last year. "They wanted to get rid of me, badly ... until I saved their daughter one day."

Kathryn's eyes widen, and I continue, "Hester had gotten caught in the ocean current. She went under. Steve dove in and got her, but she wasn't breathing. I saw the whole thing and ran over to help," I explain.

Kathryn listens, capturing my every word as if the story I'm telling impacts her directly. "At first, Steve wouldn't let me near her. Finally, he let me help while he called 9-1-1. I cleared her windpipe and started CPR compressions. Hester gagged, spat up some water, and was as good as new," I recount. Relief washes over Kathryn's face. "Ever since then, we've been like family," I say.

"Crimony. Thank God you were there, Dre." Kathryn says, beaming at me.

"It really wasn't that big of a deal," I shrug. "I like them. Their dog, Tim Johnson, and I have formed a pretty solid bond. Sometimes, I even feel like he's my dog."

"Their dog's name is 'Tim Johnson' and their daughter is 'Hester?' That's priceless," she laughs, snorting twice. "The literary agent in me loves that."

"Yeah, Steve's a writer, and Ava is a literature professor at the College of Charleston, so it fits them," I say. "Sometimes, when the storms are going to get really bad, Ava sends Hester out to beg me to come inside for the night. Ava fights dirty; she knows I can't turn that little girl down."

"Storms? I never thought about that," Kathryn says, her eyes filling with worry.

"Nothing to worry about. Between Rory and the McAllisters, I'm safe. It's the people who don't have anyone to look out for them that it's really scary for … and sad," I say.

My stomach clinches as I think about all the people who are out there alone, day-after-day, penniless and starving. "I've really learned a lot being out here, living like this. I spend a lot of time down at the shelter, lending a hand. I don't accept their offerings or anything like that, but I do like to help … to talk … be their friend."

Kathryn's silent for a while, probably processing everything I just piled on her. "Remember when Dave at the Fair was thanking you for something? What'd you do for him?" Kathryn asks.

I feel guilty, realizing Kathryn must've been thinking about that since the moment it happened. I blew it off like it was no big deal, but she obviously saw through it all, knowing I was hiding something all along.

"Nothing all that earth-shattering. Dave's not really a part of the fair, ya know; he just goes and helps out to get free tickets. He works down on the docks actually," I explain. "I know him pretty well. Anyway, his son was climbing on the ferris wheel when nobody was watching and fell. Dislocated his shoulder—"

"So, you heard about it and ran down to fix it?" Kathryn finishes. I nod, shrugging my shoulders.

Kathryn crawls over to me, staring at me as she does so. "I can't believe you thought I'd leave you after hearing all of this. Don't you know that a woman's libido is tied directly to her heart strings?"

"Huh? Whattya mean" I ask, brushing her hair away from her face.

"You know, when a woman sees a man she's dating play with a little kid or do something over-the-top nice, it immediately wets her panties and makes her want him even more," she explains, kissing my neck and biting lightly on my earlobe.

"Darling, where I'm from, women only get wet from money and prestige," I counter.

"Well Dre, you're in Charleston now, the friendliest city in the country, and I for one ... am one hot mess right now," she whispers, licking the corners of my mouth. "If you don't start touching me, then there's going to be Hell to pay," Kathryn says, climbing the rest of the way up on to my lap and kissing me hungrily.

I've missed her touch, her taste, so much; my body just burns with desire and need for her. I can feel the want from my heart to my groin, pulling on my spine, pushing on my stomach. Groaning, I say, "The beach is pretty private right now. Wanna make love to me in the sand under the moon?"

"You're incredibly romantic, but Dre, I don't need romance right now. I need you inside me," she pleads. Everything tightens inside me; the yearning is almost deadly.

"Fuck Pebbles, I've missed you," I moan into her ears running my hand up the back of her shirt, reveling in the feel of her bare skin.

"Then flip me over and show me how much," she begs, sending heat straight to my groin. Flip her over? Fuck yeah.

"How in the world can you possibly be okay with all this?" I ask, confused.

"Oh my God, did I just ask you, no tell you, to turn me over and do me from behind and we're still talking? Did you grow a vag since the last time I saw you?" Kathryn asks, laughing.

Taking off her shirt, she says, "We'll talk about this too, I guess, but we're going to get started at the same time." After she unfastens her bra and it slides slowly down her arms, she says, "I decided on my way here that nothing was going to keep me away."

I nod, taking her nipple into my mouth. "I realized that I wanted you, and we'd get through whatever had your panties in a bunch … together," she moans as I tug lightly on her hardened nipple. The pressure she's putting my on head, urges me to suck harder; I acquiesce. "Oh God … yeah …"

"Keep talking Pebbles," I chuckle, squeezing both of her breasts together, looking up at her with heated desire.

"Nothing was keeping me away," she pants truthfully. "But then when I got here, I thought … thought … Oh Dre … that … that …"

I stop, lifting her up. Kathryn stands as I unbutton her pants, pulling them down. Her hot pink lace panties remind me how sexy and confident she is, confirming how lucky I am to have her. "That what?" I ask, shimmying her underwear down over her hips, slowly, as I soak in the beauty of her body.

"That Ava was your wife," she admits, as my hands massage her thighs. With each stroke and knead, I maneuver her body closer to me; her sexy scent captures my attention, and my body weakens with need.

"Did you say 'wife?' Fuck Pebbles, what kind of asshole do you take me for?" I ask, realizing how hurt she must've been. My chest aches, knowing the pain and torture I put her though, all while not wanting to ever hurt her.

"I'd never do that to you … to anyone. That's un-fucking-forgivable." My fingers find her desire, wet and slick, slippery and sensual. Her knees buckle; I hold her into place.

"But you still came back here after you thought I was with Ava?" I question, quickening the pressure and rhythm of the tiny circles I'm manipulating within her.

Her breath catches, "Dre, I was so hurt, so pissed." Kathryn rounds her hips, swaying into my touch as she says, "Ready to fight, but the truth is … I just … just … I want you. I can't stop." Kathryn's body tenses; I can feel the mini quakes inside of her as she clutches my head grabbing fistfuls of my hair. "Oh God, Dre, I'm … I'm … yours."

I yank her body down onto the blanket, laying her on her stomach. Grabbing a condom out of my wallet, I rip open the foil packet and glide the thing over my straining cock. I trail my tongue up her calves, along her thighs, and on her beautifully rounded tight ass. I knead the flesh, filling with unbearable need and desire.

"Please … now Dre," she begs, lifting her body onto her hand and knees, pushing back against me.

"Holy shit, you are just sexy as Hell," I say, placing my hands on her hips as I slide between her legs. Her body welcomes me, enveloping me in wet, slick warmth. The feeling is incredible; reality floods through me. Everything that I questioned all these months finally seems so clear. The truth. The answers. Myself. I'm nothing, nobody, insignificant, if I'm not with Kathryn Howell.

She rocks back against me; I'm soaring, growing, grinding, and yearning. This is everything. She is everything. I can feel my need for her deep within my body, my soul. This is right. It's perfect. Kathryn rolls her hips; I mimic her rotations. Her moans send me to the edge. I'm climbing—almost over the top.

"Adrian! Adrian!" Rory bellows, coming through the tent.

"Fuck dude!" I scream, as Kathryn lunges into the blankets, and I fall on top of her, covering her naked body, pulling the blankets over us. "What the Hell?"

"Sorry Kathryn," Rory apologizes, looking away. "Adrian, I'm sorry buddy, but I had to come."

"Adrian? Ummm ... Dre?" Kathryn asks, looking between the two of us.

"There's no time for that. Sorry buddy," Rory says, walking over to me, looking solemn and frightful. "Piper's in the hospital," Rory explains, tears filling his eyes. "It's bad."

"What? What happened? How bad is it?"

"I booked you ... both ... on the next flight out," Rory explains. Looking at Kathryn, Rory says, "Syd's at your apartment packing you some shit. She's meeting us at the airport."

"Holy fuck Rory! Is it that bad that I've gotta go home? Now?" I ask, feeling my stomach lurch. "Like how bad? Is she gonna ... gonna—"

"Adrian man, I don't know. Lafferty just called me; he doesn't know much," Rory said, averting my eyes.

My entire body convulses; my eyes betray my strength, filling and spilling with tears and pain. "Oh God, Rory. Oh no," I cry, hitting my knees. "I left her. I fucking left her."

Tears streaming down Kathryn's face, she looks at me, terrified, and says, "Who's Piper?"

"My baby sister."

~ Kathryn ~

Relief and pain battle each other inside my heart. Piper is his sister, his baby sister; crisis over her title, their connection averted. But pain and worry overtake my heart. Dre, or I mean, Adrian, is crushed. Why would he lie about his name, too? Maybe that explains why I couldn't find him on Google, Twitter, Facebook, or anything. Not that I spent hour after hour, day after day searching. Maybe that's even why there was no "Dre Donley" registered at Brown, too. Dre really wanted to get away from his previous life, alienating himself from every part of who he used to be.

Feeling concern and helpless, I eye Rory, looking for guidance. Rory shrugs, shaking his head, as worry splays across his face. Rubbing Dre's shoulder, "Man, come on, we need to get to the airport. Syd's on her way."

Glancing up at me, Dre pleads, "Go with me. Please. Come to New Hampshire with me?"

"Of course Dre, Adrian, anything … anything you need," I comfort. New Hampshire? Dre's from New Hampshire?

Grimacing, he says, "Dre, please, God Kathryn, please, please don't call me 'Adrian.' I don't ever want to be 'Adrian' to you, Pebbles."

I nod, extending my hand for him to take. "Whatever you want, Babe," I comfort.

The three of us walk in silence across the beach to the McAllisters' walkway. Crossing the walkway, Rory says, "I got everything out of your safe. It's in the car. I charged your phone on the way here." Rory hands Dre an iPhone, a phone he swore he didn't have or use.

"Thanks," Dre nods, squeezing my hand. "Lafferty didn't say anything? Didn't tell you what happened?"

Rory hesitates. Dre and I both realize he's not telling us something. Dre stops, turns to Rory, and pleads, "Man, you've gotta tell me if you know something. I can't get there ... be fucking around ... them ... and hear whatever it is all at once. You know that. Come on, you've gotta tell me."

Rory wipes his eyes, nodding. "Alright Buddy, alright, she's in ICU. Pipe's lost a lot of blood. They've given her a transfusion already, but the rare blood type is a concern. You're gonna need to donate when you get there."

"God, fuck, of course ... what else? Is that it?" Dre asks, looking distraught.

"If ... I mean, when ... when ... she wakes up, they're gonna monitor her ... before ... before ..."

"Before what?" Dre grabs Rory, shaking his shoulders, urging him to disclose everything. I'm standing there, watching all of this unravel, feeling nothing but pain for Dre and an overwhelming sense of uselessness to him and his family.

"Before they move her to the psych floor for evaluation," Rory finally explains.

"Psych ward? Why the fuck would they—" Dre stops; his eyes widen, spilling over with tears all over again. "Piper didn't … she wouldn't …" Rory grabs Dre as he begins to sway, his knees buckling from the weight of the situation.

"Come on Buddy, ya gotta pull it together. Ya gotta be strong for her right now. She needs you," Rory begs, trying to give Dre the strength he needs to go forward.

"Kathryn, why don't you go start the car and tell Syd we'll be at the airport in twenty minutes?" Rory says. I nod, taking Rory's keys and heading to the front of the house, knowing there's more that Rory and Dre are keeping from me.

Walking to Rory's car, I notice Warren's truck, and my stomach falls. It's amazing how life still seems to go on for others when someone else's life comes crashing down. I get in the car, start it, blast the air conditioning, and text Warren, praying that Syd and Rory will take care of getting Warren's truck back to him tomorrow morning. Rory must have some effect on Sydney. She's not usually one to step up to the plate when tragedy hits. I'm lucky to have her. I'm lucky to have everyone in my life. It's crazy how something awful makes you realize just how blessed you really are.

Warren's truck is his pride and joy. How ironic? One man loves his truck, an inanimate machine, while another fights adamantly against material love—only to discover that his baby sister lies fighting for her life in a hospital bed, a life she may have wanted to end herself. Holy heck, life is one confusing and agonizing turn after the next. Life sure doesn't make sense; there's no rhyme or reason to what's thrown at you.

Dre and I sit in silence, fingers interlocked in one another's hand, waiting for the flight, boarding the plane, and all throughout take off. After the flight attendant fills our drinks for the second time, I finally speak, "Dre, I don't know what to do—for you."

Dre looks at me, bewildered, as if he just realized someone was actually attached to the hand he's holding. "Just being here is everything to me," he says.

"I just … I … I've never dealt with anything scary or hard before," I confess, feeling worthless. "I'm afraid I'm gonna say or do the wrong thing."

"Kathryn, I'm not gonna lie or sugar coat this. It's gonna get really intense. I'm so sorry for what you're gonna see and hear," he explains, kissing my hand. "I wish I could just protect you from it all, but Baby, having you with me is what's going to get me through this."

"You're kind of scaring me, Dre." I say, feeling a sense of doom looming.

"I wanted to get away, to start over, because of my family," he begins. "They're awful, horrible fucking excuses for human beings."

"Piper?"

"Oh God no, she's the best we've got," Dre swoons, his face lighting up. "Unfortunately, she's only seventeen, so she's stuck there until fall."

Shaking his head, he continues, "Growing up, I always knew my parents were assholes, but it wasn't until last year that I really saw them for whom they really are."

"Doesn't everyone have problems with their parents?" I ask, wanting to appease his anger and resentment. People shouldn't give up, turn their backs on their families, no matter how screwed up and dysfunctional they are.

"Not to the degree at what the O'Donnells have," he confesses. "The money, power, control, it's all the O'Donnells want or need—they'll stop at nothing to get it too."

"O'Donnell is your real last name?" I ask, wanting to fill in all the holes in the stories, fabrications, downright lies he's told me. Dre's lies pile higher than any skyscraper I've ever seen, but there's something about him that allows me to still trust him, forgive him, want to be with him. God, I pray I'm not making a monumental mistake flying to his hometown with him.

"Yeah, I became 'Dre Donley' to sever the ties to them—as well as hide from them," Dre admits, shaking his head. "They're pissed that I'm ruining their reputation, destroying their perfect family image by going into medicine, refusing my place in the O'Donnell status hierarchy."

"I just don't understand why it matters. Who cares? You're a grown man; you can make your own decisions—live any way you want." I question.

"You'll get it once you're there, and you see first-hand how they operate," Dre says, his face falling. "I just fucking hope they let me in to see Piper."

"Of course they'll let you in. She's your sister!" I exclaim.

"No Pebbles, it's not that easy with them. You haven't met them. Nothing is ever that easy with them."

As we ride the elevator to baggage claim, Dre faces me and says, "Promise me that all of this, what you're about to see, hear, and discover won't change how you feel about me right now."

"Dre, wow, I—"

"Just please, promise me," he says, his eyes pleading with urgency, as he grips the railing with one hand and my hand with his other.

"Okay ... okay Dre ... I promise," I relent, hoping that I never have to break this vow.

Once we exit the airport, Dre sighs languidly, his shoulders falling. "Hi Lafferty," he says, greeting an older gentleman. The man takes Dre's bags, while reaching for mine.

"I'm happy to see you, sir. Unfortunate circumstances for this reunion. Forgive my intrusiveness. Jada, Piper's friend, knew she was in contact with you ... Piper's phone had your friend, Mr. Carlson's, number in it." Lafferty explains, apologetically. "I would never disrespect your wishes otherwise."

"Of course Lafferty, I'm glad you called," Dre says, hugging him stiffly. "Rory was a big help getting me here, so calling him was definitely the right move."

"Thank you sir," Lafferty says. "Excuse my manners, Ma'am. I'm Niles Lafferty, the O'Donnells' butler and driver." Lafferty extends his hand, shaking mine professionally and formally.

"Kathryn Howell, Dre's friend," I reply, smiling nervously. Chauffeur? Butler? Understanding his confusion and discomfort, I clarify, "Adrian's friend from South Carolina."

"She can say she's my 'friend' all she wants Lafferty, but this woman here is undoubtedly the best thing that's ever happened to me—quite possibly even the love of my life," Dre states, beaming at me. My heart flutters; my mouth goes dry. He really does take my breath away.

Smiling warmly, Lafferty nods, while opening the hatchback to the black Escalade parked in front of us. "I didn't know how much you'd have with you, so I brought this car. Sheldon has the limo at the hospital with your parents," Lafferty explains, motioning for us to get in the car.

"Would you care to go straight to the hospital or to the house to freshen up a bit first?" The look on Lafferty's face tells me that he thinks we should be stopping at the house before heading to the hospital.

"Nope, I'm good like this. If they have a problem with how I look then they can take it up with someone who gives a fuck," Dre confirms, slamming the door harder than necessary. Lafferty flinches and grimaces, at either the door slam or the vulgarity of Dre's words; I'm not sure which.

Driving to the hospital, all three of us are silent, engrossed in our own thoughts and worries. I've never really visited anyone in the hospital before, not counting my co-worker who had a baby over the summer. Hospitals creep me out. They're buildings where people suffer and die, for God's sake. Granted, sometimes, people recover and go home, but that doesn't change the fact that there's a storage room for corpses. No thank you. Machines and doctors and injuries scare the heck out of me. Luckily, I've never been faced with tragic, debilitating pain or fear. Currently, fear is enveloping me, suffocating me. I'm terrified for Dre. I'm scared of what will happen to his little sister. I'm afraid of what I'll actually witness. And I'm frightened of the truth that lurks within Dre's past and family.

- Dre -

I'm not an overly religious man. But, I've been known to ask Him every now and then for a favor or two. I should probably do my part a little more—show more gratitude, especially since all I've been doing since Rory walked into my tent is pray to my ever-loving Lord that Piper comes out of this. How could I have left her? I knew better than to leave her alone with them, let them try to corrupt her, change her. Piper is the only person worth anything in my family, my past. She's the only thing that's good in my life—until Kathryn. God, please don't let her—

"Are you okay?" Kathryn asks, holding the door for me. I hadn't realized I stopped at the threshold. My entire life I've loved hospitals, been enamored and amazed by what occurred within the walls of them. The medical profession has always mesmerized and awed me, intrigued me. For the first time in my life, I'm scared to death to walk through the door.

"Yeah, I'm okay. Just a little spooked," I admit.

"I'm sure," she says, offering her hand. "I'm here, Dre. Don't forget that."

Smiling weakly, I grab her hand as we walk into the hospital.

Piper is still in intensive care. Naturally, I'm not on the approved list of visitors. Rory called the hospital en route to the airport to ask what I already knew. I had the foresight to see this one coming. They could only give information to people on the "in the know" list, due to privacy laws. I knew my parents would never put me on that list—just to spite me. They'd know that Piper's well-being was an integral part of my happiness and existence.

Approaching the reception desk blocking the doors to ICU, a strikingly beautiful woman with soft features and flawless black skin stops us. "Excuse me, do you have your visitors' badge?"

There are times when I'm thankful that I was blessed with this face and this body; it often gets me what others couldn't get, makes things easier. I'm not proud of it, but I've repeatedly used it to my advantage. By the way she's devouring me with her eyes, this is going to be too easy.

"No, I'm sorry. We just got here," I explain. "We're here to see Piper O'Donnell."

"Oh yes, of course," she says after recognizing the last name.

As she looks over the list of names, she asks for mine. "Tristan O'Donnell," I reply amicably and confidently. This is Jada Montgomery."

The receptionist is clearly appraising me, calculating my net worth. I can almost hear her "carrying the one" in her head. It's nauseating really. When people hear my name all they really ever hear is "jackpot" or "walking wallet." God, I want to fucking throttle her, but I know my anger is misplaced, misdirected—all she's done is ask me my name.

"Oh splendid Mr. O'Donnell, I know they've been eagerly awaiting your arrival," she coos, batting her lashes at me, as she bites seductively on the end of her pen.

I'm not at all shocked that Tristan hasn't graced them with his presence yet. I knew that whatever, or whomever, he was doing right now would absolutely take priority over Piper. Fucking typical. Goddamn selfish-ass bastard.

The receptionist buzzes us through the double doors. "Who's Tristan? Who's Jada?" Kathryn asks, running to keep up with me. "Dre, wait! Hold on."

"I'm sorry. I just can't believe he isn't here. Son-of-a-bitch, what a fucking prick," I seethe. "Where does he get off not being here?"

"Who? I don't know what you're talking about," she says, staring at me, her eyes searching my face.

"Tristan, my brother. I knew he wouldn't be here. I also knew they'd be waiting on him like court waits on the fucking king," I say through gritted teeth.

Kathryn nods, stepping back. "Okay, ummm … but if he were here, we wouldn't get in, right? So that's kind of a good thing."

I shouldn't be yelling at her, taking this out on her. I sound like an envious, petulant child, but she hasn't met Tristan. Kathryn has no idea who or what he is.

"Who's 'Jada? I should know who I'm impersonating."

"Jada's my sister's best friend. I knew she wouldn't be here this late, so it's cool to use her name," I explain, relaxing a little, thankful that Jada and Piper are close enough that she knew to notify me.

"You're a pretty smart cookie," she says, giggling, as she loops her arm through the crook in mine. "For a homeless dude."

I stop, turn toward her, and kiss her softly on the lips. Relishing the sensation of her lips on mine, the taste of her tongue as it twirls around mine, and the feeling of her body pressed against mine.

Freeing herself from my embrace, Kathryn touches her lips, eyelashes fluttering, and says, "Whoa, what was that for?"

"I needed a little 'Kathryn-courage;' kissing you gives me strength," I explain, grinning at her.

"I'm glad that I give you strength, because you ... those kinds of kisses ... weaken me," she admits, sighing.

I take Kathryn's hand in mine, heading down to room #202 to see my baby sister. Turning the corner of the corridor, the sight I'd been dreading all along slaps me in the face. My father and mother are standing outside of the room. My mother is wildly tapping away at the keyboard of her cell phone; my father's pacing back and forth, talking quietly, but dramatically into his phone. They're dressed impeccably. My father's suit jacket is gone; his tie loosened around his neck. My mother is in a tailored pants suit and heels, her hair perfectly styled and flawless. The only indication that things are amiss in their lives is the small smudge of mascara on my mother's face.

Luckily, they're too engrossed in their own lives, they've yet to notice us. It's quite possible my parents wouldn't even recognize me anyway. Their clean-cut, well-groomed, and well-dressed son left over a year ago, and who's returning does not even remotely resemble the same man. I motion to Kathryn, indicating that we're standing in front of my parents.

Her eyes widen; she stares at me in disbelief. On cue my parents turn simultaneously, noticing us for the first time. My father is stoic and cold, saying nothing as he turns back to his phone call.

My mother puts her phone into her Louis Vitton handbag, clears her throat, and asks, "How did you get back here? It's restricted for anyone … but family."

Closing my eyes, taking a deep breath, I say, "Come on Mother, don't do this. You gotta let me see her," as I try to maneuver around my mom to the hospital room.

"You made your decision, young man, when you left town," she spews the words venomously at me, blocking my way into Piper's room.

Finally, my father disconnects his call, walking over to us. "Well, well, well, look who finally showed up."

"Hi Dad, can you let me around … please?" I ask, trying to get through.

"Don't 'Hi Dad' me. You can't come waltzing in here after being MIA for over a year, and expect to get your way," he says, respectfully, not to mention surprisingly. Then, he pulls me by the collar, growling quietly in my ear, "You spoiled little fuck." My father—always the gentleman in front of the eyes of strangers.

"I'm getting in there … with or without your consent," I say. Squaring off my shoulders, staring at my father, nose-to-nose, I threaten, "I left, and you both know damn well why. I kept your fucking ugly secrets. Don't make me use them … now … after all this time just to see my fucking sister."

"Listen hear you little—"

"Look who the mother-fucking cat dragged in!" Tristan bellows from down the hallway. My parents are diverted for a moment, which gives me enough time to yank Kathryn's arm, pulling her through the doorway with me.

The lights are dim; the rhythmic beep of the monitors fill my ears, shattering my heart. I walk through the dark, cold, stark room, concentrating on my steps, feeling the weight of each foot as I step one foot, then the other toward her bed, willing myself to move closer. It's paradoxical how much the one place that typically gives me the greatest sense of self-worth and confidence suddenly fills me with dread and an overwhelming sense of worthlessness.

My eyes adjust to the light and the limp, small body of my sister looks frail and helpless. Piper's hooked up to an Electrocardiograph machine, monitoring her heart and other vitals. An oxygen tube is in her nose, assisting her with the breaths she can't or won't take on her own. I'm relieved that she doesn't need an Endotracheal tube and ventilator. Small victories.

I look around, taking in the dark, dank, cold room, wishing it had some of the vibrancy and effervescence that typically surrounded my sister. But it doesn't. This room is filled with gloom and fear, as most sterile ICU rooms are. There's even a faint smell of dried blood and urine wafting through the room, churning my stomach, knowing it's the blood of my family, our coupled pain and deceit.

I remember the first time I ever let her down. She must've been about five or six-years-old; I was 16 at the time. Some friends and I were going to go sledding on a Snow Day from school. Piper begged me to let her go. I didn't want her tagging along, but my mom insisted I take her. My mom hated Snow Days, because that meant we were home with her, distracting her, disrupting her time, and destroying her house. If I wanted to go, then I had to take Piper with me.

It was cold; snow was still coming down in a whiteout. My friends were all at the park, having a blast, sledding, drinking whatever they scored from their parents' liquor cabinets. I was fucking pissed. My kid sister had just ruined my whole day. The snow was wet and packing easily, creating a slick, icy hill.

I took no caution in going down the hill, accelerating considerably. Piper was on the front of the old runner sled. We were going so fast; I couldn't control the rusted-out runners. We were headed straight for a pole by the pavilion. I screamed for her to jump. I jumped off, not realizing I should've grabbed her too. I rolled down the remainder of the hill. Piper slammed right into the pole, cutting her head open, getting a severe concussion.

Carrying her home, Piper cried in my arms, blood pouring down her face. I felt so helpless, so guilty. My mom was nowhere to be found. I took Piper into the bathroom, bandaged her head the best I could and waited for my mom to get home. When Kathryn started vomiting, I panicked. But, I still waited.

After an hour of waiting and soaking three towels in blood from Piper's head, I knew I had to take her to the hospital. I drove there while she was dozed off. I thought that was a good thing. If she could sleep, then she must be okay. That's what I kept telling myself, anyway. Little did I know at the time, it wasn't a good thing.

The doctors stitched her up, 29 stitches in her head. They were more concerned with the concussion. Piper stayed the night in the hospital for observation. My parents were livid, rightfully blaming me for everything. I stayed with her, not leaving her bedside. My parents were relieved that they didn't have to stay. Typical.

I knew that night that I'd do anything I could to protect her. I was never going to let anything happen to her again. I promised her and promised myself. Fuck, I hated not living up to my promises. Here it is 12 years later, and I'm staring at the same little girl in a hospital bed, knowing that I'm probably to blame for this too.

I reach for her hand, only to discover the bandages that are blocking my hand from holding hers. Glancing down, I'm submerged in agony as I understand why both of her hands and wrists are wrapped with gauze and medical tape. Oh Pipe! No! God no! Piper wasn't "crying for help", wasn't trying to "make a point." My beautiful, tormented, seventeen-year-old sister was trying to end her life. A desperate act of finality.

Kathryn quietly and delicately wipes my cheeks with a tissue; I hadn't even realized I was crying, couldn't even feel the stream of tears roll down my face, dripping onto the hospital bed's rail. My shoulders shake; a sob escapes me. Kathryn wraps her arms around me, giving me support and strength. Burying my head in her hair, I cry in her arms, allowing her to see me at my weakest, needing her to be the strength that holds me together.

Wiping my eyes, I clear my throat, and say, "Thank you … thank you for being here … for everything."

A faint smile appears on her face, her eyes glistening in tears. Kathryn places her hand against my cheek; her thumb lingers over my lips. I turn into her hand, kissing her palm, and then holding it against my heart. "It means everything to me that you're here."

The door busts opens. The switch flips on, blinding the room in bright fluorescent lights. "This one here?" asks a security guard, followed by two husky, angry nurses.

"Yes, that's him," my mother confirms. "He's not permitted in this room … not anywhere near our daughter."

"Dude, you pissed off the 'rents. You're gonna need to do some serious ass-kissing to fix this shit," Tristan jokes, sidling up next to me as the security guard roughly escorts me to the door.

Ignoring my brother, I say, "I'm a goddamn doctor. How can you not let me in? I can read her charts, talk to the doctors for fuck's sake. Let me help," I argue, trying to free myself from the guard's grip.

"You're not welcome here," my mother states, turning her back on me. "And neither are you … whoever you are."

"Yeah, who's this chick?" Tristan asks, drinking in every inch of Kathryn's body with his eyes. "Ya need me to keep you warm while Ade's being detained?" Tristan asks, wrapping an arm around Kathryn. I see her grimace and flinch. Losing my shit, I shove the guard back, barreling toward my brother.

"You son-of-a-bitch, don't touch her, don't look at her, don't you even fucking think about her," I threaten, "I will fucking destroy you."

"Looks like the streets have been real good to ya, kid … turned you into the hot-blooded loser we all knew you'd be," Tristan sardonically says, just as the security calls for backup.

I protectively wrap my arm around Kathryn's waist, pulling her against me. "No need to call anyone. We're leaving," I announce in utter disgust. "I'm walking out on the one and only person in this family who's actually worth anything. Thanks y'all ... thanks a fucking lot."

Walking out the door, I hear the smallest muffled sound; the sound stops me in my tracks, warming my heart. "Adre-annie." I turn, along with everyone else, as Piper's eyes flutter.

I plow through my family to the hospital bed, "I'm here, Pipe. I'm here." Her eyes flutter and roll back into her head. Her mouth opens, but nothing comes out. I stroke her head, wiping her hair off of her forehead. "Come on honey, wake up. Talk to me."

The security guard grabs me. Shrugging him off me, I growl, "Get your hands off me." I glare at my parents. "Piper's waking up ... she wants me. Do this for her—not me."

They look at each other, then at me. Both of my parents narrow their eyes. My father addresses the guard, "Let him be." Turning his face back to me, he says, "Until she's awake."

Her eyes flutter again. A small smile reaches her lips. "Annie," she croaks. Coughing and gagging, she adds, "You're home."

~ Kathryn ~

I'm in over my head. I am one hundred fifty-two thousand percent in over my head. When Piper finally spoke, relief washed over the room, drowning out the anger and hostility that was flowing so roughly between everyone. I for one was thrilled for the break in tension, especially since it meant that Piper was out of the woods, as the doctors said.

Luckily, when the doctor came in to check on her, and realized that she awakened to talk to Dre, he overrode Dre's parents and insisted that he stay with her throughout the rest of her stay in the ICU as well as when she's moved to the psychiatric floor for evaluation. The doctor believes that Dre's presence lightens her darkness. He wants Dre to be there to talk to her, listen to her, and comfort her. The O'Donnells didn't want to besmirch their name by refusing to do whatever was the best for their daughter. Dre dodged a cold, ostracized bullet. Thank God, his relationship with Piper was strong enough to penetrate her catatonic state. If anything, they should be grateful to him for that.

After he sits with his sister a while, Dre and I go downstairs to donate blood for her. I wasn't a match, but I still felt like donating for someone who may need it in the future. Dre was obviously an exact match. Watching him, understanding how much she means to him, my heart breaks and warms at the same time. I love how much Dre cares for Piper, would do anything for her. But, I also hate watching him endure this pain, knowing he can't protect her, do anything for her, other than donate his blood to her. After the nurses, tape our arms up with hospital gauze, Dre heads back to Piper's room. I just head to the couches to watch television.

Sitting alone in the waiting room, I start flipping through the television channels, wishing Syd would've grabbed my Kindle or Jose's manuscript from my nightstand. I feel terribly for canceling on him so much lately. Jose is never going to publish his book if I don't get my butt in gear. Poor kid.

Looking for something to watch, I'm floored when I see Chet O'Donnell, Dre's father, plastered all over the television screen on each channel, with the scrolling headline: "Chet O'Donnell, multi-billion dollar real estate mogul's daughter fights for her life after a failed suicide attempt."

I knew he looked familiar, but I couldn't place it. They posted a family picture of the O'Donnells. I don't even recognize Dre, the clean-cut, obedient young man on the screen. The picture depicts them as the perfect family: attractive, well-groomed, close-knit, and loving. A picture is worth 1000 words, but the words that this picture tells is full of lies and deception.

Feeling his hands on my shoulders, kneading my sore muscles, deliciously, I moan, "Mmmm … God, that feels so good." As his hands mold and roll over my shoulders and down my arms, he kisses my neck, nibbling on the back of my ear. "Man, do I want you, but you know how I feel about … mmmm … public displays of … mmmm … affection."

"Come on Baby, you know you want it," an unfamiliar voice growls in my ear, making every hair on my arms and neck stand up, sending terror and disgust throughout my body.

Shooting up off the couch, I knock Tristan's hands from me. "Easy Baby, I know you've been slumming lately and all, but I'm willing to do some slumming of my own to show you what it's like to swallow a real man," he says. His sleazy, condescending, taunting voice makes my skin crawl and stomach heave. "You'd like that— wouldn't you?"

"What I'd like is for you to walk away—walk away and never speak to me again," I say, desperately trying to sound poised and collected, but the quaver in my voice betrays me.

Knowing I can't make a scene in this hospital, I turn to walk away. Tristan accosts me, grabbing my arm. His breath is hot and heavy on my neck, "I don't mind dipping my dick in some sloppy-second filth. I know how much Ade likes his whores."

Tristan doesn't realize that my father forced me (and I mean the kicking, dragging and screaming kind of forced) to take self-defense my entire senior year of high school if I was moving away to a strange campus.

Realizing my pride and Dre's honor are at stake and a heck of a lot more important than what some hospital nurses and orderlies think of me, I grasp his hand tightly, allowing Tristan to believe I'm relenting. He comes in closer, giving me the angle and grip I need, I yank his arm up around my head, bending over with full force as he flips right over the top of me, landing on his back on the hard, cold hospital floor with a thud and a groan.

"If you ever effing touch me again, I'll rip your tiny penis off and shove it down your throat, you douchebag!" I threaten, kicking him in the thigh with all my might.

"Ya know Pebbles," Dre says, draping an arm around me, "sometimes it's a lot more effective if you actually do throw around some hard-core, vulgar profanity every now and then."

I hadn't realized Dre'd come up behind us. I feel a mix of my own selfish pride and even guilt for flattening Dre's brother in the same hospital his sister is in, fighting for her life.

"Dre, I'm sorry," I explain, hoping that he doesn't think I was leading Tristan on.

Bending over Tristan, Dre glares at him. "Don't you think it would've been a lot better saying 'fucking' before the whole 'touch me again' or even 'dick' if you're gonna shove it down his throat?" Dre asks, standing back up and kicking his brother in the side, "or better yet, how about up his ass?" he adds, kicking him in the stomach.

"Don't come near her again, you asshole." Kicking him again, he threatens, "Ever."

"Why'd you and this cunt even come here?" Tristan groans, doubled over on his side on the floor. "Nobody wants you around anymore."

Bending over and punching Tristan in the mouth, Dre hisses, "Don't ever call her that again."

"Alright Dre … enough …" I plead, pulling on his arm. "This is getting all a little too *Lion King-y* for me."

Still staring down at his brother, venomously, Dre starts laughing, hysterically, and finally turns toward me. "Did you just say '*Lion King-y?*' I'm pretty sure that isn't an adjective, Babe. But I get it … I got ya."

"Brothers really shouldn't kill brothers; I got a big problem with that," I explain. "No matter how much they effing deserve it."

"Again, 'fucking' would've been a lot stronger there," Dre argues, dragging me into his arms. "How in the eff did I ever get this lucky?"

Dre went back into the hospital room to sit with Piper, willing her to awaken again. His parents wouldn't permit me, under no certain circumstances, to enter the room—especially after the whole Tristan in the waiting room rigmarole. Gratefully, I'm allowed in the ICU waiting room—just not room 202. Feeling antsy and trapped, I decided to stroll around downtown, taking some time to clear my head and process everything I'd come to learn in the past twenty-fours.

Dre lying to me was one thing. Dre being homeless "by choice" was another. But his family being multi-billionaires was something completely different, and quite honestly, hard to swallow. I didn't exactly grow up in squalor, but Dre's upbringing, social, and financial status were intimidating and overwhelming.

From what I've witnessed, I'm pretty positive that I never want to step foot in New Hampshire again, and most definitely do not want to come face-to-face with any member of the O'Donnell clan again after this trip—excluding Dre that is.

Over the years, I'd always prided myself on how well I judge people and their characters. Still, I don't think I'm wrong about Dre. Understandably, I'm a little leery and hurt by all the lies he fabricated and how he couldn't trust me, as well as **my** character, enough to disclose all of his secrets. I'm not going to sugarcoat it; I felt isolated and betrayed when all the half-truths and even the whole truths started spewing forth.

Honestly though, I'm glad they're out in the open now. It feels as if a vice wrapped around my lungs has been released, allowing me to breathe. Truthfully, it also feels like a weight has been removed from my heart too, encouraging me to feel what I've felt all along for Dre. I'm in love with him. Destitute or affluent, penniless or wealthy, Dre has my heart and I have his, making me feel like the richest woman on the planet.

After calling Sydney and even phoning my mother, I'm soaring, floating, happier than I've felt in a long time. Both Syd and my mom agreed with me, despite all the deception and weird, wicked lies. Dre's still "a keeper," according to them. Sydney's excited that we're dating guys who are friends—she'll always be a middle school girl at heart. My mother's elated that she'll get to see Dre more; she really is schoolgirl-crushing on him.

I also called Leif, my slimy, two-timing, megalomaniac boss at Seaside to tell him that I wouldn't be in for the rest of the week. I explained that I was "working at home." Leif knows that I know too much and don't approve of his "extra-curricular" activities. Therefore, he won't give me any crap about my absences. Some lies and deceit are just unforgivable and unacceptable. We've just agreed to work together, understanding that we don't see eye-to-eye on common morality.

Putting in a call to Jose, explaining why I can't make it again, actually puts me in a chipper mood. Jose is the sweetest little kid. Granted, he's a senior in high school, but his outlook on life, his open-minded and accepting nature make him one of the greatest guys I've ever met. When I first met him at Seaside after agreeing via email to let him pitch me his manuscript, I couldn't believe he was only in high school. Jose's mature, insightful, and nearly brilliant. I think initially he was crushing on me, but we got over that pesky obstacle. Now he views me as a superior, someone who can make or break his writing career. I really am quite blessed with the hand I've been dealt in life and with the people who've come into my life. I just wish Dre had a bit of my luck.

I decide that I'm going to pick up a few things to brighten Piper's room, and maybe even some of the O'Donnell family spirits. Typically, I know that ICU rooms aren't allowed to display flowers, balloons, and other cheery "get well" paraphernalia. But something tells me that the hospital would make an exception for Piper O'Donnell, Chet O'Donnell's baby girl.

Walking down the corridor to the ICU waiting room, I overhear Dre's voice in one of the private conference rooms. Then, I hear the unmistakable contempt in his father's overbearing tone. Knowing I should continue down the hallway to the waiting room,

I begin walking away. But the words that come next stop me abruptly, piquing my fear and curiosity.

"You're already dead to me—don't force to make it official," Chet O'Donnell threatens. "I know people Dre. People who don't give a flying fuck whether you're dead alive."

"Shut the fuck up, Dad. You don't fucking scare me anymore. I'm over the days you control everything. This is bigger than you—that's why you're grasping at straws to shut me up," Dre retorts.

"Listen here pretty boy—"

"No, you listen here. I can destroy you—all of you. And I will … if you force my hand," Dre seethes, raising his whispered voice. "Just leave us the Hell alone. Leave me alone. Kathryn alone … and fucking leave Piper alone … when she wakes up."

"You don't scare us, you little fuck," Chet hisses.

"I don't? Are you sure I don't Dad? Seems to me you're pretty fucking scared that I'm gonna squeal, ruining all that you've ever worked … or shall I say cheated and lied for," Dre says, smugly.

"How much, Dre? What's it gonna take to make you get over this?" Dre's mom asks, her voice bitingly bitter.

"God, do you fucking people ever listen? This is not about money. I could give two shits about your goddamn corrupt money," Dre bellows, storming out the door, running straight into me, knocking the vase of flowers right out of my hand. He and I stare silently as it shatters to the floor, spraying glass, water, and cheery hues of yellow and orange everywhere.

Dre shakes his head, closes his eyes, and continues down the hallway. Putting the balloons and stuffed piggy on the nearest table,

I run after him just as he enters the elevator. "Dre wait!" I beg. "Are you okay?"

"No Kathryn, I'm fucking awful. This … all of this … just sucks the fucking life out of me. I gotta get out of here," he states, breathing deeply.

"Baby, you've got to tell me what's going on. That was pretty intense in there," I say, rubbing my hands up and down his arms. "Let's go check in to a hotel. We'll use my credit card and just hold each other. You can tell me everything."

"Alright Pebbles," he acquiesces, solemnly. "It's time you knew the whole truth."

- Dre -

All along, I had a sneaky suspicion that Kathryn was open-minded and non-judgmental enough to look past my "homeless" status. Ever since I watched her selflessly fill parking meters and tap her chipped, un-manicured nails on the hood of her rusty Volkswagen Bug, I knew she wasn't an uppity, socialite, ladder-climbing bitch. Hell, she carries a knockoff purse, willingly eats hot dogs and noodles, and uses gift cards and coupons. If those weren't clues enough, the whole wearing lost and found clothes should've tipped me off. I could tell that whenever she discovered the truth about my living situation that she'd find it admirable and respectable. Kathryn would never consider herself "too good" or even "above" others for the possessions they had or didn't have. At least, I hoped. I was just too damn chicken-shit to tell her.

It's the story that's she waiting on now that fills me with dread, could quite easily redefine how she feels about me. Kathryn has a bleeding, sympathetic heart like I do. This reality may put her over the edge. Truthfully, it makes me question my character, and even my overall goodness. Basically, I stopped looking in the mirror, caring about my family, my future, anything when I agreed to shut my mouth and look the other away. Plain and simple, I'm a coward, nothing more, nothing less.

Guiltily, I must admit that I was very much like my family until everything went down. I basked in the lifestyle money and recognition brought forth. Summer excursions in Europe, spring breaks in Palm Springs, Christmases in London or skiing in Vale were all a part of my childhood, a childhood I never questioned, but enjoyed and flaunted at each and every opportunity I could. I'm not proud of this, but it's ultimately who I am—who I was—who I'm so desperately trying to forget. Adrian O'Donnell's shell is one I'm more than willing to shed.

Settling on the bed, surrounded by pizza, breadsticks, and wings, Kathryn groans, closing her little Weight Watchers app. "Again, I'm over my points." She puffs her lips out, pouting like a child. "I hope you're into the fluffier woman, because I'm on the verge of getting there."

"Oh Hell," I say, staring at her body, "don't you see how gorgeous you are?"

I will never understand women. They're never satisfied with their bodies. I wouldn't be head-over-heels fucking whipped over this chick if I weren't stupidly attracted to her. When I look at her, I go dumb, losing all intelligence, because she's so damn sexy.

"Uh no, I don't. I know each and every one of my imperfections, and each one is far from gorgeous, but thanks for the compliment. Does make me feel better," she says, smiling bashfully.

Taking my hand in hers, she says, "Alright, enough stalling Dre, dish the goods. Tell me the story that you think will scare the crap out of me."

"Or … check this out … we could have hot, crazy, mind-blowing sex and forget everything," I offer, stalling longer. Looking at Kathryn, I just don't want to let her go, and I'm afraid this saga is going to seal the deal and make her hightail it home without a second look or thought.

"Oh we're gonna do that … positively. I believe we left off at a pretty crucial moment last night. But first … first … I want full disclosure," she confirms. Smiling, with a cute little wink, she adds, "Then, you'll get full exposure."

Conjuring up the image of her naked ass in the air last night, and Kathryn on her hands and knees, offering herself to me makes me instantly hard. Adjusting myself groaning, I relent, "Alright Pebbles … just prepare yourself. What you're about to hear isn't pretty … it's not pretty at all."

A little over a year and half ago, my father started molding Tristan to be the second-in-command at O'Donnell Industries. They spent a great deal of time together, and Tristan was really proving to be quite the businessman. Clients trusted him, confided in him, and relied on him. My father was in his glory, because his eldest son, his pride and joy, was following quickly and successfully in his well-formed and highly acclaimed footsteps. At this point, my parents had already given up on me; the idealistic son who "wanted to heal the world." Tristan loved the limelight, devoured it and reveled in it, really.

My father had to have an emergency surgery due to an infected gall bladder. The operation couldn't wait, because he was in excruciating pain. However, he was needed in Chicago for a major business meeting with a large corporation; both sides were pining for a merger. The merger would change the lives of many employees and make more millions for O'Donnell Industries. Feeling optimistic, my father sent Tristan to handle the merger.

Tristan wined and dined the clients, charming the pants off of everyone involved. Tristan finally rose to the golden-boy status he'd always coveted. I was no longer his competition; he was my father's exclusive right-hand man. Tristan sat proudly at the top, paramount over all other employees.

Months went by and more and more people were enthralled and impressed by Tristan's business mind. It was as if he had the Midas touch. He could do no wrong. Until he did.

One night, after a long business dinner, wine and champagne flowing freely, Tristan left the expensive restaurant and decided to hit an old, local dive bar that we frequented in our early 20s, playing pool and throwing darts with our buddies. After a few shots of Jack, and a couple of Jack and Cokes on the rocks, Tristan started chatting up the cocktail waitress, Leah Franchetti, a former schoolmate of mine.

After sharing a few laughs and a lot of drinks, Tristan invited Leah to spend the night with him. She declined, but he was persistent—just as he always is. Tristan offered to take her to the most expensive and swanky hotel in town, figuring she'd never been someplace so elaborate before. Leah caved, falling prey to my overly aggressive and bombastic brother.

At the hotel, there was more alcohol and plentiful flirting and foreplay. Sometime in the evening, Tristan became argumentative and volatile—just as he always is. Leah decided she'd made a horrible mistake and attempted to leave his room. Apparently, he lost his cool, punching her in the face and violently raping and abusing her.

Tristan remembers none of it, claims Leah's full of shit. No part of him would own up to his crime, or "indiscretion" as my parents refer to it. Leah stopped to see him one night at our house, explaining that she was going to go to the cops and the news channels if he didn't compensate her for her pain and suffering. Throwing her out on her ass, Leah did what she had to do. When my family least expected it, she pounced. Confronting my father in the parking garage, Leah retold the whole sordid affair, explicitly describing the violent and unforgivable behavior of my disgusting brother. Leah had the bruises to prove it.

My father wouldn't hear of it, begging her to quiet down. With each urgent denial from my father, Leah's voice grew louder and louder. Finally, my father took her into his limo, exchanged threats and ultimatums. After driving around for over an hour, Leah Franchetti was $300,000.00 richer and gagged with a promise of "skipping town." Three days later, Leah showed up again, wanting more money. My father refused, ordering her own of town. The ball was in her court, and he knew it.

Leah took my dad for another 20 grand, signed a confidentiality contract, and left. Nobody's heard from her since. My brother committed a heinous, despicable, and completely unforgivable crime, and my parents used their money and power to make it go away, saving my brother from a future of imprisonment, as well as saving themselves from public ridicule and embarrassment.

"Holy crap, this is the junk that soap operas are made of," Kathryn states, incredulously. "And they told you all of this?"

"Tristan and I went out one night, drank a few too many, and he told me everything—what he remembers of it anyway." I confess. "My parents were frigging ballistic when they realized I knew. They were more pissed at Tristan for telling me, their bleeding-heart son, than they were with the fact that their son fucking raped some innocent woman."

"My God, so what happened? What'd you do?" she asks, her face full of wonder and worry.

"This is what I never wanted you to know, Pebbles," I admit, knowing that whatever positive light she's seen me in was now going to darken drastically. "Nothing," I admit, pausing to let the fucking truth sink in, penetrate her mind, break her heart.

"My fucking brother raped a girl. My asshole parents paid for her silence, and I did nothing," I confess, hating myself. Running my hands over my face, trying to hide from the reality of my cowardice decision, I finally say, "I got mad, began to loathe everything my about my entire family, and just up and moved the fuck away, leaving them to deal with all their inner demons on their own."

"God, I'm no better than any of them," I continue, not being able to look Kathryn in the eyes. "My heart can bleed all it wants, but my actions speak louder than my words and wants. I did nothing. I'm a yellow-bellied coward, who easily could've wronged a right but chose to look away and get the fuck out."

Silence fills the room; it's deafening and shattering at the same time. I want her to speak, to tell me how disgusted she is with me. How my lack of courage proves that Tristan and I are more alike than I would ever like to admit.

"So what're you going to do about it?" she asks finally, patiently awaiting my answer.

"What can I do? What's done; is done," I respond. By the reaction on her face, it's far from the response she was hoping for.

"Uh, no, not a chance, Dre," Kathryn states, crossing her arms over her chest, shaking her head. "You're seriously considering letting let him get away with that crap? Even worse, you're gonna let that poor woman suffer, never getting redemption for what he did to her? No way … not gonna happen, Dre. Not on my watch."

"I don't want to sound like a dick here or anything, but it's not my fight. I washed my hands of the whole thing a long time ago," I argue, hoping she'll see my side of this. "Plus, Leah got all she wanted," I add.

"Okay, let's start with Leah, do you think she's really over the abhorrent violation that she endured? Do you Dre?" she asks, not really wanting an answer, but obviously making a strong case. Continuing, she says, "Do you really think that money, any amount, can be compensation enough for that kind of victimization?"

"God Kathryn, you know I don't. That's why I've been living in a fucking tent for over a year. What the fuck am I supposed to do?" I question. "Like I said, it's not my fight."

"Oh Dre, you couldn't be more wrong. That's what's wrong with the damn world today. Nobody wants to take a stand against the bullies," Kathryn pleads, her face contorting in frustration.

"Why let Tristan win? Why do the bad guys always get to win? People like you, like me, we have to fight against the cruelties in the world, help the underdog ... otherwise nothing ever changes," she argues.

Kathryn groans in frustration and anger. "When the weak can't fight for themselves, we absolutely have to fight for them."

"I know. Stop. Jesus Christ, I know. This is exactly what I've been telling myself for that past year," I say, caving to the inner battle I've been having with myself every day. "What am I supposed to do? Call the police. Narc on my own brother? Turn my parents in? What?"

"Ummm ... that ... I don't know," Kathryn admits, crawling over to me, lying her head down in my lap. "I know what's right ... just like you do ... but I don't really know how to go about it."

"Neither do I ... neither do I," I mumble.

I'm shocked that she's touching me, holding me. It doesn't make sense why someone as compassionate and kind as Kathryn Howell is still snuggling up against me after learning who I really am and what I really am—a coward.

I run my fingers through her long, dark hair. "Well Pebbles, that's everything. There are no more hidden skeletons in the Adrian O'Donnell closet of lies, " I joke feebly, still playing with her hair.

"Should I book you on the next flight back to Charleston?" I ask quietly. The question's out, but I didn't realize how anxious waiting for her answer would make me. My stomach ties in knots as what seems like an interminable about of time passes.

"Not unless you're going with me," Kathryn says, reaching up and stroking my cheek. "Dre, I think you've been dealt a crappy hand, a horrifying one … but I understand your torment. You love them, but hate them too … for being the immoral jerks they are. I'd worry more and wonder more about you if you **weren't** so torn and confused. They're your family. Like it or not."

"Not," I groan, banging my head back on the headboard.

Sitting up, Kathryn leans in and begins kissing my neck. "We're gonna solve this dilemma … together." She strokes my cheek again.

Smiling, "But first, I need a long, hot shower," she explains. "My body aches and it's been a long day. If we're being totally honest, a little soap and shampoo would do me some good."

"Alright Babe, I'll clean up the food and mess. You go take a shower."

"Man, sometimes you really are off your game," Kathryn complains. "Let's try this again … I'm going to take off all my clothes, get completely naked, and stand in the hot stream of water, while it beats down on my wet, hot, naked body," she describes perfectly, staring deeply into my eyes. "Then, I'm going to soap up my hands and wash every inch of my body with my lathered up and wet—"

Shedding my shirt and pants, before she finishes, "I say, "Race ya." Kathryn laughs, scrambling to get off the bed, kicking the pizza box to the floor.

By the time she gets to the bathroom, I'm naked and already have the water running. "It's too cold still," I explain, leaning on the wall, drinking in her beauty. Aroused, I watch intensely as she removes her shirt and bra, tossing them aside.

Walking over to Kathryn, I draw her nearer, tugging on the top of her jeans. Not taking my eyes from her hers, I unbutton her pants, running my hands along the inside of her jeans until they begin to lower off of her hips. Kathryn wiggles her hips, forcing the jeans to fall faster to the floor. Still wearing her hot pink panties from last night, Kathryn wriggles out of them quickly. Her body is breathtaking; the sight of her womanly curves fuel the fire inside me, sending heat and need straight to my groin. Just looking at her, wanting her, being near her, washes away the pain, fear, and worry of the day's events.

"Fucking exquisite," I moan, wanting to bury myself deep inside her. "Come here."

Confidently, Kathryn approaches me, her eyes directly on my arousal. She reaches for me, enclosing both of her hands around my erection, slowly sliding her hands up and down its length, willing it to grow and strain. "It should be ready now."

"It's been ready—always ready for you, Pebbles," I reply, my breath catching.

Giggling, Kathryn smiles and says, "The shower … the water should be hot enough."

Chuckling, I pick her up as she wraps her legs around my waist and step into the stall. The feel of her body pressing hard on mine stirs and heightens my desire. "You're all that I crave," I murmur into her ear, sliding the tip of my tongue along the collarbone.

Water splashes and drenches my shoulders and back. Kathryn looks more tantalizing and tempting as stray droplets fall down her hair and face. I turn her into the direct stream. She throws her head back, arching her back, as the water washes over her face and hair. I get lost in her magnificence as I bend my head and take her nipple into my mouth.

Moaning, Kathryn grinds her hips against me, generating a slow, rhythmic friction between us. I squeeze her ass, holding her closer, gyrating my pelvis with hers. Backing her up against the wall, I tangle my hands in her long, wet hair, tugging her head back, giving me more access to her neck and mouth. The taste of her skin coupled with the water has all my nerve endings screaming.

Kathryn unwraps her legs from my waist, and slides, slowly down my body. Reaching for the soap, she removes the plastic from around the tiny, hotel bar soap. "Fits perfectly in my hand," she grins wickedly, and begins caressing my body with her hands and the soap. The mixture of her hands and the soapy lather traveling along my skin, my body, and my length is the equal epitome of torture and pleasure.

I want nothing more than to pound away deep inside her, pushing her roughly against the wall with each thrust and grind. But, I don't. I'm taking it slow, allowing her to sexily explore my body.

Kathryn's tender touch, combined with her irresistible body, selfless heart, forgiving nature, and intelligent wit make her the answer to my prayers, the reality to my dreams, and the only sanity in my psychotic and crazy world.

Hungrily, I kiss her delicious lips, devouring her tongue, holding her slippery, wet body secured tightly against mine. "Baby, I need you now."

"Not yet, Dre," she whispers, "not yet."

I moan in defeat, knowing Kathryn's taken control, control that I don't want to regain. Her exploration of my body has my insides on the edge, ready to react and explode at any minute.

Finishing, her seductive cleansing of every inch of my body and hair, Kathryn glides her hands over my body as the water rinses the foamy suds. Kathryn's lips, tongue, and teeth follow her hands' lead, trailing all over my body, sending me to the brink.

Kneeling, Kathryn closes her eyes as the water beats down on her face and breasts. She runs her hands along her breasts, pushing them together, kneading the water-soaked flesh. My hands replace hers as I revel in the vision below me. I'm captivated and rendered speechless by her sensuality.

Bending my knees slightly, I slide my erection between her breasts as she stares up at me, mischievously. Her tongue flicks out, greeting me as I rotate upward toward her mouth. Kathryn's hands find me, pumping rhythmically. In one quick motion, she engulfs me, taking me all the way into her mouth.

"Oh … fuck," I groan, trying to maintain balance and control. I just want to drill into her, pound away at her tight little body. "Jesus—" Holding back, I slow my hips not wanting this to end.

Pulling back, "Dre, you need to let go … go ahead and finish," Kathryn urges, still expertly controlling me with her hands and breasts.

"I wanna … be … inside you," I moan, breathlessly.

"Condoms and showers don't get along too well, Sweetheart," Kathryn reminds me. "You get me all night in that king-sized bed. Let's worry about you for now." Kathryn is perfection. Every last thing about her is what every man has ever wanted and yearned for—especially me.

Kathryn guides me back into her mouth, willing me to surrender to my desires. Her hands grip tightly on my ass, urging me further in. As she hums softly, the vibrations put every nerve ending in my body on alert. The pressure builds, climbs, filling me with pleasure and frustration. The sensation is bliss; I rock my hips, preparing for release as I try to pull back.

"Babe, I'm … gonna …" I warn between pants.

Nodding, Kathryn doesn't retract, but continues faster and harder, hitting the back of her throat with each thrust and pump. Kathryn wants this, wants me, wants all of me. This is her conquest, her way of owning me. I'm hers. Every last part of me belongs to her. The thought empowers me, warms me, overtakes me, it's what sends me over the edge of euphoric ecstasy.

Regaining my strength and balance, I pull her up, kissing her softly. After our lips part, I grab the soap, lathering my hands with soapy bubbles. My hands travel her body, cleansing her skin in soft, sensual strokes. Her lips part; her tongue glides over her upper lip. I watch, mesmerized by her reactions to my touch. When Kathryn's chest heaves, offering itself to me, I accept, exploring her breasts with my hands and mouth.

When her breathing quickens and her body weakens, I slow my movements, paying attention to the task at hand. After rinsing her body completely, I fill my hands with shampoo. Turning her back to me, Kathryn lets her head fall back into my hands as I massage the shampoo into her hair, caressing her scalp.

"Feels so good," Kathryn murmurs, rubbing her head against my palms.

"Pebbles, I'm just washing your hair," I explain, grinning at the effect I have on her.

"It doesn't matter how you're touching me, it's pure erotic magic," she coos. I chuckle at her words. "I'm serious, Dre," she says turning toward me as the water washes over us. "I've never experienced such pleasure before. When I'm with you … it's … it's everything."

Placing my lips on hers, I whisper into her mouth, "Everything."

"My God, Dre, that … that … was incredible," Kathryn pants breathlessly, lying on her back, staring glassy-eyed at the ceiling. "I'm mean, I've had some good sex before … mainly with you … but that … that was … unbelievable." Just the thought of her having sex with someone else tenses my muscles, making my heart constrict.

Shaking the image from my head, "Earth shattering? Mind-blowing? Toe curling?" I boast teasingly, trying to erase haunting visions of Kathryn and Theodore from my mind. Running my hand along her bare stomach, I say, "Use all the words you need to describe me Pebbles."

Kathryn's right though. I've had my fair share of sexual experiences, and sex with her is above any I've experienced before, by far, especially just now. The connection was magnetic. I don't know if it was that the deception and guilt were finally gone or that we've hit a new level of intimacy and emotion, but either way, it was phenomenal.

"I'm not even kidding. I feel like I should give you some kind of an award ... standing ovation ... I don't know," Kathryn marvels. Smiling, her faces lights up, "I know! Maybe I should write a song, a poem, or something," Kathryn says, giggling.

"How about a limerick?" I joke, entwining my legs in hers.

"Ha Ha. Very funny, John Irving," she says, smacking me on the arm.

My phone rings, surprising me, since I haven't used it or needed it in over a year. We glance at each other, shocked by the disturbance. When I make no move to answer it, Kathryn says, "You have to get it. It could be news about Piper."

Hearing Kathryn refer to Piper, I spring to my feet, grabbing my phone off the hotel dresser. Relieved when I see Lafferty's name on the screen, I answer the phone. His words flood with me relief and an overwhelming sense of love for my little sister. Beaming, I tell him that we're on our way, as I punch the air in triumph.

"Piper's awake; she's asking for me," I announce, tearing up.

Kathryn jumps off the bed right into my arms. "Oh thank God. Oh my God, that's so wonderful," she squeals, squeezing me and kissing me all over my face. It's almost as if every last thing she does confirms even more how much I love her.

"Before we go to the hospital, I wanna say something." I walk Kathryn over to the bed and sit down with her on my lap. "Pebbles, I never could've faced any of this without you. I couldn't have come back here … faced them … or anything," I admit, tracing her jaw with my thumb. "You give me strength and courage I didn't even know I possessed. I just want to thank you … thank you for being here … for being … everything."

Smiling, Kathryn's eyes glisten, and she kisses me lightly. With her lips on mine, she whispers into my mouth, "Everything."

I wanted to tell her how hard I'd fallen for her, but I didn't want to look into her eyes, hold her close, say, "I love you," and then jet to the hospital to see my sister. I've never told a woman that I loved her before. Well, I told Waverly, but I never meant it. I never even thought I meant it. It's just what she wanted to hear, so I pussied up and said it, never once feeling anything but slight tolerance for her.

Fuck, most of the time with Waverly, I just wanted to gag her—and not in a sexual way. Waverly is the epitome of high maintenance and frustration. I spent the majority of our relationship praying for earplugs or that a meteor would shoot out of the sky, hit me directly in the head, and put me out of my goddamn misery.

Since I'd never experienced true love, true passion (until now), I think that's why it'd been so easy to give up women for the past year. Sure I had urges, desires, but nothing overpowered me, made me long for something—until now. Being with Kathryn makes me feel like I'm connected to my lifeline. I know she feels it too; nobody has ever looked at me like she does. It's almost as if I can do no wrong, and let's be clear, I'm not sure I've done anything right lately—except find her. Holy fuck, talk about pussying up! My vagina's gonna start bleeding if I keep this shit up.

Bottom line, I'm in love with Kathryn. My brother's a dick. My parents are assholes. My sister is the best my family has to offer. And me, I'm a total pansy. Alright, now that we're all up to speed, and my head is clear; I'm ready to see Piper.

"And you made fun of me for talking to myself," Kathryn kids, in the elevator. "Anything in that head of yours that you'd care to share, Mr. Deep-thinker?"

"Don't you worry about what's in my head," I say, holding her hand, tugging her toward me. "You just worry about what's in my pants."

"Classy. Real classy. I'm swooning here … but seriously, don't start shutting me out, again," she warns. "I don't like it."

"Trust me, I won't." I promise her. "I was just going over the last 24 hours in my head."

Kathryn wraps her arms around my waist, resting her head on my chest. "They've been a pretty crazy 24 hours," she says. When the elevator dings, Kathryn kisses my cheek, grabs my hand, and we step out onto the hospital floor. We walk silently, hand-in-hand, down the hallway to the waiting area. Kathryn squeezes my hand, a token of encouragement and support as I head into the room alone.

My entire family turns to look at me when I enter the room. Both of my parents scowl at my arrival; Tristan glares irately at me. Although I'm nearly suffocating from family drama and obvious detestation, I've got a shit-eating grin sprawled across my face. Piper is sitting up in her bed, fully awake, and sipping an apple juice.

"Hey kiddo," I say, kissing her forehead and then cradling her in my arms. "You gave us ... all ... quite a scare," I whisper in her ear. Tears fall down my face as I think about what could've happened if my "always-successful" sister were successful this time around.

"Mom, Dad," Pipers calls. My parents bolt over to the bed, all ears to whatever Piper wants. "Can I talk to Dre alone for a minute?" My mother's eyes squint, glaring at me. My father huffs and walks out the door with my mother close behind him. Tristan leaves staring at me the entire time.

After they leave, Piper's loses it, uncontrollable sobs escaping her. "Pipe, what is it? I'm here, Baby; I'm here."

"I'm so sorry. I'm so so sorry, Adre-annie," Piper says through sobs. "Please, please, please forgive me. I didn't mean for them to find out. It was an accident."

"Who? Find out what?" I can hardly understand anything she's saying.

"Mom and Dad, Ade, I didn't mean it. I swear. I was being so selfish, I guess," Piper cries.

"Honey, slow down ... relax ... I don't know what you're talking about," I explain, stroking her hair, trying to console her. Seeing my sister like this guts me.

Not being able to protect the people we love the most is fucking bullshit. I want to save her, help her, protect her, and just fucking make damn sure she never hurts like this again. But I can't. And that's the problem with loving someone so much. Their pain so easily becomes your pain. Their suffering is yours.

"Charleston. They know. Mom and Dad know you live there ... and it's all my fault," she confesses, crying harder. "I'm so sorry. You trusted me Ade and ... and ... I blew it."

"Whoa ... hold on ... Piper, it's okay. No ... no ... stop that," I soothe, shaking my head, wiping her tears away. "So they know ... who cares? All that matters is that you're here ... you're with us. Piper, none of that shit matters. You matter," I say, holding her tightly in my arms. "You matter."

"But, I promised you ... and I couldn't keep that promise," Piper says, trying to catch her breath. "Adrian, I even remembered to write 'Dre' in every letter I sent. I was being so careful. I didn't mean to let you down," she wails between breaths.

Realizing her pain and finally understanding her words, my heart crumbles, and my gut wrenches. "Piper, you didn't ... Oh God Piper! You didn't do ... do ... this ... because of ... of ... me? Did you?" I ask, feeling like I'm going to be sick.

Her face contorts; her body quakes. "Ade, they won't let me go." Piper's crying so hard now that I'm worried for her. This can't be good for her. She's still recovering, still weak, and still so vulnerable.

Holding her, I just say, "It's okay, Baby. It's okay," rocking her back and forth, careful of the bandages on her wrists.

"Don't you get it? It's not okay. I'm stuck here … with them. I can't do it. I can't, Ade. I just can't," she cries into my shoulder.

"Piper, it's alright. You're going to college next year. You'll get away—just like I did."

"They won't let me!" she explains. "I was gonna surprise you. I was so excited." Her voice quivers; her body shivers as she tries to calm herself down. "I applied to College of Charleston, Ade. I got in. Early admissions." Piper can't fight the smile or gleam in her eye. "I could start classes in June."

"Piper! That's fucking incredible. That's … that's … great news," I exclaim, feeling excited for the future for the first time in a long time.

"But … see … it's not! That's what I'm trying to say," Piper groans, leaning her head back on the pillows.

"They said I can't go. They won't pay for school if I'm going anywhere near you. At first, they couldn't understand why I wanted to go to Charleston in the first place … and then … then, I guess they just figured it out."

My parents are fucking nutcases. To think that they can hold their daughter back from where she wants to go to college is absurd, especially since it's only because they want her away from me.

"Piper, first of all, not going to the college of your choice is no reason to … to …" I don't even know how to say the words.

"Adrian, please, ***please***, can we not talk about that now? Not yet. **Please**." Piper pleads, her eyes weary and scared.

Relenting, I nod, rubbing my hand down her leg, squeezing her foot. "Absolutely. Of course," I say, respecting her wishes, "but Pipe, we're gonna talk about it."

Piper nods her head, averting my eyes. She wipes her cheeks and brushes her hair out of her face. "Ade, what am I gonna do about Mom and Dad? I can't be in that house with them any more. I just can't!"

"Don't worry about them, Hon. You just worry about getting better, stronger; I'll take care of them," I promise, having no clue how we're going to rectify all of this.

"Would you ... would you ... **want** me to live there?" she asks, nervously, "like ... near you ... or **with** you?"

"I'm sure we can add on to the beach tent," I kid, grinning at her.

"Adrian! I'm serious. Would you?"

"I wouldn't want it any other way, kid," I say, realizing I mean every word of it. Having Piper with me would be like having part of my family back—the part I actually want.

When the nurses came in to change Piper's dressings and remove her old bandages, I took the materials from them and handled her care myself. My breath caught and sobs escaped when I saw the vertical scars along her wrists. Looking at her and the agony on her face, I knew at that moment that there was no fucking way I was going to make her go back to my parents' house, enduring their scrutiny and ridicule for one more minute. I finally understood. My sister's right; she can't go home.

A psychiatrist came in to meet with Piper, so I had to step out. She wasn't ready for me to hear all that she'd bottled up and hidden away. Walking out into the hallway, I didn't see Kathryn anywhere. Feeling guilty for leaving her alone so long, I started to search for her. I didn't have to search long; I turned the corner and heard the unmistakable chide of my father.

"Listen here Missy," he said, "I don't know what game you're playing or what you know, but I want you to walk away … walk away and forget you ever met my son."

"My name's Kathryn—not Missy," she corrects firmly. "And I'll tell you the same thing I told him the day I met him, 'I don't play games.' I'm not walking away. A woman doesn't walk away from a man like Dre."

"For Christ's sake, his name is Adrian," my father bellows. "Don't you understand? You're outta your league here. People like us don't fraternize with riffraff like you, Honey," he patronizes. I hear Kathryn's gasp, and all I want to do is rip my father's fucking head off.

"That's right, Dad. We sure don't. We just pay them the fuck off, so they can go hide somewhere far away from us high class civilized people?" I seethe, ready to take him down with every eye in the hospital on us.

"Aren't we just the upper crust? Look at us everyone … we're the fucking O'Donnells and we're just above it all."

"Now son—"

"Son? Oh that's just goddamn priceless. Now that you're fucking terrified of what I'll do … or say, I'm suddenly your son again. Fuck that," I say, wrapping my arm around Kathryn's waist, guiding her to the elevator. "Let's go, Babe."

As we walk away from my father, he calls, "How much? How much Adrian?"

I stop, turning around slowly; my fists clenched. "What?"

"Name your price. I'm sick of this holier than thou bullshit," my father states, walking toward us. "Surely your girl here would like a little something. What is it; Princess, ya got student loans? Old, beater car?" he patronizes, leering at us. "What about your parents? Wanna buy them something real nice?"

Kathryn's stunned, completely speechless. My father's abhorrent behavior infuriates me. "Are you fucking kidding me? What happened to you? What happened to that guy … to the man I looked up to? Where the Hell did he go?"

"Don't give me your shit, Adrian. Everyone's got a price," my dad says, coming in close to my face, nearly nose-to-nose. "So what's yours, Golden Boy? I'll write you a check, and you and your whore can go live happily ever after in whatever white trash town you want."

"Don't you ever—"

"Dre! No!" Kathryn screams, stepping in front of my father, stopping me. "Look at me," she demands. I take a deep breath, dropping my hands, unclenching my fists.

"Dre, it's not worth it. Don't … don't even think about it … let it go … let's just get out of here," she says, rationally and calmly, stroking my cheek, running her thumb along my jaw.

My teeth clench, jaw sets. I nod, breathing deeply. "You're right; you're so right. He isn't worth it."

~ Kathryn ~

"Holy fucking, mother-goddamn shit! Your family is ass-butt nuts crazy!"

"Easy Pebbles, 'mother-goddam' and 'ass-butt nuts' aren't real phrases," Dre laughs, holding me in his arms, his face beaming. "And you're right, swearing doesn't become you—not one bit."

"I mean, what the Hell, Dre? Your dad seriously just tried to pay me off! Who the fuck does that?" I ask, feeling rage and embarrassment boiling together inside of me. "Nobody! That's who. I mean, I guess people do that crap ... like on *General Hospital* or *Desperate Housewives* ... not in real life!"

"Alright, calm down, deep breaths," Dre says, stroking my arms, firmly.

"How can I calm down? One of the richest men ... like ... ever ... just offered me money to go away. That's ... that's ... just crazy. I need ... I need ... a drink. Can we ... can we go somewhere?" I ask hopefully. "I'm a little edgy right now. Can we please?"

"Anything. Anything you need," Dre replies, kissing my forehead.

Everything is just whacko in this state. I don't think I'm going to be making a return visit anytime soon to New Hampshire. The short time I've spent here has been long enough to know that this is not anywhere that I want to be. These people, Dre's family is just out of control, manipulative, aristocratic, criminal nutjobs. When we leave here, I'm never looking back. Now, I finally understand how easy it must've been for Dre to just pack up and bail. I would've too if I were him.

Leaving the hospital, sucking in the fresh air, I finally feel like I can breathe again. I know that Dre's agonizing over what to do about Tristan's heinous crime, but I just want to get the heck out of here. I have to come up with a solution, help him through this, so we can leave the second Dre's ready to go home. Because right now, I'm ready.

Walking into a small corner tavern, I'm relieved that we're finally going to be able to sit and drink without all this stress suffocating us. We take a small table in the back, and Dre gets us two draft beers. Normally, I'm a wine or mixed drink kind of girl, but right now, an icy cold beer in a frosty mug is just what I need. For the first time in my life, I wish I had a siphon; I'd just down this thing in two seconds flat, begging for a refill.

Chugging my beer, I look around the bar, taking in the clientele. The people in this establishment are really well-dressed, perfectly groomed, and carrying designer handbags.

"Dre, what is this place?" I ask, feeling completely out of my element.

"Executive Tavern on the Green," he says, drinking his beer. "It's kind of like a country club, but with no pool or golf course. It's members only."

"Why'd we come here?" I ask, wondering why he'd choose a place like this. "I thought you were 'so over' this lifestyle?"

"I wanted to see if Tristan was here," he says, grabbing my hand across the table. "I'm gonna try to convince him to turn himself in."

"Uhhh Dre, do you really think **that's** gonna work?" I ask, rubbing the back of his hand with my thumb, enjoying the feel of his fingers interlocked with mine.

"Not one bit," he admits. "I just don't know what else to do. I just can't see myself calling the cops and reporting them. I know they fucking deserve every last thing that happens to them … I just can't be the person who puts all that shit into motion."

"Is this your roundabout way of asking me to do it?" I ask, anxiety setting in.

Chuckling, Dre kisses the back of my hand and says, "Not even close. That's funny though. Pebbles, I'd never put you in the middle of this. You're too pure and good to be involved in this shit."

Thinking about Dre's plan gives me an idea. "Dre, have you ever talked to Leah? Gotten her side of the story? Offered your support? Sympathy?"

Shaking his head, he says, "No. I tried once. Went to her apartment even, but she wasn't home." Motioning to the server to bring us two more beers, Dre adds, "After I left, I never really got the guts to try again. Why?"

"I don't know. I was just thinking—what if we go to her and try to convince her to come forward and … maybe even press charges?" I ask, weighing the pros and cons of this plan in my head. "Wouldn't that be the best of both worlds, really? Leah gets justice—and it doesn't have to be you who does it?"

Dre's mulling it over, ruminating the probability of my idea actually working. His mind is clearly considering my suggestion. "I don't know. Seems like a long shot … but it's a thought."

Taking his hand in both of mine, I say, "I know it's hard—and just sucks—but you know you have to do something." Dre nods, scraping the frost off his mug with his other hand.

"But … but … if you decide to do nothing … I'm gonna do nothing with you." He looks up at me, sadly. "I'm not going anywhere, Dre. You're pretty amazing. The way you take care of people, help people, and even find ways to try to forgive people is remarkable. My mom's right. You're a keeper."

"She thinks I'm a keeper?" he asks, sheepishly. I nod, winking at him.

Then he says, "Just wait until you tell her all this crap—she'll be changing her tune then."

"She already knows Dre. We're keeping you—as long as you want to be kept," I joke, feeling the unmistakable flit of butterflies in my stomach.

"Pebbles, ever since that damn carousel ride, I've been sold," he confesses.

"Oh riding behind me on that horse did it for you?" I reply, rolling my eyes.

"Although that was pretty nice being up against your ass like that, riding that horse up and down, it wasn't that ride that did it. Not even close," Dre admits.

"Oh really, what was it then?"

"It was two things. One was watching you stare at that little girl riding the carousel. When you watched her, you looked so happy, a happiness beyond any I've ever experienced," Dre says, his face grim, remorseful.

Shaking his head, he adds, "I thought 'shit if some strange little girl does that to her, what would her face look like if it was … was… Fuck, just forget it."

"Dre Donley, are you getting shy on me?" I ask, smacking his hand playfully.

"Let me make this easier for you … yes … if she were mine, then I'd be that happy every minute of my life. Having kids really is my ultimate fantasy." Dre looks away, definitely shyly, obviously a trait I didn't know he possessed. "So what was the second one?"

"That's easy. Watching your face on the ride. It just glowed," Dre recalls. "Lately, I've dreamed of meeting someone who didn't care about money and all that. When I saw how excited you were, how much fun you were having … I just knew … knew I could never let you go."

Dre takes my hand and brings it close to his lips, but stops when we hear, "I heard, but I didn't fucking believe it. I can't fucking believe you'd come back here, Adrian." Dre's eyes widen. Then his head and shoulders fall as he drops my hand quickly back onto the table.

I turn only to see the most beautiful, well-put together, classy woman I've ever seen. I'd never tell Sydney this, but she makes Syd look like—like—me. Her Burberry trench coat is cinched tightly around her tiny waist. Her legs are long and thin, and look like they were made for her leggings and riding boots. Her long blonde hair is tied back in a slick ponytail. This chick's got the biggest, bluest eyes I've ever seen. Dang, if I weren't straight, I'd take her home with me.

God, whoever this person is has quite the effect on Dre. He's staring at her as if he can't see anything else in the room. I wonder briefly if my skin is turning the dark shade of green that I'm feeling wash over me.

Dre averts his eyes, shaking his head. "Hi Waverly," he says, resignedly, "it's good to see you."

"Who's your friend?" she asks, never glancing my way. Dre was right; he dated some stunning women.

"Waverly Harrington, this is my ... my ... friend, Kathryn Howell," Dre answers wearily.

Oh no. He just called me his "friend," the kiss of death. I thought we'd just covered this. Crap, he's always going to be the unattainable commitment-phobic drifter, no matter how hard he tries. Frankly, I'm getting discouraged with all this.

"Friend?" Waverly says, snidely. "If that's all—"

"Well, it would've been more," Dre offers, "but you showed up and interrupted us. I was about to tell, Pebbles, here how she is the most beautiful, loving, forgiving, and incredible woman I've ever known."

Dre picks my hand back up, massages my palms, and says, "No one holds a candle to you, Babe. You're all I ever wanted."

Waverly's eyes narrow, glaring at us angrily. Dre continues, "I was going to say all those things to her, but you came over. I guess she'll never know that I'm completely in love with her—have never loved anyone more."

"You're a fucking prick, Adrian. No wonder your family disowned your ass. I dodged a goddamn bullet when I dumped you and your limp dick," Waverly seethes, before storming away.

We watch her walk away, both of us smirking devilishly. Turning to him, I say, "She must not be all that good in bed if she couldn't get you hard. I think it's pretty easy."

Laughing, he says, "Pebbles, you're too much."

"By the way, Dre," I say, taking a deep breath. "I fell for you on that carousel too—if we're being honest."

"You liked the feel of my di—"

"Yes, that was nice. It was more like the added bonus, not the deal-sealer for me though." I confess.

"So what was?"

"That's easy, when you stood up on the moving horse and started singing while everyone was staring at us, I was smitten," I admit, taking a long slow drink of my beer, trying to figure out how to explain this to him.

"I'd spent so much time with Theodore, wishing he was more fun, more spontaneous, but he never was," I complained. "Just once, I wanted him to shock me, make me laugh … anything, but it never happened. I knew I didn't want a 'predictable forever.' I want surprises, moments of magic."

Laughing, Dre says, "Well damn Pebbles, I guess I nailed that surprises part."

"You sure did," I agree. "But, you've pretty much got the magic nailed too."

"Baby, don't you worry. I got a few more tricks up my sleeve."

The next morning, after finishing our coffee, we exit the café, holding hands. "You're sure you wanna do this?" I ask, feeling like I'm going to puke.

"No, I don't want to … but I'm going to," Dre confirms, as we walk across the street to the apartment building. "I can't believe how easily you got her address."

"Hey now, Syd and I have some serious stalking skills," I boast, squeezing his hand tighter as we walk into the building. "I'm not gonna tell you how many nights I 'Googled' you and came up with nothing. I can't wait until I get home, and I can 'Google' Adrian O'Donnell."

"Remind me to destroy your computer when we get back," he says, glancing at the numbers on the elevator. "Well here goes nothing."

In the elevator up, neither of us speak. My heart is pounding so hard in my chest; I wonder if Dre can hear it. I really wanted him to come here alone, let me stay back at the hotel and catch up on some work. Last night in the hotel room was incredible—and we didn't even have sex. Dre and I talked all night, revealing secrets, telling stories about our childhoods, connecting on a whole new level, a level I thought I'd never reach with him.

We hashed out the entire plan—everything. The first step to our game plan was on the other side of the door. As Dre knocks, I swear my heart is trying to compete with who can pound harder. Finally, there's movement and rustling from inside the apartment. I grip his hand firmly; Dre squeezes encouragingly back.

The door opens, and Leah Franchetti stares at us. Recognition registers, and she tries to slam the door. Dre puts his foot in the door, "Leah, wait. Please, I just wanna talk to you."

Pushing on the door, Leah argues, "Fuck, I swear to God, Adrian, I'll call the fucking cops." Dre won't let her close the door; she's shoving it pretty hard against his foot. "I always thought you were the 'good one' Adrian. Never thought you'd sell out like the rest of those assholes."

"Leah, please, you know me. I'm not here for them … I'm here for you."

"Nice try, I know your Daddy sent you—just like he sent his lackeys last month." Leah says, struggling with the door. "I know the deal … I haven't forgotten. I'm not gonna squeal."

"Leah, that's exactly what I want to talk about," Dre begs, looking at me with frustration. I nod, encouraging him to go on. "I … I … think you should tell someone Leah."

There's complete silence. The pressure Leah was applying on the door subsides. "Just go home Adrian," Leah says quietly.

"Not until you let me in … not until you talk me, Leah." Dre explains. "We need to talk."

Seconds that seemed like hours pass; then Leah lets the door open, as she walks to the couch. She sits down, lights a cigarette, and turns her television off. Leah's an attractive tall bottle-blonde with a short pixie haircut. Time had hardened her, but it was obvious that she was once a beautiful girl.

The apartment is cute, quaint, and artsy. "I love that mirror. Did you paint it?" I ask, before realizing that we're not here for pleasantries.

"Yeah, I did," Leah said, taking a long drag from her cigarette. "I made most of the shit in here from junk I found on the street—out on curbs."

"It's really beautiful." I compliment, putting my hand on Dre's knee. "I'm Kathryn, Dre's … Dre's girlfriend." I say, trying it out for the first time.

"Are you sure about that?" Leah asks, "You don't sound so sure."

Laughing, I say, "Well, it was just established about seven hours ago. It's pretty new. I kinda liked saying it though." Leah looks at me curiously.

A smile grows on her face, softening her features. "Damn, that was one honest fucking answer."

Dre laughs, "Kathryn's middle name is honesty. It's fucking crazy, I tell ya. Chick can't lie."

Leah visibly relaxes, finding a small semblance of comfort with us. "Oh I get it O'Donnell. Ya gotta start flying straight now that you met Miss Perfect here."

Dre squeezes my leg, "Yeah that's about right."

Dre and Leah talk about some old high school classmates and where each of them ended up. From my vantage point, it almost seems like two old friends catching up, sharing stories and laughter amicably. They chat for nearly half an hour before Dre brings up his brother again.

Leah dodges the question and offers us some drinks, absconding into the kitchen. As Dre and I sit on the couch, I take in the modesty of the apartment. It's exactly the type of apartment I'd have if I didn't have a good job, money to play with.

After getting us some drinks, Leah suggests we move to the kitchen table. She stirs a shot of something into her soft drink and says, "You're a good guy, Dre, but I can't give you what you're asking for."

"Leah, I don't understand. You're so badass. You've never taken shit from anyone. Why now? Why let Tristan get away with this?" Dre asks, pounding his hand on the table, making Leah and I startle.

Leah shakes her head and sighs deeply, exasperated. "Because I am badass."

Smiling she says, "I don't know why I'm about to tell you this. Maybe because of that time in tenth grade, I don't know, I've always thought I owed you for—"

"What happened in tenth grade?" I ask, looking between the two of them.

"Nothing really, Dre kind of saved … or Hell … maybe ruined my reputation. I don't know," she laughs. "What do you think it was O'Donnell?"

"Ruined, definitely ruined."

"Fucking hoity-toity cheerleaders decided that since I'd never blown a guy before that I must be a fucking dyke—"

I gasp, hating that word. I despise when people get judged for their sexual orientation. It's downright ludicrous, completely unacceptable.

"What's the matter?" Leah asks, staring at me.

"I'm just not a fan of that word," I admit.

"Oh fuck, me either. Especially the way they used it—like it's a bad thing. Who cares what or **who** I do? Ya know?" I nod, really warming up to Leah. Actually, she's the first person in this whole town that I've actually liked.

"I know Adrian here hates that shit too." Leah says.

Dre nods, "Remember when I went to that gay pride parade in college?" Leah laughs, evidently recalling the incident.

"Oh yeah, it was the talk of the town. I was so frigging proud of you," Leah compliments.

Confused and feeling very out of the loop, I ask, "Gay pride?"

Dre laughs and recounts a story that has Leah and me mesmerized. It will never get old listening to him open up and share his life with me. Although the story was appalling, I enjoyed hearing him talk, learning more about him.

In college, Dre and Rory went with a few of their homosexual friends to a gay pride parade. The parade was televised on the news; therefore, his parents and their snobby friends saw Dre walking down the street in all his glory, in support of his friends. The O'Donnells were mortified. They ended up refusing to pay his college tuition for the rest of the year and stopped payments on his car and automobile insurance. It didn't faze Dre at all. He just got a part-time job, washing dishes in the dining commons to pay for his car and insurance. Two scholarships and student loans took care of the rest of his tuition.

The idea of one of their children washing dishes on campus was too much for his parents to endure, so they caved on the car payments and insurance, deciding that washing dishes was beneath an O'Donnell. It was the first time Dre realized that his parents and their financial status were ridiculous, beginning to believe that it all meant entirely too much to them. Therefore, he secretly kept the dishwashing job, oftentimes just donating the money to his fraternity to help pay for their wild weekend parties.

"And wow ... just wow," I say, "You never cease to amaze me."

Grinning, Dre says, "Thanks Pebbles," kissing the inside of my wrist.

"Anyway, back to the tenth grade story? What happened with those girls who were making up crap about you?" I ask.

"Oh Hell, they spread that rumor all around the school. Everyone treated me like my 'lesbianism' was contagious," she recalls, grimacing and narrowing her eyes. "Man, high school can be brutal. Fucking cuntbags."

"So later that month, your boyfriend here, told everyone ... like fucking everyone ... that I blew him, and it was the best blowjob he'd ever gotten," Leah laughs. "Mind you, I'd never even talked to him—let alone touched him. Adrian did it all on his own."

Dre picks up where Leah left off. "And I hadn't gotten blown yet either. Basically, it was a win-win lie. I got status, and Leah was suddenly straight with guys beating down her door," Dre explains, holding my hand on the table.

"I didn't know if I should thank him or kill him," Leah admits. "It's crazy how it was okay for me to be a tramp who'd blow a guy I'd never met, but it wasn't okay for me to be in love with a girl," Leah says disgusted.

Continuing, "I mean; I wasn't. I'm straight. But still, high school's stupid. They were both fucking lies. One got me isolated; the other got me social status. Teenagers are fucked up."

Laughing, Dre says, "I mean, if you don't wanna make a liar out of me, we could always—"

"Hey!" I scream, hitting his arm. "Down boy."

"Can't blame a guy for trying," Dre jokes, winking at me.

Leah puts her head in her hands and groans. "I know I'm gonna regret this," she says, sighing again. "Jesus Adrian, you're just too damn cute-"

"Thanks Leah, so you'll do it? You'll turn him in?" Dre asks.

"I think it's for the best Leah … for you … for everyone," I add, wanting her to know that we really are on her side.

"Whoa, whoa, hold on guys. I said I'm going to tell the truth," Leah says, pausing and rubbing her forehead. "Alright, fuck it; here goes … your fucking brother didn't rape me. I'd cut off his dick if he even tried."

Silence.

Silence.

"What?" we both exclaim together.

"It's blackmail. Extortion 101. Your parents, although rolling in cash, aren't too bright, ya know?" Leah explains, as she begins to tell us the events of the night she was allegedly raped by Tristan O'Donnell.

According to Leah, she and Tristan had drunk all night together, getting pretty loaded up. Quite willingly and eagerly, she accompanied him to the hotel. Apparently, they had pretty incredible, mind-blowing sex. Leah pointed out that they'd consumed so much alcohol she was beyond shocked that Tristan could even perform so well—or even at all.

At one point, Tristan was behind her, being rather rough. With one overly powerful thrust, he knocked her off the bed, and she lunged forward hitting her face on the small writing desk in the room. At the time, they both thought it was hysterical. Tristan even went down the hall to get her some ice.

After another round of kinky crazy sex, they both fell asleep. The next morning, Leah rolled over, reached for him, and he was gone. Leah'd waited for him to call her, come see her, anything, but he never did. Then, she devised the plan to get herself out of debt, open her dream art gallery, and get revenge on yet another douchebag who "dicks deep and ditches."

"Are you fucking kidding me?" Dre asks, incredulously, knocking over his chair as he stands. "So, you just made it all up?"

"Technically … yes," Leah admits. "But, I'm pretty sure Tristan's done his fair share of dastardly deeds. He could use a little penance."

"But it's my parents who are paying—not Tristan," Dre argues. "This is fucking—"

"Wait, wait, wait Dre," I soothe, rubbing his arm. "Babe, this couldn't be better news."

"How can you say that?" he asks in disbelief.

"Well, first of all, Tristan didn't rape anyone. Your asshole brother is a lot of things, but he's not a rapist. That's pretty good news if you ask me. He's probably even learned his lesson at this point."

"Unlikely," Dre says gruffly.

"Leah's out of debt and able to start her own art gallery," I add.

"How does that even—"

"Dre! Don't you get it? Your brother didn't rape someone! You're not covering up a crime, an unforgivable, heinous crime!" Dre rubs his forehead, scowling and pensive.

Continuing, "Unfortunately, you learned who your family really is through all of this, which sucks, I know, " I explain. "But, you've completely evolved this year, thanks to the lies and deceit of this one woman. Do you really want to turn her in for extortion? Aren't you better off in your life now? Isn't everyone better off now?"

Dre stares at me, anger draining from his face. "Except for one person," he says, his face lighting up. "But I just figured out how to fix all of this. Pebbles, you're a genius."

- Dre -

As Lafferty pulls up the driveway to my house, I watch Kathryn's face as her eyes bulge and her jaw drops. "You grew up here?"

"Nope, I grew up in Charleston this past year," I smirk, pulling her onto my lap. I kiss her neck, running my tongue along her jaw. "I can't wait to get you back to the hotel. We'll have nineteen hours of uninterrupted time until our plane takes off."

"If ... the plan works," she says, brow furrowing.

"So far, everything you and I do together turns out incredibly," I say, biting lightly on her bottom lip until she opens her mouth, giving me full access to tease her tongue. "And I mean everything."

Lafferty opens the door, "Excuse me sir, we're here." Like I didn't know that. Like he didn't know that I was back here fooling around with Kathryn. Jesus, I could not wait to get out of this damn stifling state.

"It's go time!" I say, kissing her excitedly. "Are you sure about this? You're on board? Completely?"

"For the five thousandth time, YES!" she screams, grabbing my head with both of her hands and kissing my forehead.

Angelisa Stone

"Dre, I'm head over heels, crazy in love with you. I've never wanted anything more." Hearing her say it, watching her face shine as the words settle over us, I know that this was the best decision for everyone.

Walking out to the patio where my parents and Tristan are having brunch, I start immediately as to not lose my courage, "Glad to see nothing's changed—even with your daughter in a suicide watch psyche ward."

"Drop the drama, Ade," Tristan says, shoving a croissant in his mouth. "She's fine now."

Picking up a crueler, I pull a bite off and pop it into my mouth. My parents aren't amused. My mother taps her long, manicured nails on the glass-top patio table, while my father sits back, and crosses his arms over his chest.

I sit down next to Tristan, pulling Kathryn down onto my lap. "Kathryn, these are my parents, Chet O'Donnell and Tamara O'Donnell. You've met Tristan, my dickhead brother."

"What do you want, Dre?" my father asks, sternly.

"Well, ya know that 'pay off' we talked about? I've decided what I want." I say, glancing at Tristan. "Ya know for my silence."

"Your father and I talked it over, figuring that this little gold-digging hussy would talk you into trying to get something out of us. We decided you're getting nothing from us. Not one penny Adrian," my mother states firmly.

"Really? Is that so?" I ask, hating whom my family has become. "Babe, do you have your phone?" Kathryn nods; smiling, she takes it out of her bra and hands it to me. My mother gasps at the sight of Kathryn taking a phone out of her undergarments. I laugh, loving how perfect Kathryn is.

"I think that before you decide against bargaining with me, you should probably hear this," I say, hitting play.

There isn't a sound or word spoken as my family watches the video on Kathryn's phone. They are speechless when they see Leah's face, but are destroyed when they hear her words:

"Hi Mr. and Mrs. O'Donnell and assfuck Tristan. I'm glad you're all together. As you can see, I'm outside the police station. In this folder, I have the pictures of my face when Tristan beat the shit out of me. See? Also, you can see the bank statements of when you paid me for my silence. Anyway, Adrian and Kathryn, Hi Kathryn, anyway, they convinced me to turn you in Tristan, and I'm going to ... if you don't give Adrian what he wants. He's got my number on speed dial. I'm going in to the station the second he calls. Thanks Adrian. Good Luck. Kathryn call me!"

"Such a sweet girl," I say, grinning. "How could you let that one get away T?"

"Why you little—"

"Are you sure you wanna do that, Mr. O'Donnell?" Kathryn asks, taunting him with the video on her phone.

"Chet, let him go," my mother commands. "We've got enough to deal with right now. Just write the bastard a check and be done with it ... with him."

"I'm glad we're all in agreement," I say, smiling. "It's so much better when everyone just gets along." Kathryn giggles, covering her mouth.

"How much?" my dad asks defeated, as Tristan storms off.

"Funny you should ask that …"

~ Piper ~

It's been exactly two years ago today when Dre changed my life, gave it meaning. (I call him "Dre" now, too.) Dre walked into my hospital room as I waited for my parents to come get me to take me back to my Hellish family sentence. He wasn't alone. As soon as I saw her, I knew she had to be the *Cider House Rules* girl. Dre had explained her to a tee. She was more beautiful than I'd imagined. I often imagined him finally happy, finally in love, and away from the constraints of our lifestyle. Dre was not meant for our lifestyle; he's too good for it, if we're being honest.

"Hey kiddo," Dre said, walking in holding her hand. "I want you to meet Kathryn."

Kathryn was sweet, kind, and intelligent. I loved her instantly, especially the way she dressed. I've always just wanted to wear jeans and a t-shirt with my hair in a ponytail. But my mom would never let me. WTF? Who doesn't let their teenage daughter wear jeans and t-shirts? My mom, that's who!

"It's good to finally meet you," Kathryn said, smiling sweetly. Kathryn even has a dimple. I always wanted a dimple. My mom once told me that I should be glad I didn't have one, because she would've gotten me plastic surgery to get rid of it. A dimple people! Do you see what I've been dealing with?

"We just booked our flight back to Charleston," Dre explained. "We're leaving first thing in the morning."

The words broke me. I tried to be strong, pretend like I didn't care, but it didn't work. I caved. I cried and sobbed like a damn baby. I couldn't stop myself; at that point, I didn't even want to stop myself.

"Please Dre. Please," I begged. "You just can't. Please. You can't go home. Not yet. Not without me. Please."

Wrapping me in his arms, he kissed my head, and said, "You're right kiddo, I can't go home ... not without you."

And that's it. Dre and Kathryn flew back to Charleston the next morning, getting things ready. Then, Dre came back to New Hampshire the following week when I was released from the hospital. Dre took me to our parents' house to pack my stuff, while my mom bitched and moaned about this and that.

My dad pounded me on the back, and said, "Good luck at boarding school, young lady."

Oh yeah, that was the lie. My parents couldn't bear to tell their friends and frenemies that I'd chosen my drifter brother over them, so they fabricated a Swiss Boarding School that specialized in troubled adolescents. As much as they tried, they couldn't keep the suicide attempt under wraps.

My psychiatrist was thrilled that Dre was taking me in. He'd heard enough to know that living with my parents and Tristan wasn't a healthy environment for me. My doctor was pleased that

Dre had a medical background and the connections in Charleston to find me a good therapist.

Dre and I have been living in a two-bedroom apartment near the beach. He screwed around for a year as a "homeless" guy, but what he never told anyone is that in the safe at Rory's hotel he had almost 500 grand. Dre's not an idiot. He may not like money and what it stands for and all that jazz. But he knows damn well that people need it. Dre pays for my college, my health insurance, and for basically anything else we need.

I like to think we're rolling in the dough; he gets pissed when I say that though. Dre and Tristan both got 250 grand for high school graduation and another 250 at college graduation. That's where I got screwed. I got a card that said, "Congratulations Graduate, move back home and you'll get your money."

Screw the money. My parents never got it. Money buys a shit-ton of things, but it doesn't buy happiness, never came close to buying my happiness. It never bought me friends who looked beyond my clothes and designer labels. Money never bought me a boyfriend who didn't want to grope and claw away at me any chance he got. It never bought me parents who cared more about me than their precious fortune.

Living with Dre, I've learned so much. It's amazing whom he's become—especially since I know firsthand where he's from. Kathryn, Dre, and I help out at the homeless shelter a lot. I don't go down there as much as Dre does, but when I do, I learn something new, something valuable every time. When he first told me that he spends his Tuesday and Friday nights at the homeless shelter, I laughed at him for being a loser who scooped soup and swept floors.

Dre looked at me like he was going to cry, disappointment flooding his face. He shook his head and said, "No amount of work or kindness is beneath me, Pipe."

Well, that was it for me. I couldn't have the only person who ever inspired and loved me to be disappointed in me. I started going with him. It was the most incredible and worthwhile learning experience. In my lifetime, I've met some of the richest, most privileged people, but yet they're still so pessimistic, negative, and sometimes downright ruthless. On the other hand, recently, I've met people who have nothing, virtually nothing more than the clothes on their backs, and they are the most kind, generous, and hopeful people I've ever encountered. It's truly amazing.

My friends, back home, used to ask me how I could've tried to end my life when I had "everything." Like I said, money can get you a pretty, shiny, plush exterior, but it certainly doesn't matter what the outside looks like if the inside is empty and alone.

Many times when I first got here and Dre went with me to therapy, he constantly asked me why. He really wanted to know why I did it. My answer never satisfied him; it still doesn't. Honestly, I just didn't know what else to do. People always talk about how suicide is selfish and that the person wasn't thinking about their family at the time. That's just a stupid thing to say. Obviously since the person committed suicide, he's dead, so you never honestly get the real answer. The real answer for me was that I did think about it—a lot—for months on end.

I thought about how my father wouldn't have to pay for my college, my wedding, or anything else. I thought about how my mom wouldn't have to wake up each morning when I went to school to make sure I was really going. I thought about how she wouldn't have to compare me to Tristan and Adrian every chance she got, being disappointed in who I was. I thought about how I needed to do it in the guesthouse bathroom, so my mom wouldn't have too much to clean up and that the blood wouldn't ruin anything.

I thought about how Tristan would finally be the center of my parents' world—something he's always wanted. I thought about how my friends at school wouldn't feel like they had to compete with me anymore and try to "one up" me every day. I thought about how I wouldn't be such a drain and burden on my friends and family anymore. I did think about them; I wasn't being selfish at all. I thought I was doing them all a favor.

The only person who made me pause and try to reconsider this escape was Dre. I knew it would crush him. As far as brothers go, Dre's the greatest anyone could ever ask for. But when my parents denied my dream of moving to Charleston for college, I knew I needed out—out of the Hell that was my life. I just couldn't find a way out. I was desperate for a way out, and I didn't know how or where to get one.

Being seventeen, I didn't realize there was one. I didn't know Dre was going to give me that way out. I just knew I was suffocating and felt like I was trapped.

That night, when I broke the razor apart from the plastic container, and I held it to my wrist, I knew one thing: I wanted out.

But there was so much I didn't know. I didn't know how connected I was going to feel when I sat at dinner nearly every night, laughing with Rory, Sydney, Kathryn and Dre. I didn't know how special it would feel when the three of us got the word "Everything" tattooed on the arch of our foot. (Dre wouldn't let me get it on my lower back.)

I didn't know how at home and loved I was going to feel when Dre let me hide at the fair, taking pictures of the moment he proposed to Kathryn on the carousel. (I told him that the pictures would turn out blurry since the ride was in motion. He didn't believe me.)

The proposal was hysterical. She screamed and batted at his hand, freaking out and crying. The ring went flying off the carousel. The ride controller had to stop the ride. People everywhere were on their hands and knees looking for the ring. Some little boy found the ring, knelt down, and put the ruby ring on Kathryn's finger, while Dre smiled, proudly. (I got pictures of all of that.)

The ruby ring with diamonds all around it is beautiful. Dre and I together decided that since Kathryn was one-of-a-kind that the ring had to be too. We've all come to realize that you don't get to choose your family, but they're a part of you, your past, your present and your future; you just have to learn to accept them for who they are—and love them the best that you can. That's why we chose the ruby—after Kathryn's mom. Sure, they've had their ups and downs—just like any carousel of life. But Kathryn and her mom are connected forever—just like Dre and Kathryn will be.

There were so many other things that I didn't know that night, alone in that bathroom with the razor blade in my hand. I didn't know how much I'd love helping Kathryn shop for a wedding gown and my bridesmaid dress, feeling like she was the sister I never had and couldn't wait to have. I didn't know what it would feel like to spend long weekend afternoons shopping and bonding with her while Dre was at work. I would've missed out on all of that. I wouldn't have gotten to see true love and true beauty up close.

I didn't know how bashful I was going to feel the first time Kathryn introduced me to Jose, and my heart like literally stopped for a second. (I still haven't told my parents about the wonderful Hispanic boy I'm dating. I'll save that for later—much later.) Jose has taught me so many things. I've not only learned how to love someone unconditionally; I've learned how to let him love me.

I didn't know how magical it was going to feel the first time Jose kissed me by the waterfall at Ariss' Oasis, with water splashing over us. I didn't know how beautiful I was going to feel when Jose and I danced at our senior prom under the moonlight.

I didn't know how excited I was going to feel when Lanette gave me my first hostess paycheck. I didn't know how proud and intelligent I was going to feel when my college professor told me that my paper was the most profound piece of writing he's ever read. I didn't know. Had no idea. I didn't know there were small snippets of wonderful that made life worth fighting for, worth living for.

I certainly didn't know how completely happy I'd feel every night I went to bed and could hear Dre and Kathryn talking in the other room when he got home late from his shifts at the hospital. I didn't know what happiness felt like. I know now. And I'll tell you this, it's incredible. I'll never go back to that isolation, that pain. I know what the other side looks like now. It's a place I never want to go back to. I used to think that I couldn't go home, but the truth is, I can go anywhere as long as I have happiness and love. But geez, was that a hard lesson to learn.

The End

About the Author

Who is Angelisa Stone?

Angelisa Stone is a typical Midwest wife and mom, frazzled by parenting and housework, and overwhelmed with sports schedules, doctor appointments, and three-dimensional creative projects due "tomorrow morning." Angelisa dreams of white sandy beaches, clear-blue waters, and Midori coladas in hand, but realizes that her loving husband and four not-so-perfect children are her real dreams-come-true. Writing and reading are her passions, and she hopes (and prays with her fingers tightly crossed) that readers will find enjoyment and escape through her words and characters.

Email Angelisa for fun chatter and banter, giggles and chuckles: angelisaauthor@gmail.com

Follow Angelisa on Twitter: @Angelisaauthor
https://twitter.com/Angelisaauthor

Find Angelisa on Facebook:

https://www.facebook.com/angelisa.stone

Check out Angelisa's profile on Gooreads:

http://www.goodreads.com/book/show/18176355-can-t-go-home

Heartfelt Gratitude To:

My family: Thank you for bearing with me and understanding when I spend hours on end tapping away at the keyboard, responding only with random "uh-huhs" and what not. Your love, support, and patience helped make this "Midsummer's Fantasy" a dream come true. Having a family who believes in you and loves you throughout all of your journeys makes everything worthwhile and possible.

The Book Enthusiast: Thank you for all of your promotional expertise and advice. The only following I have gained is because of you. Please contact Debra at The Book Enthusiast Promotions if you're looking to market your novels.

Fictional Formats: Thank you for making my book so beautiful and visually pleasing. Thank you for bearing with my technological inferiority. Fictional Formats is an incredible company, creating the most gorgeous books and eBooks. Check them out! You won't be sorry. https://www.facebook.com/FictionalFormats

Sophie Chamberlain: Thank you for your artistic eye and talent in creating the lip-biting, desirable cover. It's stunning and exactly what I wanted. If anyone is interested in using Ms. Chamberlain as your cover artist, email me at: angelissaauthor@gmail.com and I will connect you to the finest cover designer around.

My friends and beta readers:

Stephanie Bailey: You rock my life, 100 times over. Our chats, our laughs, and our vulgarity brighten many of my days. Thank you for always reading whatever I send your way and offering your kind words. You are insightful and wise. I'm lucky to be one of your "quarters." I can't wait until the day we watch a football game together.

Michael Burhans: You truly are "the bomb," even though it's an outdated phrase. It fits you literally and figuratively. Thank you for helping me with my technological inadequacies and always reading whatever junk I send your way. It's nice to have a male perspective on my writing.

Debra Celentano: You are a Godsend, my little butterfly. To think that I had a whim, an idea to do a blog tour and cover reveal, and then WHAM, you took it all over and spent so much time and energy organizing an event for someone you'd never even met. You are truly a remarkably generous and thoughtful person. Thank you for all that you do and have done.

Shannon Girard: Thank you for always offering advice and ideas, and for always making me laugh. I'm grateful for your encouragement and compliments.

Mallory Grant: Thank you for pushing me and forcing me to do writing sprints with you when it's the last thing I want to do. Readers: Remember the name "Mallory Grant," because her upcoming book, *My Real*, will knock your socks off.

SK Jean: Your pictures inspire me, keeping me going for the "fun" parts. Thank you for your support.

Skye Jordan: I love your spunk and fire; it inspires me. (And scares me a little.) I love that friendships can occur miles and miles away through type strokes. Readers: You need to read *Reckless*, by none other than the spitfire, Skye Jordan. You will heat up when you read Jax and Lexi's story.

Tiffany Kasmetskie: Your last name sucks. It's way too hard to spell! But I love you nonetheless. I'm grateful for your help and encouragement. I feel like Harper Lee when you're around; you're always praising me and making me feel confident in my writing. Thank you.

Aine Kelley: I love spending our evenings writing and sharing. It makes it so much more personal and enjoyable. Readers: Again, remember the name "Aine Kelley," her debut novel is due out very soon. You'll love *Finding Home*.

Joy Kriebel-Sadowski: You make me want to write. You make me feel like my writing is worthy. Thank you for always reading whatever I write and giggling with me over what I write.

Angela McLaurin: Friendship occurs even when distance separates those two people who are destined to be friends. Your friendship means the world to me. I'm not too fond of the distance though. I love that I was able to hug the person who means so much to me. I hope it happens many more times in the years to come.

Kim Box Person: You are the most selfless person I know— always helping and cheering for the underdog. Thank you for the Release Day Blitz.

Lisa Rutledge: You were the first person to ever make me feel like a "real author." I think I'm going to name something really special after you. It's the least I can do.

Chrissy Sharp: You are one fun lady. I'm a "laughier" person when you're around. Thank you for the fun.

Stephenie Thomas: Thank you for your encouragement and for agreeing to check out my book for The Indie Bookshelf. I so wish our lives were not so parallel. You deserve happiness and joy.

Denise Tung: You are my sweetness; the one person who understands what writing and creating means to me. My heart belongs to you. Thank you for being there for me through everything.

Christine Zolendz: I've decided that if anyone ever decides to read *Can't Go Home*, and if I gain any sort of following, then I want to be a writer/author just like you. You are kind, gracious, and an inspiration. You write from the heart with feeling and purpose. I'm lucky to have met you. Now, if I could just do it in person … Readers: Please check out Christine Zolendz and her Mad World Series, starting with *Fall From Grace*. You won't be sorry. Shane Maxton is a dream.

Please check out the following blogs and their wonderful bloggers! They are integral in the success of any indie author. Thank you to the blogs and bloggers who were a part of the *Can't Go Home* BLOG TOUR, organized by **Debra Celentano** at *The Book Enthusiast*:

2 Friends, Promote
Abigail Books Blog
Chapter Break
Christina's Book Reviews
Crash the Party
Crazies R Us Book Blog
Dawn's Reading Nook
Dirty Girl Book Club
Flirty and Dirty Book Blog

Give Me Books

Hooked on Books

Keeping It Real Book Blog

Kim's Book Blog

Life Becomes Me

Mia Bella Luce

Mia's Point of View

Rachael Orman's Writing

Raw Books

Read and Share Book Reviews

Rumpled Sheets Blog

Sarah's Book Shelf

Shh Mom's Reading

So Many Books, So Little Time

The Book Enthusiast

The Book Hangover

The Book Obsessed Momma

There's This Book

The Two Brains of Book Reviews Adults Only

Tiffany Talks Books

Whirlwindbooks

Thank you to those blogs who blasted my RELEASE DAY with a Promo Blitz, organized by **Kim Box Person** at *Shh Mom's Reading Book Blog*:

Book Addicts Not So Anonymous

Bridger Bitches Book Blog

Flirty and Dirty Book Blog

Kindle Crack

Shh Mom's Reading

Smardy Pants Book Blog

The Book Blog

The Book Hookers

True Story Book Blog

Who You Callin a Book Whore

A special shout out to the blogs/bloggers who participated in the *Can't Go Home* Cover Reveal, organized by Debra Celentano at The Book Enthusiast:

A Cauldron of Books

A Generous Helping of Romance

Diary of a Book Addict

Bare Naked Words

B's Beauty and Books

Bella

Best Sellers & Best Stellars

Book Bliss

Book Geeks Unite

Booked On Romance

Books and Their Seven Deadly Sins

Books, Coffee, and Wine

Christina's Book Reviews

Crash the Party

Dalene's Book Reviews

Deb Deb Reviews

Escape Reality with a Book

Flirty and Dirty Book Blog

Guiseppe Del Medico

Haloangel Reads

Indie Brits

Jelena's Book Blog

Jess's Book Blog

Jessica Loves Books

Keeping it Real Book Blog

Life with Lesley

Lisa Writes

Literary Lust

Literary Nook

Lynn's Book Blog

Made For You Book Reviews

Mean Girls Luv Books

Mom of 2 Book Reviews

Mommy's Late Night Book-up

Mommy's Reads and Treats

My Daily Romance

Obsession is a Book

One More Chapter

Orchard Book Club

Penelope Syn

Rachel Orman's Writing

Read and Share Book Reviews

Read That

Reading Bliss

Reading is Dreaming with Open Eyes

Romance Schmomance

Room with Books

Rose and Beps Blog

Sarah's Bookshelf

Scandalous Book Blog

Sunshine & Mountains Book Reviews

Swoonworthy Books

The Book Enthusiast

The Book Obsessed Momma

The Phantom Paragrapher

Tiffany Talks Books

Whirlwindbooks

Who You Callin A Book Whore

Made in the USA
Charleston, SC
28 September 2014